Slater's Tempest

T.J. Jones

Slater's Tempest

Chapter One

SEALS spend a lot of time in and under the water. I'm not talking about the cute ones at the zoo with the puppy-dog eyes, but the elite group of Naval combatants called SEALS. It's an acronym, but that's not important to my story. Everybody has heard about the incredible exploits, some true, some complete fabrication, and some sensationalized by the news and a self-aggrandizing few willing to talk about their service. I was fortunate enough to serve as a SEAL for four years, which was enough.

Don't get me wrong, I loved it, and would go to blows with anyone who had anything bad to say about the outfit, but it was grueling. There were times during the training when I was sure I wouldn't make it, that I would either wash out or die from shear exhaustion. I managed to make it through, only because I was young and too stubborn to give up.

We trained in every circumstance imaginable. We jumped out of airplanes in the black of night, crawled for miles through snake infested swamps, and fought mock battles twenty feet underwater without Scuba gear until your lungs felt like they would explode and your vision blackened. After the training, I finished the four-year commitment, then asked for reassignment. Part of it was fatigue, and part of it was the realization that I might be asked to do things that I couldn't or wouldn't want to do.

But the reality was that I was never truly afraid, and that was the most important part of the training. We were a team, a single fighting force, and everybody had a partner. If you got into serious trouble, and some did, your partner would pull you out of whatever mess you found yourself in or give his own life if necessary, to save yours. No matter how bad it got, being afraid wasn't an option. Your partner was there for you, and you had to be there for him. Dying wasn't an option either, it just wasn't part of the mission statement.

That was probably the reason I was able to stay calm, trapped as I was with my leg pinched by the mangled boom of the Caroline, pinned thirty-some feet under water with about fifteen minutes of air left in my tank. It had been a lot of years since I'd admitted that I couldn't last as a SEAL and given my spot to someone younger and more fit for the mission, but the training was still a part of me. I wouldn't die, I had a partner.

These days, my partner was my girlfriend and roommate, Maggie Jeffries. But like my partner in the Navy, I had every confidence that she would do whatever it took to pull me out of my latest mess. It was a perfectly clear day topside, and I could see the outline of the dive boat above me and the shadow of Maggie's long legs as she reached it, undoubtedly frantic to find the rope she needed to pull the mast from my leg. As I watched, the six-foot Bull-shark that had become our belligerent companion circled the boat a couple times, then dove directly back at me, avoiding a last second collision that I would have been helpless to defend against.

The shark was only curious for the moment, but Bulls can be aggressive and unpredictable. Given time it might decide I was defenseless enough to attempt a kill. Decide was a poor choice of words. That would imply some logic behind those prehistoric orbs that stared blankly at me as it circled. Sharks, in my opinion, only understand kill or be killed. But, like most carnivores, they are only dangerous when they're hungry. This one wasn't, yet. Luckily, the rigging that had trapped my leg was lying flat when the mast shifted and only trapped, not cut my calf. Fresh blood would have changed the scenario, possibly attracting more, larger sharks, the hungry kind. But I wasn't worried, I had a partner.

***

When I retired from the Navy after twenty years, I expected to spend my retirement quietly, selling cars or being a security guard for some outfit that really didn't need one. I thought I'd fly my airplane a lot and maybe take up fishing. I didn't plan to become a private investigator, and I didn't plan to fall for my best friend's little sister. I sure as hell didn't expect her to fall for me, but that's what happened.

Most mornings, when I opened my eyes and looked at the beautiful woman on the pillow next to me, I had to think twice about pinching myself. If this was a dream, it was the best kind, and I really didn't want to wake up.

My business partner and girlfriend, Maggie, is the younger sister of Angie Jeffries. She was the blond-haired, blue-eyed obsession of my teenaged years, and the person I always hoped I would end up with. It turned out, life, and the Butterfly had a better plan.

Maggie Jeffries stands about five ten, an enchanting combination of red-haired beauty and sarcasm with a knack for knowing when people are lying, and a third-degree black belt in Tae-kwon-do. After getting shot, I thought twice about turning full-time detective, but it was hard to look into those blue eyes and deny her anything. As was usually the case, Maggie knew best, and now I was looking forward to our next predicament.

This particular morning when I opened my eyes, the second pillow was empty. I rolled over and swore softly when I looked at my phone, nearly eight o'clock. By now the redhead was already back from her run and in the shower. I'd grown accustomed to sleeping in, and there'd been too many days on the couch, watching television.

7

Not working full-time was making me lazier by the day.

 We stopped the man who had killed Maggie's half-brother, but he had shattered my fibula with a well-placed shot that was intended to cause me a lot of pain. He had succeeded in that, it still hurt like hell. He would have killed me, as well as Angela, had Maggie not stopped him with a well-placed shot of her own.

 Before a bullet shattered it, I didn't know where my fibula was or what it did. Turns out, it's important for things like walking and standing, neither of which I had been able to do for the past few weeks. The doctors said I had been lucky, but I didn't feel that way. I felt useless. Being useless is time consuming, and gives you the opportunity to think. Thinking leads to worry, which is also useless, and time consuming. It's a vicious circle.

 Lately, I was worried about Maggie. I had killed a couple of men, both recently, both Dinar's assassins that had been sent to kill innocents. I was confident that the men I had shot, deserved it. That's what I told myself, and I'm a very practical guy. But sometimes at night when I couldn't sleep, their faces came back to me. I wondered if Maggie ever saw Dinar's face when she closed her eyes, and if that was why she cried out in her sleep sometimes.

 I hoisted my bad leg out of bed and eased myself up onto the crutches that I had become adept at using during the last month. If there was any plus side to having a bad leg, it was that all the time on Maggie's weight machine had increased my upper body strength considerably. When I got bored, it was that or Judge Judy.

Maggie was showering in the Master, so I carefully worked my way across the slippery tile floor to the kitchen on the other end of the great room and nuked some day-old coffee. It was a beautiful Florida morning, unusually cool for the end of August, and the doors facing the Saint Johns river were wide open. From the television over the microwave, a political commentator ranted about the latest controversy, and in the front of the house, a flock of seagulls cackled noisily as they fought over some carrion along the shoreline. Both battles sounded equally interesting to me. I turned the television off and pushed the French doors shut.

Our house, Maggie was calling the place, which I thought was generous. No sailor on a pension could afford such a spread. Her father's estate had funded her dream home, and luckily, she was willing to share it with me. I tried the coffee, dumped it, then thumped across the tile into the half bath for my morning ritual. By the time I did my business and navigated back across the kitchen to a chair, the redhead was brewing a new pot of coffee and making breakfast.

"Slater, if you fall off those damn sticks, you're going to be back having more surgery. Why didn't you use our bathroom this morning?"

9

"I don't care how long we live together, there are some things you will never see me do."

"Glad we agree on that, but these are special circumstances. You didn't complain about the sponge bath last night."

"I will never complain about those. Sorry I over-slept, you should have poked me before you went running."

"I was pretty sure you wouldn't want to go with me."

"Hard enough when everything works. How's your sister?"

"How'd you know I stopped there?"

"Gabriela's birthday, isn't it? I figured you would have to stop by and at least say hi."

"Family party is this Saturday. She's having her girlfriends over tonight. Hard to believe that kid went through what she did. As far as anyone knows she's just a normal thirteen-year old girl with a rich mother that spoils her rotten."

"Who would have thought Angela would ever be someone's Mom? She's come a long way in the last year."

"Your appointment is at two, isn't it? I'm teaching a class, so Jasmine volunteered to drive you."

"Okay, but if I fall on her, it'll be just a tiny pile of blue hair and broken bones. She isn't big enough to catch me." I loved Jasmine, which was why it was so much fun to pick on her.

"Then you better not fall over, she'll leave you right where you land."

"Why isn't she bringing McCade? He's back on the job, isn't he?"

"Young guys heal a lot faster than you old timers, Slater. He was back at work a week after getting shot. But she's flying solo today."

"Forty is the new thirty," I reminded her.

"And sitting is the new smoking. Once you're off those crutches, you need to start moving around. Jasmine or I can help you if we need to, but the doctor said any kind of exercise is good. You can walk the shoreline. The soft sand will build up your leg strength and none of the neighbors are likely to shoot you. They all know you belong to me."

"Maybe if you get a leash, you can walk me mornings and we can meet up with Gabriela and Duchess. I doubt I could outrun that Lab, so I won't be retrieving anything."

"The leash sounds good, and maybe a muzzle," She quipped.

"Luis is coming over later this morning to go over some plans with me for the two new remodels. There's no exercise involved, but at least it'll keep me awake. I have to admit, I am getting out of shape."

"Sounds like McCade is going to be leaving, or already has. He's taking a different job."

"Why is that? I thought Jasmine was just getting him trained in?"

"Too much stress for him. Being that girl's bodyguard and boyfriend is more than he can handle."

"I manage."

"Jasmine doesn't have the patience I do. Maybe those pain meds affected your brain, Slater, it was me saving your butt this last time, not the other way around."

She put a plate in front of me and grinned. It was nice, having a quiet breakfast and sparring with the redhead. For once, I wasn't wondering if someone was plotting to kill us or the people we loved. Most of the men that had tried that were incarcerated, or dead.

"I'll have the cast off today, then I can get serious about rehabbing. Another week and I should be getting around pretty good. Doc Hays said I can start running in a couple weeks, if I'm careful and don't get shot again."

"She knows her stuff, especially leg injuries. She helped one of the guys at the club when he crashed his bike. He had multiple fractures and he almost lost his foot."

"Crashed his bike? A big Harley?"

"Nope, a small Schwinn. Brake cable snapped and he sailed through a stop light, got broadsided by some geriatric in a Caddy."

"Lot of ways for the Butterfly to get you," I mused.

"Are you still on that kick? If the old guy wasn't half drunk, he could have stopped."

"Was it fate or bad luck that he had to have that third drink? Sometimes it's the little things," I paused for effect, "or is it?"

Maggie didn't share my fascination with the Butterfly Effect, and she enjoyed mocking me. "Very deep, Slater. Or is it?"

My phone buzzed and I held up a finger. "One minute and I'll explain the finer points. I'm thinking about writing a book, now that I have free time. This is Tommy Ackerman." Maggie raised a brow, but didn't comment. "How's my favorite lawyer?" I asked.

"I'm great. How many lawyers do you know?"

"There's Jarrod, but he's not really a lawyer. Maybe by the time he gets out of prison, he'll have his license. I do like you better than him."

"Never would have guessed that little bastard was capable of a kidnapping."

"Yeah, hard to believe he was right there under all of our noses the whole time. Turns out kidnapping is a lousy way to get a girlfriend. That kid is screwed up. He's lucky Maggie didn't shoot him in the foot, like she did RJ."

"Part of why I called. As his lawyer, I'm privy to things that are confidential. There's information that I can't share with you about one of his visitors."

It wasn't hard to guess who he was talking about. "Could it involve a tiny girl with questionable choices in hair coloring?"

"Can't say, but I can tell you that a young woman with very blue hair was seen at the prison this week on visitor's day. That's not breaking privilege, it's just an observation."

"I have a friend with a soft heart and a short memory, who happens to have very blue hair. I was just telling her the other day how it would be a really stupid idea to hang around with a kidnapper. She didn't thank me for sharing that."

"I also advised my client that communicating with his former victim was unadvisable."

I chuckled into the phone. "Is this really necessary? We both know we're talking about Jasmine and Jarrod."

"I can't discuss a client's indiscretions, but nothing good can come of it."

"She won't listen to me, but maybe Maggie can talk some sense into her."

"I don't see how it's good for him either, but he claims his therapist is okay with it. No point in my asking, those guys won't tell you anything."

"Must be an ethics thing, like when you're a lawyer." I laughed at my own joke, he didn't.

"I was going to talk to you about a job, but maybe you'd rather try being a comedian."

"Any work would be tough right now. I think I get a walking cast today, but unless the perp is a little old lady in a wheelchair, I'll never keep up."

"I'm working on something that might be a perfect fit, since you can't do much else. The client is coming in later in the week. I told him about you and Maggie, and he wants to meet you. He has kind of an unusual proposition, but he also has a boatload of money. After I talk to him, I'll set up a meeting."

"Sounds good. I need to do something. I'm getting fatter by the day." Maggie glanced over and nodded silently. "I have to go, Tommy, my roommate is being especially difficult this morning." I ended the call and studied the redhead.

As usual, she feigned innocence. "What? Is he talking about another case already?"

"Nothing for sure. If it's just surveillance I could handle it. If someone needs chasing, that'll be on you."

"I'm faster than you anyway," She stated confidently.

"Baloney, we've never put that to a test. Once my leg is healed, it's on."

"Name your poison, Slater, a hundred yards, a mile, a marathon? I'm game for anything."

"Are you going to be able to get away from the gym if we get a case?"

"I have two back-up teachers. I told them the PI thing comes first."

"Obviously I'm worthless to Luis right now, even more so than usual."

"You said it, not me. Have a good day, and don't be too hard on Jasmine. And please don't harass her about visiting Jarrod. He's locked up for at least five years. By the time he gets out, she'll have forgotten all about him. I have an early class, a beginners' class for Mom's. Stacey Lane got a bunch of women together and they want basic self-defense training. That woman needs something to keep her out of trouble."

"That'll be a blood-bath. I've never met anyone that likes to gossip as much as Stacey Lane. It's never good, and she makes most of it up."

"Be nice. She never has anything but good things to say about you. She asks about you every time I see her."

"Don't volunteer any extra facts."

"Facts aren't important to Stacey, she just likes a good story. I'm told she talks about us constantly."

"We're fake news?"

"News is something people care about, Slater. Other than Stacey, nobody wants to know what you and I are doing. She probably has an ulterior motive. I think she has a little crush on you, and word is she may be getting a divorce herself. No doubt she'd be willing to forget our friendship for a shot at a big ginger like you." That amused her more than it did me. "I have to go. Tell Luis I said Hi." She kissed me quickly on the forehead.

"That was romantic."

She laughed and gave me a proper kiss. "There, happy now? Have a good day and don't give Jasmine too much trouble."

"I'm always nice to Jasmine, but she's a poor listener."

After I met with Luis, Jasmine came to give me a ride to the doctor. It didn't take long for me to say the wrong thing. "I thought you were going to let your hair go back to its natural color. That is the brightest blue I've ever seen. Cerulean, I think they call it."

"Blue is my natural color, it matches my eyes. I could go green if you like. Hard on my hair, but if you don't like blue, lime green is always an option."

"I know, I should keep my opinions to myself. I just think you'd make a pretty blond. I've seen pictures. You were only five, but cute as a button."

"It makes me look too much like my Mom, but you're right." I looked at her quickly and she laughed. "You're right, you should keep your opinions to yourself. Why couldn't Luis drive you to your appointment? Do you question his fashion choices?"

"Luis and I don't talk about our hair, Jasmine, we're construction workers. Real men don't do that." That got me an eyeroll. "He had to get back to the jobsite, and besides, I thought you volunteered for Slater duty. Are you having regrets?"

"Regret is a strong word, and I'm obligated to be nice to you after you demolished your airplane rescuing me." Jasmine held the door open as I pulled my bum leg into her car. She slammed the door behind me, then ran around and got in the driver's seat.

"It was an old airplane anyway." I looked out the window, fighting the impulse to say more. That didn't work. "Speaking of kidnappings and kidnappers, how is Jarrod?"

"I'm going to kill Tommy," Jasmine growled. "Jarrod needs a friend right now, Slater. He's really messed up."

"I agree. He kept you captive in his basement for two weeks, chained to a post. That is by definition, really messed up."

"I know, but I can't help feeling sorry for him."

"After what he and RJ did to you, and all of us?"

"That was the worst of it, all of you thinking I might be dead. I don't think those two morons would ever have hurt me, but RJ threatened to more than once, and Jarrod made him behave. Skinny little bookworm that he is, he stood up to RJ and threatened to kick his ass if he disrespected me. Can you imagine him saying something like that? It was so stupid and corny, but so damn sweet. I couldn't hate him, even when he left me chained in that smelly basement all day watching TV Land."

"That whole time, you were never afraid he might do something to you?"

"I was never afraid of Jarrod. He looks at me like Angela's Lab looks at her and Gabriela, total

18

love and loyalty. I know what he did was wrong, and more than a little crazy, but deep down he's not a bad person. He's just confused, and needs help."

"I repeat, he chained you to a post...for two weeks."

"Truth is I was really scared, Slater, but if not for Jarrod I would have been terrified. I was never sure that RJ wouldn't rape me, or shoot us both after he got the money. But Jarrod stood up to him for me, so if I can make Jarrod a little happier by going to visit once in a while, I'm going to do that. I know you and Maggie risked your lives to save me, and I really appreciate that. I love you both very much. But that doesn't mean I have to hate Jarrod, does it?"

"No, I guess it doesn't," I admitted. We rode in silence for a few blocks, then I looked over and pretended to inspect her hair. "Blonde is nice, but I guess the blue is okay. You know what works for you, and you're a pretty smart kid."

Getting a cast off is exhilarating. Janet Hays was a few years younger than me, with a ready smile and a wall full of Diplomas. She used a battery-operated saw to remove my cast. It looked a lot like the saws we used on construction sites to hack holes in sheetrock and plywood. Smaller, but undoubtedly sharper. I had managed to hurt myself on more than one occasion with the bigger saws, but thankfully, Doctor Hays was more proficient and careful than I'm capable of. She removed the old cast without any bloodshed in a matter of minutes.

Doing a little dance seemed appropriate and feasible, as well as some serious scratching, and the new cast was tiny in comparison. The reality was that the leg still hurt when I put weight on my foot, and although there was vast improvement, I definitely wasn't ready for a marathon with Maggie.

"Don't throw the crutches away yet, Slater. You can start putting some weight on the leg, but don't push it. The bones will meld with the titanium screws and continue to tighten up. You can move around, but pain is an indication that you need to back off. You can use just one crutch, or some people prefer a cane."

"A cane? Maggie would love that. She and Jasmine are always teasing me about being old. A cane will just give them more ammunition."

"A cane is less of a hassle for getting in and out of a vehicle. You shouldn't drive, and try to keep most of the weight off that leg for another week or so. We'll pull the cast in ten days. From what I saw, the surgeon we called in did an incredible job. You're lucky to be walking at all."

"I'm lucky to be alive, Doc."

"That's what I understand. One of my friends at the club was telling me the whole story. She made it sound like Maggie was the big hero."

"She was, actually. Neither Angela or I would be here if she hadn't showed up when she did."

"Stacey said she took on several men with automatic rifles, and took them down with just a handgun."

"Your friend is Stacey Lane?"

"Yes. You know her?" I must have made a face. Doctor Hays laughed. "She does embellish on the truth from time to time, but really, she has a heart of gold. We go back a long time, middle school as I recall."

"She's stretching it a little, but she's mostly right. Maggie was amazing that day, like every other day. I'm a lucky guy. But hopefully neither one of us has to get shot, or shoot anyone ever again. I'm ready for something boring, lost dogs, or a cat up in a tree."

"No climbing trees for you." She chuckled, then paused and gave me an odd look. "But, what would you say to handling a delicate matter for me, as my investigator. It would have to be absolutely confidential, just between us."

"Maggie and I are a team, I can't take any job if she isn't on board."

She shrugged. "That's okay, as long as it's completely confidential. How does it work? I have more patients waiting, so I can't go into it now, but soon would be good."

I pulled a card from my wallet. "Text or call and we'll set something up. Maggie is teaching at the Club part-time, but obviously I'm available anytime. Is it urgent?"

"No, but I want to resolve it pretty soon. Sooner would be better for everyone involved."

"I'll give Maggie a heads up, and you two can figure out a time that works for both of you. Her number is on the card. I've been hobbling around the house watching soaps and doing crosswords. Any kind of a case will beat that."

"I would say careful what you wish for, but I don't want to scare you off. It's possible I could do it myself, but that would get complicated."

"That's what we do, try to uncomplicate things. You have me walking again, more or less, so hopefully we can help you."

"Where did you find that cane?" Maggie asked as we got ready for supper. "You could have walked out in the yard and just cut down a tree from the looks of that monstrosity."

Jasmine shook her head. "He wouldn't buy a regular one, claimed they were for old people. I can just see Slater lying on the floor like in one of those commercials. 'Help I've fallen and I can't get up'."

"Don't make fun of the elderly," I cautioned. "If you're lucky, you might be one someday."

"I wasn't making fun of old people, Slater, I was making fun of you. Most of those canes had three legs, so they would stand up by themselves.

Slater had to go old school, like he's John Steed. Is there a switchblade in there?"

"Who's John Steed?" Maggie asked. I had heard the name, but I wasn't sure either.

Jasmine looked back and forth between us. "John Steed and Emma Peel? The Avengers?"

"Isn't that Scarlett Johansson and Chris Hemsworth? Man, that guy is good-looking," Maggie said, digging glasses out of the cupboard.

"Not those Avengers," Jasmine scoffed. "This was back in the day, the BBC's answer to James Bond. You don't know what you're missing," She said earnestly. "When I was locked in Jarrod's basement for two weeks, I watched a lot of old shows, and the Avengers was the best. John Steed was this badass British guy that beat people up with his cane, or maybe it was an umbrella. Doesn't matter, it had a secret knife, and sometimes he stabbed people with it." She looked at our blank faces. "All right, I was really bored, but it was a good show."

I hefted the cane. It was a substantial piece of hickory, with a crook where there had been a knot that now served as a handle. It was easily twice as heavy as it needed to be, but there was no knife hidden anywhere. I made a pass in the air for Jasmine's benefit.

"Careful with that thing, you're going to break a glass," Maggie said. "Did Janet say what she wanted to talk to us about?"

23

"No, just that it was extremely confidential and delicate."

"Delicate?" Jasmine asked.

"Hey, I can be delicate, just ask Maggie."

Jasmine curled her lip. "Spare me."

"I'll bet your Grandmother misses you," I tried.

"Maryanne went to Washington," Maggie explained. "We have custody of Jasmine for a few days, or weeks."

"McCade quit and the other bodyguard needed some time off." Jasmine went on. "I'll be staying in the guest room for a while. Maryanne doesn't want to have to worry about me getting swiped again."

"You and McCade are done? I liked that guy, and he did help save my life."

"He's a little old for me. Basically, I was just using him for sex."

"Stop that! I don't want to hear about that," I admonished. "And don't tell me it's sexist, you're too young to talk about stuff like that."

"Wow. I'm glad you just pretend to be my Dad. We would really butt heads if I was forced to listen to you. I hope Maryanne hangs on for a few more years, until I'm twenty-one at least."

"Hangs on?" I panicked. "What's wrong with Maryanne?"

"Nothing. I'm just messing with you. What do you think the Doc wants? She's not married, so it isn't a divorce case."

"We don't do those, and I couldn't tell you what it's about even if I knew. Part of the PI Code of Ethics."

"As if," Jasmine snorted. "Isn't that the point of hiring a private investigator, to do the dirty jobs the real cops won't? That's why I keep trying to sign up. I'd be good at conning people into telling me their secrets. I do it to you all the time."

"You're too young. Besides, aren't you starting college pretty soon?"

"Not until the winter term. I convinced Maryanne I was too traumatized to go back to school. Stalkers everywhere."

"Maryanne is too smart to fall for that," Maggie objected.

"Yeah, but Slater isn't, you ruined it." Jasmine laughed. "Actually, I just asked her if I could wait until winter semester, or maybe even next year. I missed half of high school because I was partying and getting stoned all the time. Maryanne said she would find me a tutor. Hopefully one that's young, and good looking."

"I'll talk to her about that," I said. "I'm sure we can find some mean old woman that smells like mothballs and has a long ruler to crack you on the knuckles when you aren't paying attention."

"Sounds like your fantasy, Slater, not mine."

"Stop, you two," Maggie spoke up. "Slater, what do you say we look for another airplane tomorrow? We can use it for the business and write it off."

"I can't afford another airplane. I have two houses that haven't sold, and that money needs to go back into the construction business."

"I said we. I just got my pilot's license, and I want to use it. We both love flying, and the river is right there. I know where we can buy a really nice amphibian for a great price. I would have to get certified for floats, but you already are, aren't you?"

"I am. You already looked at one, didn't you?"

"Chip Daniels has a Cessna 172, and he asked if we were interested. I know you don't like the high-wingers, but it's a hell of a buy."

"And the water is soft, in case you crash again," Jasmine added.

I ignored that. "I've seen that airplane, it's nice, like new."

"I can make the down, and we can split the payments, or lease it to the business." Maggie insisted.

"What business? We haven't investigated anything for weeks."

"So, you think we can buy it?"

"You keep saying we, like it isn't your money. I'll admit, I miss the Piper. I can pay you back for the down when one of my houses sell, but we need to investigate something, or I'll have to go back to pounding nails. And that isn't going to happen real soon." I lifted my new cane as evidence.

26

"You know Maryanne will back anything you want to do," Jasmine pointed out.

"She has done enough, and I don't like the idea of using Maggie's money either."

"Once you two get married, you won't have to feel guilty about spending her money." The blue-haired girl said casually.

"I still won't be comfortable spending her inheritance," I said, without thinking. There was an awkward pause as we all looked at each other, then it dawned on me what I had just eluded to. "Okay, I meant, if we get married."

"Too late, Slater. That sounded like a proposal to me," Jasmine roared. "Might as well drop to one knee right now."

"Stop tormenting him, Jasmine." Maggie blushed. "Things are great just the way they are. I already tried the marriage thing and I'm not doing that again anytime soon." She looked at me awkwardly. "Not saying never, just no time soon."

"I'm sure the Butterfly has it all worked out," I said confidently.

Jasmine cocked her head. "You are so weird."

Chapter Two

Roland Dunbar stood when we walked into Tommy Ackerman's office and swept the odd looking, plaid hat he was wearing from his head. Pretty sure they're called flat-caps, the kind newspaper boys used to wear, or displaced Irishmen trying to hold onto their heritage. I don't know why, but I disliked him immediately.

I guessed him to be in his late fifties, tall as me, but rail thin, with curly red hair that was starting to disappear in the front. His bushy eyebrows nearly touched and were sorely in need of a trim. He was wearing a brightly colored, expensive looking silk shirt and a pair of tiny red suspenders that struggled to hold up his pants.

He held his funny hat in one hand and extended the other to Maggie first, then to me. Thin as he was, his hands were oversized claws that didn't seem to fit his frame, gnarled and twisted with arthritis, and he squeezed my hand roughly, like a kid with something to prove. Despite my irrational aversion to the man, I had to acknowledge that he was roguishly good-looking for his age. His eyes, clear and blue, shifted back and forth between us, then settled on Maggie.

His voice was a raspy deep baritone, pleasing to the ear. "I see what you were saying Tommy. The hair's right, and her eyes are very blue. Beautiful eyes you have, Lassie." He tossed the goofy hat on the desk and sat back down. I dropped into a chair and leaned my cane against the wall, then looked over at Maggie. She was as confused as I was.

"Roland has an idea to help with your investigation, Slater," Tommy explained. "I told him a little about you, and he wants to try passing you two off as relatives. That's presuming you decide to take the job. It would mean spending some time in the Keys."

"Tom told me that you'd been shot." Roland peered at my cane. He had just a whisper of an accent that could have been Irish, Scottish, or fake. "That's a clatty bit of luck. But a week or two on my beach and you'll be sound as a dollar." I was a sucker for accents, but I still didn't like him.

"A week or two? That's a pretty big commitment."

"I have a pretty big checkbook, Mister Slater. Sorry Maggie, of course I don't mean to leave you out of it. You are the pretty one. You look to be more my kin than your man here. We'll say you're my cousin's daughter. I don't have a cousin, just an ungrateful bastard of a brother. He lives in Atlanta, and he never goes down to the Keys anymore. It's not likely he'd show up and blow the story."

"You have a home here, and in the Keys?" I asked.

"Aye, yes I do." His eyebrows bumped against one another briefly. "I'm sorry, it's a force of habit, talking the way I do. Sometimes the little bit of an accent works for me. I use it to charm wealthy clients, and it gets to be a habit. I was born in Chicago, so it's phony as a tent-preacher, but I am full-blooded Scottish. Some people find it enchanting when I talk like Ed Sheeran."

"I sure as hell do." Maggie blushed, and giggled like a Bieber groupie. "Maybe I have a type."

"Sheeran's not even Scottish," I grumbled.

"Exactly, but people eat it up," Roland said. "My wife, that is my first wife, she really was from Scotland. She was the fiery one, let me tell you. Hot blooded and hot headed. Incredible woman. Drowned in our swimming pool, four years ago. That's when the trouble started with Isla."

"Pretty name, Isla," Maggie said.

"Pretty as her name, she was." Dunbar dropped his head and stared at the floor for a few seconds. His voice cracked, but he coughed and continued. "Pretty as her mother, and that's saying a lot. We named Isla after her grandmother from the old country. She died young, and I met Caroline shortly before her father passed away too. I was in the Army and I brought her back to the States with me. Easy back then, we still welcomed immigrants."

"What you want us to do, it has something to do with your daughter?" I asked.

"It does. When my wife died there was an investigation because the circumstances were considered suspicious. I was a person of interest. For business reasons, her life insurance was ten million dollars. Mine was twenty, in order to protect our assets. I'm a wealthy man, was then, and much more so now. But at the time my investments were struggling and to some people it might have looked like motive. As I said, Caroline could be a hand full at times, and we weren't getting along very well when it happened. I can admit, it might have looked bad.

"Isla, she claimed to see things, like she had psychic powers or something. She told the police that she saw me swimming with my wife the night she drowned. I wasn't home that night and I was able to prove it, but it got messy. Isla eventually recanted her story and claimed that she hadn't actually seen me. She said that Old Eli told her about it, even though this all happened here in Jacksonville, not down at Big Pine Key."

"Old Eli, who is he?" I asked.

"He's the ghost that came with our beach-house. I never saw him until after Isla died, so when he couldn't talk to her anymore, I guess he started coming to me."

I peeked at Tommy, then at Maggie. It didn't seem like he was joking.

"Old Eli, is he from Scotland too?" I asked with a poorly concealed smile.

"He was a fisherman from No Name Key that went to the bottom during the hurricane of thirty-five. They say he still haunts the neighborhood. Supposedly he was having an affair with the woman that lived in the house that we tore down to build ours, and he stops in sometimes, still searching for her."

I'd heard enough. "Sorry Roland, but ghosts? If you expect us to spend a bunch of our time and your money going all the way to the Keys, you have to be serious about this."

"Have you ever seen a ghost, Mister Slater?" He asked levelly.

"No, I've never seen a ghost, because they don't exist."

"Nobody's ever seen God, but a hell of a lot of people think he's up there. It's not like I've had a real conversation with Eli, but I've heard the stories, and I've seen things; shapes drifting across the room, furniture and knick-knacks rearranged. One night, I'm sure I saw him in the kitchen, looking out over the bay and steering his ship."

"I think you need to talk to a someone else about this Roland. Maybe a professional." I was hoping Maggie or Tommy would end the meeting. Surprisingly, neither of them said a word and he continued with his story.

"Anyway, even after the police concluded that Caroline's death was an accident, my daughter and I kept having trouble. She pulled away from me. I met someone, a younger woman, and remarried. No surprise that Isla hated my new wife. She started spending more time down in the Keys, partying, and I think she was doing drugs. Part of

Caroline's insurance money was hers, and she ran through a small fortune in a hurry. My wife and I went down that first winter and it was tough. Isla was hanging out with the locals and managed to turn most of them against us. Often as not when we were there, she would sleep on the boat. No matter what I said, she held onto the belief that I had killed her mother somehow. I let her live down there, and Ginger and I came back here on a more or less permanent basis. We went down for the occasional weekend, but Isla would barely speak to us."

"When did she pass away?" Maggie asked.

"Every year, all the neighbors up and down the beach have a Labor Day party to end the summer season before people leave to get their kids back in school up north. There are a lot of people my age that have their kids and grandkids with them for the summer, so it's kind of a sendoff. It's turned into a three-day beach party, and we all take turns hosting. Our place is right in the middle of it. Caroline loved to play host, and she was good at it.

"We had an old water tank, the kind cattle drink from?" I nodded, and he rambled on. "We would fill it with ice and beer, pop for the kids, roast a pig and set up a volleyball net. Have one hell of a time. Next night, we'd just slide down the beach to the Jackson's place and do it all over again. Lot of drinking and shenanigans, maybe some skinny-dipping after the kids went to bed, but

33

nothing too wild. There was the time someone got caught in the bushes with JT's wife, but that was a while back, and all's been forgiven." He smiled stupidly at the memory of past parties, or possibly of JT's wife. I pulled him back to the moment.

"Tommy said your daughter disappeared shortly after Labor Day two years ago?"

"We went ahead with the beach party, even though we knew that Hurricane Irma was barreling down on us. That early on, they made it sound like Armageddon, but we said screw it, if our houses were going to get blown off the damn map, we'd make it a weekend to remember. The party started Saturday, and we went straight through until Monday night. By then, everyone was taking the Hurricane warnings pretty seriously, and starting to evacuate."

"That was the worst hurricane I can remember," Maggie commented. "Our house is pretty high up, but the storm surge covered most of the yard, and we lost a dozen trees."

"Our house in the Keys is supposedly Hurricane proof, and the fact that it made it through without much damage was unbelievable considering what I saw everywhere else on the island. If my daughter had stayed there, she would have been safe."

"She ignored the evacuation order?" I asked.

"I thought that she was going to leave with us and come up here. We waited until Thursday afternoon. They're never sure of the track, but we figured if the wind and water were as bad as they predicted, there was a chance the house wouldn't still be standing when we got back. Isla took the boat over to the little marina just west of there, but she knew if Big Pine Key took a direct hit, the Caroline might not be there either."

"The Caroline? You named your boat after your first wife?"

"Yeah, and Isla was more worried about that damn boat than the house or herself. That's why she ran off and stayed behind. She said she had to check in with some friends before we all evacuated, then she never came back. We waited as long as we dared, then drove out of there. I called a hundred times and texted her, but she wouldn't call me back. She had a stubborn streak, like her mother. If I had any idea what she had planned, I would have stopped her. The thing was, a lot of people didn't believe how bad it was going to be. Loving that boat is what got her killed."

"Isla took the boat out ahead of the hurricane, against the advice of the marina," Tommy put in. "Roland has a slip at his house, but they thought the marina would be safer. There was so much chaos, the local police couldn't watch everyone, and she slipped past the Coast Guard by staying in the shallows for as long as she could. That's what we think, we aren't certain."

"We believe she was making a run for Marco Island, hoping she could find a safer spot for the boat further inland," Roland continued. "She must have tried to stay away from the coast for as long as she could, hoping the storm might track east again. She was a wonderful sailor, but the winds would have been too much once the hurricane caught up with her. She went down about fifteen miles west of Rice Island. If she tried to call for help, it was too late. The Coast Guard had been called in by then. No one in their right mind would be out on the water in those seas."

"Did they find the boat?" I asked. I didn't ask about her body, he looked ashen, and his big hands were shaking.

"Yeah, not hard these days. The boat had a GPS locator. The Coast Guard found the Caroline and I hired divers to search for her body. Normally she would have been wearing a harness in that kind of weather, but there was no sign of one. Crazy, trying to beat a hurricane like that." He dropped his head and closed his eyes, then looked up and started again. "It takes five years to be declared legally dead."

"Did you have insurance on her too?" I knew that was rough, but I had to ask.

"Slater!" Maggie snapped.

Roland raised a hand. "No, it's a fair question. No. Mister Slater, no life insurance."

"She tried to out run Hurricane Irma and didn't make it. I'm terribly sorry for your loss, but how can we help you?"

He clawed at the pocket of his shirt, hooked something with a crooked finger, and tossed it on the desk with enough force that it careened into my lap. I slipped the gold chain over my fingertip and lifted it. A delicate broach spun slowly as the chain untangled, then a small key with a large eye slid down the tiny links and settled against it.

"Tell me, who in the hell sent me that, and why?"

"What's the key for?" I asked.

"No idea. It was never on there before, when she was alive."

Maggie reached out for the chain, holding the heart shaped locket carefully in her fingers. She glanced at Roland, who nodded briefly, then carefully triggered the catch.

I leaned over her shoulder and could see the tiny picture of a young woman with dark red hair holding a child in her lap. The little girl's hair was several shades lighter and redder, but they had the same blue eyes and tangled braids that disappeared over their shoulders. It was obvious that they were mother and daughter.

Roland extended a shaky finger and pointed at the necklace. "Since she was old enough to understand anything, the only time Isla removed that necklace was to shower or swim. Other than that, I never once saw her without it. After her mother died, it was even more important to her. Sometimes I insisted that she eat with us, and she would clutch it to her chest while she ate with one

37

hand and talked under her breath, speaking to the broach, or to her poor dead mother; we were never sure which. She was holding onto it like that the last time I saw her."

"It's possible she left it behind before she went to the boat, just forgot to wear it." I reasoned. "There's no sign of water damage."

"No dammit!" He leaned toward me, banging a fingertip on the table. "If she was drawing breath, she would have had it on. The story about checking on her friends was a lie. We found out later she went straight from the house to the boat, then took it out of there a couple days later."

"Okay. How did you get the necklace?"

"It came in the mail a couple weeks ago, with a note. All the note said was, 'Murderer'."

"They said you were a murderer because your daughter took a sailboat out in a hurricane?" Maggie closed the broach and pushed it back toward him.

"That's not what it meant. It arrived four years to the day that we found Caroline dead in the swimming pool. I believe Isla sent it."

"You think she's a ghost too, like Old Eli?" I wasn't trying to be a dick, I really wasn't sure.

"No, of course I don't think that," He spat. "Tommy?" He glanced at the lawyer, then glared back in my direction.

"Slater is understandably confused, Roland." Tommy came to my defense. "You said her boat went down in hurricane Irma, fifteen miles from shore. Anyone would presume she was dead, and you did say you believe in ghosts."

"I swear to Christ I saw Old Eli in my house," He snapped, glowering from under his unibrow. "But I don't think my daughter is a ghost. I think she may be alive, or was. I can't be certain she still is."

As was usually the case, Maggie knew when to jump in. "You think she might be dead now, because she wouldn't have parted with the necklace if she were alive?"

"Never, it was her most prized possession. If she went down with the Caroline, that necklace would have gone with her. There was no way for some random diver who might have found the necklace, to know who the people were inside of it. There is no inscription or any identification. The only people, other than Isla herself, that could have returned that necklace, would be people that knew Isla and her mother very well. Isla looks, or looked, a great deal like her mother did in that photo, which was part of the reason Isla loved it so much. The fact that it was delivered on the anniversary of Caroline's death has to be more than a coincidence."

"Isn't it possible that one of Isla's friends has had the necklace all this time? Someone who doesn't like you?" Maggie asked. The old Scotsman was more tolerant of Maggie's questions.

39

"Isla struggled with her mother's death. She had issues with depression and got into drugs, like I said. She continued to insist that I had something to do with it all. Caroline had demons of her own, which was the real reason we found her in the bottom of that swimming pool. She wasn't well. The coroner ruled it an accidental drowning, but the insurance company fought it because she had taken some sleeping pills, along with her other medications. They claimed it was intentional, that she had taken enough to kill her, even if she hadn't drowned. Suicide would have cut their obligation in half, so of course they jumped on that, and the fact that she was on antidepressants. I had to sue to get the full settlement.

"Isla called it blood money, even though part of it was hers, and told all of our friends on the Key that Ginger and I had plotted the whole thing. For the record, I didn't meet Ginger until after my wife died. Everyone took sides, and people love to gossip. But to answer your question, no, Isla would absolutely never have gotten on that boat without her necklace, and she would never have given it to anyone, willingly."

"Sorry to ask again, but you do understand that a flesh and blood human being sent this necklace to you, right?" I risked.

He drew a ragged breath and the red hue of his skin darkened. I fully expected him to end the meeting and send us packing, but he managed to control his anger. "Mister Slater, when you get to

40

be as old as I am, I hope you'll learn that you don't always have the answer to everything. Peculiar things do happen, and sometimes there is no explanation that makes any sense. I only know that my daughter took the Caroline out that day, and the next day it was at the bottom of the ocean, ripped to pieces by Hurricane Irma. I believe Isla must have went down with that boat, and I also believe she was wearing her necklace when it happened. Yet here it is. If I could make sense of any of this, I wouldn't be asking for your help."

His hands were shaking noticeably and Maggie reached out to cover them, casting a scathing look in my direction.

"My partner doesn't mean to be insensitive, do you Slater?"

"I really don't." And I didn't, but I was at a loss. "But still, that is the question. If your daughter went down with the Caroline and was wearing that necklace, how is it that it's sitting here on this table today?"

"My point entirely." He fell back in his chair. "A part of me wants to believe that she survived somehow. Contrary to what I said about Eli, I doubt the existence of ghosts. As Maggie pointed out, the most logical answer is that one of the dopers Isla knew got ahold of the necklace somehow, and is using it to torment me. Sending it to me on the anniversary of my wife's death would be especially cruel. If she were alive, I don't think Isla would do that."

"I'm sorry Roland, but if Hurricane Irma caught up with the Caroline in open water, the odds of Isla surviving are slim to none. What is it that you think we can accomplish by going down to the Keys?"

"Our parties used to be the biggest on the beach. Everyone loved Caroline, and I always made sure they had a good time, tons of food and booze. Hell, sometimes we didn't even sleep, drank ourselves sober and then started all over. But then Caroline died, and everything changed. The first year it was okay. People seemed to accept Ginger, and the Labor Day party was almost as big as it had ever been.

"But then Isla stayed down there year-round, and Ginger and I only went for a long weekend once in a while. Normally, before Caroline died, she and Isla would spend the summer there, every holiday, and long weekends. I went back and forth to keep the business running. But as I said, after I remarried, Ginger and I stayed in Jacksonville most of the time and just went down for the holidays. Ginger and Isla never really got along."

"May I ask why she isn't here today?" Luckily Maggie spoke up, I was growing impatient.

"Tennis. She thinks this is all a big waste of time. It's her opinion that Isla's old boyfriend sent the necklace, just to be a prick. He is a prick, for what that's worth."

"So, what is it we're supposed to accomplish?" I said again.

"I'm getting to it." The furry red snake over his eyes twisted at odd angles as he wrestled with his anger. He didn't like me, and I wasn't too crazy about him either.

"Last year, Ginger and I were down there for the Labor Day party again, but it was a bust. Like I said, Isla had half of them thinking I'm a murderer. But people talk, Mister Slater, and drunk people talk a lot. Most of the people that were around when Caroline died, and when Isla disappeared, will be at this year's party. My caretaker and his wife live on the property, and he's been spreading the word that I'm selling out to a relative. What better way to meet people than to give them free food and booze?"

"So, you want us to go down there and get everybody drunk, hoping someone will confess to sending you that necklace? That's your plan?" I was incredulous, but he nodded.

"My party was always on Friday night, the Jacksons next door have one on Saturday, and Murphy takes Sunday. By then, everyone is hung over and ready to head back to work. My caretaker will spread the word that you want to meet all the neighbors and continue the tradition. Practically everybody on Big Pine Key comes to these parties, and I'm guessing the person who sent me that necklace is one of them."

"Presuming it wasn't Isla," Tommy added.

43

The old man shrugged. "I realize that's unlikely." He smiled at Maggie briefly, then continued. "I'm sure you can be charming if you really try, Mister Slater, and it's obvious Maggie can. We're going to say you're buying the house because Ginger and I never have time to go down there, but that I want to keep it in the family. If we say Maggie is Isla's distant cousin, that will be a good reason to talk about her disappearance. Loose lips sink ships, and maybe someone will say enough to help you figure this out. That's a poor expression to use, considering." He looked glumly at Maggie. "Mostly, I just want to know what happened to my Isla."

"I have commitments the first part of next week," Maggie pointed out. "Slater?"

"Let us talk about it, Roland. I'm not sure I want to get involved in this, with my leg being the way it is," I said cautiously.

"I know that we got off on the wrong foot, Mister Slater. I lose my temper when I shouldn't, so if that's the issue, I apologize." He extended his large hand.

"Thanks, but it's not that. It's just the logistics and timing of it. Labor Day is a week from Monday, and that doesn't leave us a lot of time to get chummy with the locals."

"All right." He seemed pensive. "Really, I didn't intend to fly off the handle. If it would help, my wife and I could meet you down there on the pretext of getting you settled in. I can take you around and introduce you to some people. Beautiful house, beautiful beach. It will be like a paid vacation. If money is the issue, I can pay extra, whatever you want."

"Maggie and I will kick it around, and we'll let you know before the weekend is over."

He wouldn't let go of my hand, and he seemed desperate. "Tommy said that you can find out the truth of this for me. Please, Mister Slater."

Tommy Ackerman interceded. "Let's let Slater and Maggie have a day to think about your proposal, okay Roland?" I leaned on my cane and stood, since no one else seemed willing to move. Maggie assured Roland that everything would be fine, and Tommy thanked us for coming in. It was clear that I was the odd man out, and that Tommy and Maggie both thought we should take the case. If not for the fact that I had spent the last five weeks bored out of my skull, I would have turned him down flat. Maybe it was the thing with the ghost, or maybe it was the way Maggie kept smiling at him.

"I know what you're thinking." I told Maggie as she held the door open for me and I eased down onto the passenger seat.

"That would be a first." The redhead grinned. "Guys who say that are asking for trouble. Pretty soon I'll expect you to know. That's when things really go to hell."

"Granted. But this particular time, I do know. You're dying to take this case, aren't you?"

"I didn't think there was any question. That sweet old guy just wants to know what really happened to his daughter and have some closure."

"His daughter was a casualty of Hurricane Irma, like quite a few other people. And Old Eli? Admit it, you thought he was good-looking. For crying out loud, he's old enough to be your Grandfather."

She laughed at me. "I didn't think you were the jealous type, Slater. He is kind of sexy. Maybe I just have a thing for Gingers." She laughed again and tousled my hair.

"Now you're just pandering. I'll admit, he does make an impression. I'll bet he was quite the lady's man when he was younger."

Roland Dunbar walked out of Tommy's office, stumbling slightly. He gave us, or probably Maggie, a brief smile and a wave, then fumbled around with the key fob of his car. He set the alarm off, shook his head in frustration, then got the door open and the alarm turned off.

"He seemed lucid enough, talking to him," Maggie said as she climbed into the driver's seat. "But he doesn't act quite right, does he? Think it's dementia, or just the fact that he's getting up there?"

"He's not that old, but maybe he had a mild stroke or something. Might explain why someone his age believes in ghosts."

46

The black Caddy pulled away from the curb, and accelerated quickly. He was a block away when we pulled into the street. Roland wheeled to his right and out of sight, but as we pulled away from the curb a white van drove quickly out of a MacDonald's parking lot further down the street, then cornered sharply in front of the oncoming traffic. Brake lights came on, horns blew, and one car swerved violently to avoid a collision. Either it was a really poor driver making a last-minute decision, or our prospective client had a tail.

Maggie put her foot down. "Know what I'm thinking now, Slater?"

"How much you like to drive fast?" The tires of Maggie's convertible howled their disapproval when she accelerated through the next turn. We caught a glimpse of the van taking a left. "Don't get too close," I cautioned. "He may just be going the same way, and if he is tailing Roland, we're better off holding back to see what's going on."

"Roland has his foot in it. He must realize he's got someone following him."

"Or he's like you, and always drives like a maniac," I commented. We had passed into an industrial section of the city. Warehouses, a storage yard, and an impound lot flashed by as we kept going faster. It seemed likely to me that Maggie's car would end up there shortly.

Roland had to be doing seventy, and the white van looked like it was catching him. Not to be outdone, Maggie closed the gap. I don't know if our prospective client knew he was being chased, or if he always drove like a bootlegger, but he took a hard left with the white van a short distance behind him. Maggie's convertible was built for speed, and we hit the corner a second later, parting wisps of acrid blue smoke left by the tires of the two vehicles in front of us.

At this point it was an all-out road race. I don't know if Roland or the guy in the white van knew we were behind them, but it was clear the white van was trying to catch Roland, or at the very least harass him. We hit two cross streets hard and all three vehicles went air-born. It was getting dangerous.

A light turned yellow in front of us, and the redhead put the accelerator to the floor. We made the light, going like a bat out of hell. We were going too fast for the neighborhood, and too fast for the cop that pulled up just as we shot through the intersection. The lights and siren came on, but unbelievably Maggie kept the gas pedal to the floor. Ahead of us, the white van slowed suddenly. He had spotted us or the squad that was flying up behind us, sirens screaming and lights ablaze. Brake lights came on and the van took a hard right turn, then tore off down an alley crowded with service vehicles. Far ahead, Roland Dunbar's Caddy topped a rise and disappeared from sight.

Maggie finally slowed down and pulled over. She looked over at me. "No idea how fast I was going, that's my story. I'll give him my best smile."

Officer Sandberg and her radar had a pretty good idea how fast Maggie was going, and she wasn't buying any of the redhead's excuses. I made sure my cane was conspicuous, complained loudly about how much my leg hurt, and explained that Maggie was in a hurry to get me home because I needed something for the pain. That didn't stop the stocky woman from writing Maggie an expensive ticket, but at least she decided not to call the tow-truck. After a sobriety test and a thorough search of the car, as well as ten minutes of scribbling and a good old-fashioned ass-chewing, she let us go.

"You were going forty-six miles over the speed limit Miss Jeffries, more than twice what you should have been. Consider yourself lucky that I dropped it to seventy-four, or we'd be on our way to lockup. If you want to get your PI license soon, like you claim, you need to obey the law. If I had given you a ticket for reckless driving, you could end up on probation. Good luck getting your card then."

"Absolutely." Maggie was suitably meek. "Like I said, I was trying to keep the van in sight and I got carried away. Rookie mistake."

"Don't make it again." The gruff woman tore the ticket from her clipboard and handed it and Maggie's license back to her, then soften her tone. "I saw that vehicle cruising the neighborhood

49

earlier. Plate holder said No Name Key, for what that's worth. Didn't run the plate number."

"More than we got." Maggie glanced at the ticket. "Thanks, Bernice."

"Just slow it down. Another ticket like that and you won't be driving for a year. You can mail in the fine, or appear in court. Good-day."

Chapter Three

Summers in Jacksonville are warm, sweltering, if you have a cast on your leg. I had never been a beach guy; too awkward and skinny when I was young, and too busy when I got older, but I was always a good swimmer. My mother accused me of having flippers for feet, and they had served me well during the long hours in the ocean when I was training to be a SEAL. I loved the water, and I still swam laps when I could to stay in shape.

Maggie preferred running, so I had been doing a lot of that up until the time that a bullet sidelined me from both. The healing process had been indeterminately long and tedious, and it was beginning to feel as if I would never get the cast off. Now that I had, I was anxious to move around and start getting some exercise, but I was stuck with the smaller walking cast for another two weeks. I knew it was petty, considering everything else he had done, but I was still pretty upset with Rashad Dinar for shooting me in the leg.

I made a remark to Maggie about it, hoping to start the more important conversation.

"If you had shot Dinar a few minutes earlier, I wouldn't be limping around like this."

"Shooting you in the leg was the least of his crimes, Slater. Stop feeling sorry for yourself. At least you're above ground."

"Thanks for that, by the way." I took the opening. "He sure as hell had it coming."

She dropped the magazine she'd been reading and looked at me.

"You know I didn't shoot him because he had it coming, right?"

"He killed your brother and your uncle, and he was responsible for your father's suicide." I pointed out. "Anyone would understand why you would want to shoot him."

"I hope that's not what you think I would do. If I had shot him because of those things, I couldn't live with myself. I'm surprised you don't understand that. Has to be a guy thing. All that testosterone and aggression you men keep bottled up."

"I just don't want you to feel bad about having to shoot him, that's all. You haven't said a word about it. It's not like you had a choice."

"Exactly, I had no choice. I shot him because if I hadn't, if I had hesitated at all, he would have killed my sister and then you. But I didn't shoot him because he killed Davey, just like I didn't shoot RJ in the foot because he kidnapped Jasmine. I shot Rashad to save two people I love, and I shot RJ so he would tell us where Jasmine was."

"You said that was an accident at the hearing," I pointed out.

"Kind of it was, and kind of it wasn't." She laughed. "If I'm completely honest, hearing RJ yell about how much his foot hurt didn't make me feel all that bad. It turned out well, so my story is that it was a complete accident. I was borderline crazy at that point, and that's not okay. But I've thought a lot about it, and I know shooting Dinar was the right thing."

"And no part of you wanted revenge for what he did to Davey?"

"I would have preferred to see him stand trial and go to prison for all the things he did, but I took no pleasure in shooting him. If killing someone ever makes me happy, I'll get out of this business."

"You're a better person than I am. He's one of the few people I think I would have enjoyed shooting, given the chance."

"Guys are programmed to think they want revenge, even when they know what they really should be after is justice. I think, given the opportunity to turn Dinar over to the police, you would have, same as me, because you're a good person. At least I hope you would."

"I hope that too, but we'll never know." Maybe it was a guy thing like she said, but given the choice between sending Dinar to jail or shooting him, I was pretty sure which way I would have gone. It was enough to know that Maggie was at peace with what she had done. "I still say you're a better person than I am, Red."

"I doubt that, Slater, but thanks."

The airplane was a steal. If it had been my money, and I had more of it, I would have insisted on giving him market value. The good thing about buying an airplane is that it's easy to verify the maintenance and hours of operation. Looking at it, it was obvious that it had been well taken care of.

Chip Daniels was well into his seventies, a former pro football player and real estate agent whose wife had just died of cancer. Now his only desire was to go back to Ohio and buy a house near his two kids, watch the grandkids grow up, and maybe coach their middle school soccer teams. Sooner was better than later he said, and unloading the plane was his last chore before leaving Florida. Maggie wrote him a check on the spot, and we all walked away happy.

"You realize I can't fly until my leg is healed." I cautioned.

"I was thinking I'll just pay to get my certification. There's a training facility this side of Daytona, a two-day course and I won't have to wait for you to heal up. I already have it booked for the first part of next week. That's why I said I couldn't go right away if we take Roland's job."

"Why did you ask me if we could buy the airplane? You already had the deal done, didn't you?"

She smiled coyly. "I knew you'd go for it. All right, I would have bought it either way, but isn't it better if we own it together? Like I said, we'll lease it to the business and write it off on our taxes."

"We should meet with Doc Hays on Thursday. She texted me, she has the day off and she wants to talk."

"Has to be before three, I have a brown belt class."

"Brown belt, that's good, isn't it?"

"Good enough to give me a workout. I'll be sore after that."

"Probably means you'll need a backrub." I said hopefully.

She chuckled. "Probably means I'll take a shower and fall right to sleep."

"Ninety-one, and she let you go?" Jasmine exclaimed. "If that was me, I'd be in cuffs right now, and they would have impounded my car."

"I was really polite." Maggie shrugged. "We were right in the middle of town and we would have flattened anyone that walked out in front of us. I was in the wrong, and she was pretty pissed."

"And flirting was useless," I pointed out.

Jasmine jumped on that. "That's a sexist thing to say, Slater. How do you know the lady cop wasn't gay and would have appreciated it?"

"Really? If I say something like that, anything at all, I'm a sexist pig; when you say it, it's just making up for all the inequality you women have suffered through. How does that work?"

"Pretty well." Maggie grinned. "It's two against one, so give it up, Slater."

"Did you tell the midget we're going to the Keys?" I asked.

Jasmine shot me a dark look. "The Keys?"

"Does this mean we're taking the case?" Maggie asked happily.

"Did I really have a choice?"

"You're the Slater, of Slater and Partners, you always have the final say."

"Right." I pretended like I thought that was true. "It's obvious there's something going on with Roland. That van was definitely after him. I'll talk to Tommy on Monday and hammer out the details. If it sounds feasible, I can take Jasmine with me and we'll get a jump on getting acquainted with the neighbors."

"I get to help?" Jasmine lit up. "Do I get paid? Do I get a gun?"

I snorted. "You definitely don't get a gun. I don't need to get shot again. But you should get paid, because you'll be part of the ruse. You can cozy up to some of the younger people and pick their brains, see what they know about Isla. She was only twenty-five, so her friends are probably closer to your age than ours."

"How cozy do I have to get?" She raised a brow.

"Not that cozy, Mata-Hari. And no drinking! If you're getting paid, you have to be professional. You can't disappear with the first cute beach-bum you see. You'll be helping us gather evidence."

"You gather evidence your way, I'll gather it mine. What's a Mata-Hari?"

"Once I'm certified for the Cessna, I'll fly down and join you," Maggie said.

"Solo?" I asked.

"Kind of the point of having a pilot's license and being certified for floats, Slater."

"Aw, he's worried about you," Jasmine said.

"Quite a bit of open water, and there is a no-fly zone out of Key West," I mansplained.

"Not that far north, and I'm sure we'll cover all that at the classes. Nice that you care Slater, but I'm a good pilot. I'll file a flight plan, and I know all the communication requirements. It's not as if I'm flying at night with no running lights, like someone I won't name."

"If Shorty here hadn't gotten herself kidnapped, I would never have done that." I reminded them. "And if the FAA had caught us, neither one of us would have a pilot's license."

"Is that why you crashed, to destroy the evidence? Good plan." Jasmine nodded.

"Of course." I played along. "It had nothing to do with the fact that RJ had your ransom money and was making a run for it. We could have just let him get away, but by now you'd be a sister-wife, living in a commune somewhere with your bat-shit crazy husband, Jarrod."

Jasmine tossed her head and pointed her nose in the air. "At least he doesn't make fun of my height."

"Fine. I'll go back to calling you, Blue. If you don't like that, dye your hair again."

"Quit you two," Maggie scolded. "One of these days it will get real, and someone will get hurt feelings."

"She knows I'm kidding." I yanked Jasmine in for a hug and all was forgiven. "But really Maggie, flying over that much open water is a little risky."

"So is being my boyfriend, Slater, let it go."

Janet Hays shifted uncomfortably in her chair, looking back and forth between Maggie and me. Thanks mostly to Maggie's efforts, our office was looking quite professional. We each had a desk, although mine was covered with blueprints, and a small conference table with four chairs, which was where we now sat. In silence.

Finally, I broke the ice. "My leg is still sore, but I'm going to start moving more."

The doctor shrugged. "Like I said, listen to the pain. Sorry, but this is uncomfortable for me. I find myself in an unusual position. I'm normally more cautious when it comes to romance, about mixing business with pleasure."

"Anything you tell us is completely confidential," Maggie assured her.

"It's a little difficult because you both know the people involved, difficult and embarrassing. As I said, it makes me look like a homewrecker. But there's also a good deal of money involved."

"Love and money make the world go around, and keep private investigators like us in business," I said. "Take your time, we're not here to judge."

"The money thing was foolish. I gave Derrick Lane a couple of hundred thousand dollars to invest for me. His firm has a great reputation, but he said he would be able to get a much better return if I gave the money directly to him. He put it in some high yield risky stocks, and warned me that there was a chance of a loss. Now he says that it's doing poorly, but that I need to just wait and it will come back. I've decided it's time to move whatever money's left into a safer investment, but I'm having trouble getting any money back from him. He keeps telling me that it just isn't the right time to pull it from the market, but he's been saying that for weeks. I told him I was willing to take a big loss, but he keeps coming up with reasons why he can't give me the remainder."

"I presume you can prove you gave him the funds?" Maggie asked.

"I wrote him a check. I could go after him in court if it comes down to that, but that's the part that's complicated." She looked down sheepishly.

"That's the homewrecker part of this story, right?" I guessed. "How long has it been going on?"

"It started getting serious about six months ago. We fooled around a couple times before that, but now we can't keep our hands off each other. You may have heard that they're considering a divorce, and I'm afraid I'm to blame. I didn't mean to fall for someone who's married. I never imagined myself as a homewrecker, but I want to marry the person I love, and I can finally do that once they're divorced. But the money makes it a lot more complicated."

I had said no judgement, but then I also had said no divorce cases. This was closer than I cared to get. "If you end up getting married, you'll get your money back one way or the other, right? It might take a little persuasion, but your new husband isn't going to cheat you out of that kind of money." I couldn't stop myself. "But if you think he's the kind of guy to steal your money, why would you want to marry him?"

Maggie gave me one of her looks. "I don't think that's what she's saying, Slater."

I shrugged and looked back at Janet Hays. "What are you saying, Doc?"

A wistful smile crossed her face. "It isn't Derrick I want to marry, Slater. It's Stacey."

"Oh." I was lost for words for a moment, but did my best to recover. "Sorry, I presumed that it was Derrick. Ask Maggie, I'm a Neanderthal. But Stacey?"

Fortunately, she found that amusing. "I know, she can seem like a handful. She talks too much and most of the time it's just silliness, but she's sweet and energetic, and I can't help how I feel. Like I said, I don't want to be the cause of a marriage ending, but Stacey has been very unhappy for a lot of years. Derrick is domineering and dismissive to her. Some people just connect, gay or straight, or somewhere in between. We've given up on labels, we just know we want to be together."

"Does Derrick know about the relationship?" Maggie asked. "Could that be why he's reluctant to return your money, to punish you?"

"I've always been a friend of their family, and it's been painful watching the way he demeans Stacey. He is a decent guy mostly, but she seems to bring out the worst in him. He knows she and I are close, but not that it's romantic. Sooner or later that has to come out, but hopefully it will happen after I get my money back. I don't want to go after him legally if I can avoid it. They have two children and I love both those kids. Hurting their Dad would be a terrible way to start my new life as their mother's partner. If it comes right down to it, I will write it off as a bad investment before I take Derrick to court for fraud and traumatize those kids."

"That's a lot of money." I said. "I'm afraid to look at the bill for my leg."

"Even at the rates I charge, I will have to fix a lot of legs to recoup that money," Janet exclaimed. "I'm not sure if you can help me, but I'm open to suggestions. Sooner or later I will talk to my lawyer and have him send a threatening letter, but I was wondering if it would pay to have you just go and talk to him. I keep getting empty promises, but maybe knowing that I'm concerned enough to hire help would get him to take it more seriously."

"Doesn't sound like a matter for an investigator, Janet." Maggie spoke up. "What do you think, Slater?"

"Sorry, but I would have to agree." I was glad Maggie was on the same page. "You should go see him at the office, tell him in no uncertain terms that you need that money back immediately, just so there is no misunderstanding. Tell him that you want to remain friends, and that the money is making that difficult. Once you get the money back, if Stacey goes through with the divorce, then you can confess to being in love with his wife."

"What do you mean, if?" She asked quickly.

"Sorry, but a lot of people make promises between the sheets that they won't, or can't keep. Not saying that's the case here, I just want you to be realistic."

"So, there's nothing you can do for me?"

"Try what I said. If he doesn't come up with the money in another week, talk to your lawyer. If he gets a letter from them, I would bet he'll get your money back to you right away. A guy in his position can't afford to get dragged into court for fraud."

"He and Stacey are at Bayside a lot," Maggie said thoughtfully, and I knew right away we were in trouble. "Maybe Slater and I could go out on the town Friday night and try to strike up a conversation with him, or them, if they're both there. I have heard rumors that they may be considering divorce, but people at the club are always looking for something to gossip about. Obviously, we wouldn't come right out and ask about the money, but maybe we can get a sense of what's going on with them."

Janet drew a breath. "Stacey assures me that she's going to file for divorce soon, so we can be together. I've been around those two for a lot of years and they're good at hiding their problems. They put on a show for people, but it's a toxic relationship and she needs to get away from him. He has never physically abused her, but it might get ugly when she tells him they're done." She teared up. "I just want her to be free of him, so we can be together."

"We can make some discreet inquiries, but there's no legal way for us to force him to return that money. Still, the law should be on your side. You said you gave him a check?"

"Yes, but I did make the check out directly to him, and he did say there was substantial risk."

"For future reference, don't do that." I chuckled. "It may be awkward, but you need to confront him, and explain that if he doesn't return your money, he'll be talking to your lawyer. I doubt that you and he are going to stay on good terms anyway, if his wife leaves him for you."

"Do you think I'm a horrible person?" She cringed.

"Things are seldom that black and white Janet, and we're talking to you on a professional level, not a personal one. But this is why I don't want to do divorce cases, there usually isn't any one individual that's at fault, there's plenty of blame to spread around."

"And sometimes no one is to blame," Maggie said diplomatically. "Sometimes divorce is just best for everyone involved and there's nothing to gain by blaming the other person. Except for my divorce, because my ex-husband was a philandering pig." That lightened the mood, and we ended the meeting.

Chapter Four

"Are you sure we have to do this?" It was early Friday evening and Maggie had insisted that we go to Bayside for supper.

"Janet gave me a small retainer, so we're obligated to at least try. Besides, you look nice in a jacket."

"With my cast and cane? Now I just need a bowler like John Steed." I made a pass at the air as if I were sword fighting.

"Don't tell me, Jasmine made you watch that old show?"

"Classic British television. She was right, and Emma Peel reminds me of you."

Bayside had always been above my paygrade when I was younger, and until Maggie's sister married a multi-millionaire, I had never stepped foot in the place. Angela married Charlie shortly after turning thirty, when he was sixty-seven. Tongues wagged, and everyone was quick to point to the fact that Charlie had upwards of sixty million dollars. The gossips all concluded that Charlie's money could be the only reason the strikingly beautiful Jeffries girl would marry someone old enough to be her grandfather. Considering what I knew now, the relationship made more sense, and it wasn't just about the money.

Angela's father had been abusive in every sense of the word, and never a true father to either one of his daughters. Perhaps that was what drew Angela to Charlie, some deep-seated need for acceptance and respect from an older man. At the time, I had begrudged Charlie their connection, because I wanted to be standing in his shoes. Now, having finally resolved my feelings for Maggie's older sister, I could see that he had been just what she needed, when she needed it.

Charlie had always welcomed me to spend time with them. He had to know that Angela and I shared some history, but it didn't seem to bother him. I had no idea back then that Angela was bi-polar, but during the time she was married to Charlie, she seemed happy and relatively well adjusted. I attributed her good behavior to being happy with her choice in a husband, unusual as it was. Maybe that's all it was, or maybe he just made sure she took her medications. Whatever the reason, Angela loved him, and I had grown to like the guy quite a bit myself. He invited me to the club several times, and I managed to behave myself, until I didn't.

Then there was the unfortunate incident involving a loudmouth drunk and yours truly escorting him out the door and onto the sidewalk. I'd returned from the bathroom to find a guy about my age telling Charlie he had no business being married to someone like Angela, and that he'd be happy to help out in the bedroom if he couldn't get the job done. I was used to dealing with drunks as part of my job in the Navy. Granted, we took a more direct approach than the spoiled inhabitants of Point Road were used to, and it was true that I had had my share of alcohol as well. I do remember asking nicely, once, before walking him out the door and giving him a good shove. Surprisingly, nobody thanked me. Instead, they insisted that I never come back.

The drunk was the son of a founding member, and Charley was the only one who appreciated my chivalry. My eviction held and I didn't step foot in the place again until after I retired from the Navy several years later. Now that I was with Maggie, I was welcomed with open arms, and apparently all was forgiven. I just hoped I would never run into that drunk again, because I doubted the outcome would be much different. I told Maggie the story on the way to the club.

"I must have been in Charleston back then, still happily married, as far as I knew. I can't believe it took you so long to get over Angela."

"I was just waiting for you to come along."

"That's what scares me about marriage. Things change, people change, feelings change. Look at Derrick and Stacey. Seems like they're happily married, two kids, plenty of money, and now they might be getting divorced. And Stacey's having an affair."

"Would it make any difference to you if she was having an affair with a guy?"

"No, cheating is cheating. If she truly thinks she's bisexual, that's one thing, but if she's just bored with her marriage, that sucks."

"See, this is why I don't want to do divorce cases, you're making it personal. Being in the middle of a divorce is always ugly, and I know yours was; but for all the people whose marriages fail, a lot of others don't. Look at Angela and Charlie, they made each other very happy during the time they had together."

"I wasn't okay with it at the time, but he was a good man. I need to apologize to my sister for that. Charlie was helping her through things, and I should have realized that."

"See? Sometimes marriage is a good thing." It was quiet for a long minute. "Someday I'm going to ask, you know that."

She smiled over at me. "And someday I'll say yes. But not anytime soon."

I changed the subject. "I don't know about Stacey, I'm not sure who I'm rooting for."

"She's not as silly as she acts. She kind of rules the roost at my Tae-kwon-do class, and she's slimming down, looks really good. I heard she's doing Yoga and Pilates, plus my class."

"Trying to look good for the Doc?"

"Maybe. If I was Janet, I'd be careful rushing into a marriage with that one."

"Any facts I should know, or are we just gossiping now?"

The redhead shrugged. "Call it intuition. I just think there's more to this than what we know so far."

"That's why you get the big money."

My partner didn't always share every scrap of information with me. On a personal note, it often wasn't my business. On a professional level, she often claimed that she was just showing initiative, sparing me the trouble of exhausting details. One of the more exhausting details she had left out this time was the fact that she had called Stacey Lane and arranged for us to have dinner with them. It made me wonder how small a retainer Doc Hays had given us, and if it was too late to give it back.

"Come on Slater, Stacey isn't that bad, and you like Derrick, don't you?" She said as we pulled into the parking lot of Bayside.

"He's an investment banker." That seemed like explanation enough.

"Then talk to him about financing one of your projects, maybe he'll try to swindle you too, and prove our case."

"I didn't think there was a case," I complained. "This is getting too close to a divorce for my liking. Janet needs to talk to her lawyer. Her attorney should be sending letters instead of us having to be tortured by Stacey Lane."

"Janet's worried that Stacey might be in danger, that Derrick might get violent."

"He's an investment banker," I repeated.

"Fine. Then we're going to have a very nice dinner, compliments of your doctor."

"Right, like she didn't charge enough to fix my leg." I pushed my door open and clambered out on my own. Bad move. The pain in my leg intensified suddenly, but I ignored it and hobbled forward.

"You okay Slater?" Maggie asked, as she slid an arm under mine.

"Just moved it wrong, it'll be fine in a minute." I assured her. I wasn't so sure, but after a few steps, the pain eased. Maggie helped me up the front steps of the place, and we checked in with the maître d who pointed us in the right direction.

I hadn't seen Stacey or Derrick Lane in quite a while. Derrick looked the same, possibly a little thinner and more tired. I knew Stacey had been working out a lot, and it showed. She had slimmed down considerably, and it looked good on her. Most people feel better when they're at or near their ideal weight, even if the charts are unrealistic. She was glowing.

They had a table overlooking the water and they waved us over. I hobbled carefully, still not sure if I'd done something to reinjure the break. Stacey jumped up and helped me into a chair while Derrick looked on, frowning.

"That looks like it hurts," He deduced.

"Yeah. All of a sudden it got worse." It seemed like an opening. "Doc Hays said everything looked really good, so maybe it's just a spasm."

"She's really good. She had our son on his feet in no time when he broke his ankle playing soccer," Derrick said.

"She's a really close friend of ours," Stacey said. "But you knew that, right Maggie?"

"Sure, I see you two talking all the time in class."

"She's practically family," Derrick agreed. "The kids love her."

"Are you taking anything for the pain?" Stacey asked, laying a concerned hand on my arm.

"I have some Vicodin that Janet prescribed, but I don't like to take it unless I absolutely have to. It feels better already."

"Have a drink, that'll take the edge off," Stacey volunteered. "Just don't take any of the Vicodin after you've had alcohol, we all know what that can do."

Angela Jeffries had been to the hospital a couple of times, mixing pills and booze. I was afraid Stacey was referring to that, and that Maggie might take offense, but she cleared herself quickly.

"Derrick ended up in the hospital three years ago. He was taking something for his back and had a couple here at the club. He stopped breathing, scared the hell out of me." She reached out and covered his hand with hers. "Poor guy, what would I have done without you?"

71

"I plan on sticking around darlin', someone has to keep you out of trouble." He cupped his hand in hers and they stared fondly at each other. I hadn't seen them interact much before, but the one time I had, it was him trying to stop her from talking, and her ignoring him. I hadn't seen any signs of him being domineering or threatening, back then. It seemed to me that Stacey might try the patience of anyone, and that Derick did a good job of handling it. Tonight, they were acting like a close, happy couple, not two people on the edge of divorce.

"How's the construction business holding up without the head carpenter?" Derrick asked.

"Head carpenter?" Maggie snorted. "Sorry, Slater, I'm sure they miss you."

"No, Maggie's right," I admitted. "They do better without me being in the way. My guy Luis, he's a genius at building."

"Maybe we should hire him, or you. We're going to do some remodeling soon, build a sun porch."

"Derrick is great at grilling. Once we get everything set up, we'll have you over for steaks. I love that you called, Maggie. I just admire you so much. You're like a superwoman, fighting crime, teaching Karate, and being a pilot. I'm just a boring housewife."

"You do a lot, Sugar, don't sell yourself short," Derrick put in quickly.

It continued that way all evening, through dinner and more drinks. The Lanes, after twenty years of marriage, seemed happy with each other and very much in love. If they were putting on a show for us, they were very good actors. And if Stacey Lane was planning to leave her husband soon to be with Janet Hays, she deserved an Oscar. Or so I thought.

I hadn't moved in a couple hours, and inevitably I needed to go to the bathroom. I got up carefully, balanced on my cane, and started toward the bathrooms which were in the back of the club. Maggie started to rise, but Stacey stood quickly.

"I can help him, I have to pee too. You two don't talk about us while we're gone." She giggled. She was pretty tipsy, and was absolutely no help in getting me to the bathroom.

We made the corner of the entrance, where the men and women usually separate, and things went south. Stacey smiled up at me and closed in. "You're lucky you're in such good shape, Slater, you'll heal a lot faster. Maggie is a lucky girl."

I don't get hit on very often, or ever. But there are signals everybody knows. Her voice dropped an octave, then she turned toward me and started reaching. I leaned back and tried to get my cane in position to back up, just as her hands started wandering. A lot. I grabbed her wrist and pushed her away as gently as I could.

"I think maybe you've had a little too much to drink, don't you?"

"I've had just enough, otherwise I would have chickened out. Derrick doesn't really mind if I have some fun, and I won't tell Maggie if you don't." She continued pushing against me, and her little hands were everywhere they shouldn't have been. It was hard to believe she only had the two. I knew the kitchen staff would have a pretty good view if they came out, and beyond the obvious, I didn't want everyone in the club thinking I was a willing participant.

"Stacey, I'm not interested. Go to the bathroom like you said you were going to do, and we'll pretend this never happened, okay?"

"God, you're a party pooper. Who knows, maybe Maggie would be into it." She actually tried to follow me into the men's room, and I started getting mad.

"Pretty sure she wouldn't Stacey, and if I were you, I wouldn't ask her. That wouldn't go well. I'm not kidding, just go to the bathroom and stop it!"

She finally gave up and I locked the bathroom door behind me. She didn't say anything when I came out, just smiled demurely, then started rattling on about how the club needed to fix the hot water as we got back to the table. We made it through another half hour of the charade, then I complained about my leg and said that we needed to leave.

"Well that was interesting." Maggie said after she had started the car.

"One word for it. Torture, is the one I had in mind."

"Derrick tried to talk me into investing with him as soon as you and Stacey left to go to the bathroom. Sounded like the same arrangement he offered Janet."

I grimaced. "Coincidently, Stacey offered me the same arrangement Janet has too. Not exactly like Janet's, because I'm a guy, but you get the idea."

Maggie couldn't stop laughing when I told her the details of my sexual assault. "I told you she has a thing for you, Slater."

"I didn't think it was all that funny. I was pretty defenseless, and she was trying to push me into the bathroom and have her way with me."

"See what us women have to put up with? I warned you. Big ginger like you, she couldn't resist. I knew she had a thing for you."

"Maybe."

"Sounds like a thing to me." She looked at me curiously.

"Maybe that's all it was, or maybe it's just the way they work it. She softens up the targets, like she's doing with Janet."

"She sleeps with the people he swindles, to keep them quiet?"

"Janet said if it meant hurting their kids, she'd just take the loss. They know you have part of your Dad's estate. Derrick offers you an investment and Stacey sleeps with me so I'll talk you into investing, then keep you quiet when it goes south."

"She just had too much to drink and wanted to jump your bones, Slater. I can't believe Derrick would whore out his wife like that."

"Maybe it's usually women. Maybe he gets in on it." I lifted a brow and fought a smile.

She glared over at me. "Why do you men always go to the threesome? I really doubt Janet would have any part of that. She's convinced Stacey's in love with her and they have a future."

"I don't think Stacey sees it that way. If she does, she's really putting on a show for Derrick. And if she's in love with either one of them, she shouldn't be trying to get her hands in my pants."

"Maybe it isn't any kind of scam at all. Maybe she's just a horny little slut." Maggie growled. "I hope she enjoys a little pain, because our next Tae-kwon-do class is going to be a bitch."

I grinned. "Now that's sexist."

"Did you guys break the case?" Jasmine asked Maggie as I fell into my favorite chair.

"That's confidential information." I pointed out.

"I just wanted to say break the case. Maggie says I'm on the team, so why don't I get to know what's going on?"

"I said you could ride along when we go to the Keys, not that you're on the team. Besides, there are only three of us, that's a very small team."

"You said I could help investigate. From the looks of you, you shouldn't be going down there at all. Maybe Maggie and I should just go alone." Logic wasn't working, so she switched to sympathy. "Is it hurting again?"

"Yeah, I twisted it a little getting out of the car. Maggie, did you tell Jasmine she was on the team?"

"I may have implied that. Would you like another beer?"

"I know what you're doing. You two are conspiring against me."

Jasmine ignored my comment. "So is Stacey Lane switching teams and ditching her husband?"

"So much for confidentiality." I took the beer Maggie proffered and tried to look upset. "Not a word of this, Blue, to anyone. It's part of the job description."

"Cool. That means I am on the team." She grinned. "I figured Doc Hays was queer, but I wouldn't have guessed Stacey Lane would swing that way. I'm pretty good at telling."

"I thought the word queer wasn't politically correct."

"Semantics. It's back in use, Slater. Hard for an old guy like you to keep up."

"I'm nice to everyone as long as they're nice to me, that should be good enough," I groused.

"Slater thinks it's all part of the way they scam people." Maggie laughed in my direction. "Stacey got handsy with Slater tonight. While her hubby was trying to talk me into an investment, his wife was trying to talk Slater out of his pants. Risky move for her."

"Slater, you old dog! But he didn't go for it, obviously, so why is it risky for her?"

"She forgot she's in my class tomorrow," Maggie said pointedly.

"You better not let on you know what happened," I said. "Let's let them think we might be interested, and see where it goes." Their eyes widened. "I mean pretend you might invest, of course. I'm not going to fool around with Stacey Lane, case or no case. Besides, if all goes as planned, I'll be on the beach in the Keys, far away from those wandering little mitts of hers."

"Me too." Jasmine grabbed my beer and took a swallow. "Breaking the case."

"And acting professional." I retrieved my beer. "You're too young to drink."

"You think no one will be drinking at this three-day beach party?"

I smiled back at her. "I'm sure they will be, but you will not."

Jasmine made a face and looked at the redhead. "He's not going to let me drink? I used to drink Cletus's buddies under the table, and I was only seventeen then."

Maggie came to my defense. "And you're only eighteen now. Slater and I are responsible for you, despite the fact that you're eighteen and we all know you've been around the block, as you like to say. You may have to fake it to fit in, but no getting drunk. We don't have much to go on, and the idea is to get the locals talking, let them be the ones who have too much alcohol and say something they shouldn't. I still don't know how talking to a bunch of drunks is going to help us figure out who sent that necklace."

"Isla's ghost. That's what our client thinks," I told Jasmine.

"Cool. I've never seen a ghost."

"And you never will," I assured her.

Looking back, I'm still reasonably sure I was right.

Chapter Five

Sometimes things work out the way we hope they will, the way they should. Angela Jeffries was bi-polar, had been sexually abused by her father, struggled with pills and booze for a good number of years, and was nearly killed by the same man that had shot me. Despite all of that, she had finally found her happiness.

There was a time early in my life, when I thought people like Angela Jeffries couldn't help being happy, and it always surprised me that she wasn't. Her family was wealthy, her house was a mansion, and she was easily the most beautiful girl I knew. But behind the haunting gaze of eyes so blue that they seemed other-worldly, and the ethereal beauty of her perfect face, was a young woman whose pain I misunderstood.

I had attributed her fits of anger to some failing on my part, or in moments of weakness, to arrogance on hers. But Davey Templeton had seen through the façade, realized the depth of her misery, haunted as she was by her father's abuse. I still wasn't sure of the day when they became aware that they were brother and sister. They had always been closer than most siblings, and he was the one she turned to when things were blackest. But close as they were, even Davey hadn't been able to break through the barriers Angela had erected to keep that darkest of secrets. She had confessed it to him finally, shortly before he was taken from her forever, leaving her even more broken than she had been.

Yet here she was, suddenly made whole and happy by her love for the newest addition to the Jeffries family, a recently turned fourteen-year old girl that Maggie and I had snatched from the clutches of a degenerate pimp.

Gabriela Martinez had survived gang-warfare, the murder of her parents, and a kidnapping that resulted in her being sold on the streets, just another victim of child trafficking. Like Angela, she had survived a lot of mistreatment at the hands of people who should have only wanted the best for her. In that way they were kindred spirits, Angela and Gabriela, and I wasn't surprised that the day was intended to be more than a simple birthday party.

Jasmine went over a couple of hours ahead of us and Maggie finished baking, while I sat on the couch with my foot elevated. I had called Janet and that was her suggestion, that and another prescription. I was trying to tough it out, and avoid ending up as another statistic of the opioid epidemic.

"Janet wouldn't prescribe something that you don't need, Slater," Maggie offered. "I'm sure she's trained to watch for signs of dependency."

"She doesn't think I reinjured it, so I'm going to try not to take that crap unless I have to.

I'll take it to sleep, but during the day I'll just grit my teeth."

"My hero," She said dryly. "Did she ask you about our investigation?"

"Investigation? I said we'd try to figure out if Stacey's marital troubles are real, that was it. I told her it seemed like they get along really well. Of course, she refused to believe me and said they were just good at faking it. She doesn't want to know the truth. I hate when people hire you to do a job, then argue with you. When Luis tells me we need twelve bundles of shingles, I don't tell him he's wrong, that we only need ten, I order twelve bundles, because he's the expert."

"People are more complicated than shingles, Slater. And I may have told her we'd dig a little deeper." She scrunched her nose in my direction.

"Of course you did, because you're complicated. Didn't we talk about divorce cases, and agree to steer clear of them?"

"We did, but I don't think it's as simple as that. The supposed divorce may just be part of the con. If they're swindling Janet and other people, we should put a stop to it."

"Maybe people shouldn't sleep with people that are married to someone else, Janet Hays included. We don't know that Stacey and Derrick are working together. Maybe Stacey just has trouble being faithful. It's very possible that she finds me irresistible."

"I do, so why wouldn't she?"

I doubted her sincerity. "Regardless, we're already committed to helping Roland, and he said money is no object. I like the way he thinks. I didn't take to the guy at first, but now we have an airplane to pay for."

"I like him, and not just because of his money. I don't think he murdered his first wife."

"Based on the fact that he talks like Ed Sheeran, and you happen to think he's good looking?"

"You think Ed Sheeran is good-looking? Maybe in an orphan puppy kind of way, but he doesn't do a lot for me."

"You exhaust me," I admitted, and closed my eyes for a nap.

There were more people at the party than I expected. After my siesta, my leg felt considerably better, and I was able to hobble along beside Maggie as she carried her baked goods and our present into the house that now belonged solely to Angela. I had been told that her mother had moved in with her new boyfriend, but she made an appearance at the party and talked to me briefly. Maggie claims her mother has always liked me, but I still feel like the cleaning lady's kid when I'm around her. That may be my problem, not hers.

Most of the extended family was there, and a few people I didn't know. Andrew Mitchel, Angela's sometimes boyfriend was nowhere to be seen. I had heard rumblings that he might not be returning. Some things work out, and some things don't. I feel pretty lucky in that regard.

"Slater!" Susan Foster called to me, and walked over. "I got shot a week before you did, and I'm over it. Are you sure you're not just milking this so Maggie will be extra nice to you?"

"Do you know my girlfriend?"

Susan Foster worked for a branch of Homeland security, unnamed and semi-secretive. She spent most of her time pulling kids out of bad situations; immigrant girls like Gabriela and a lot of girls from our own country that had taken a wrong turn. She and Maggie's brother had worked together before he died, rescuing young women from a variety of brothels, both in the US and overseas.

She would never divulge exactly who it was she worked for, but when she wanted something done, it happened. The FBI and the local police, no matter where she was at the time, seemed to be at her beck and call. She had extricated Maggie and me from a couple of sticky situations with just a phone call.

Surprisingly, killing Dinar hadn't raised any red flags, but shooting Randy Jenkins in the foot meant Maggie was without a permit to carry her gun for the next year. Susan couldn't fix that one. Florida's Stand Your Ground law allowed Maggie to dispatch Dinar, but blowing off two of RJ's toes was considered reckless discharge, even though it helped us find Jasmine. I had to admit, there was a certain amount of justice in the ruling, given that Dinar was a twisted psychopath, and Randy Jenkins was a bungling doofus. An eight-toed doofus that was behind bars.

"I didn't know you had met Gabriela. Not that I'm complaining, it's great to see you." I attempted a hug and nearly fell over.

"Careful, Slater." She steadied me easily, then stepped back. "I needed to talk to Angela right away, and she said to just come to the party. She introduced me. Gabriela's a wonderful girl. I'm glad I could help with the immigration interview."

"Part of the birthday celebration, I guess. Sounds like the adoption is going to go through. Angela didn't want to tell a bunch of people until it was a sure thing."

"I have a couple of kids that need a place for a few days and Angela said she could put them up. She's volunteered to foster a few kids, one or two at a time. Gabriela is on board with it too. She can translate and help make the kids feel more comfortable, being she was in their shoes not too long ago."

"There's plenty of room in this old house now that Angela's Mom moved in with her new boyfriend. It's ironic, after what Frank and his brother did, that it would end up as a sanctuary for abused children." Jasmine wandered over and I extended my arm around her shoulder and dropped my hand onto her head. "This is my pet

Smurf, Jasmine, although Maggie claims the better half. I get the rebellious, sarcastic side. Have you met Blue?"

"I introduced myself, Slater." Jasmine slapped my hand away. "And I'd be nice to you once in a while if you were nicer to me. Susan was telling me all kinds of good things about some guy named Eric, and I had no idea it was you she was talking about."

"Slater and I go back a little," Susan acknowledged, nodding her head at me. "He gets himself in a lot of scrapes. Good thing you're joining the team. Maybe between you and Maggie, you can keep him out of trouble."

"How is it everyone seems to know you work for me, but me?" I asked the smiling blue-haired girl.

"You said I was going to the Keys to help investigate, and getting paid. I'm excited, so I may have told a few people." She made a face and spoke to Susan. "He won't let me have a gun."

"That sounds reasonable, considering his other partner got a little trigger happy," Susan replied.

"RJ's a jackass and I'm glad Maggie shot his stupid foot. He talked Jarrod into the whole kidnapping thing. Jarrod is pretty weird and he maybe has some head problems, but he's not a bad guy at heart."

"Jasmine has been visiting Jarrod at the penitentiary," I explained. "He couldn't win her over by chaining her up in his basement, so he's hoping for some conjugal visits."

"Sometimes you find love in unexpected places, right Jasmine?" Susan asked.

"I'm probably going to marry Jarrod when he gets out, Slater, and make you walk me down the aisle," Jasmine said seriously.

"Yeah, right." I laid on the sarcasm. "I know for sure you're smarter than that."

"Slater, why do you have to always be so mean?" Jasmine said softly and dropped her head. Soon tears were trickling down her freckled cheeks.

Horrified, I fumbled to apologize. "Jasmine, I'm sorry, I really am. If you care about Jarrod it's none of my business. Don't cry, please."

Before I could continue, she tossed her hair back, laughed loudly, and turned on her heels. "Got you, Slater! You are such a rube."

"Wow." Susan grinned at me. "Someone has you wrapped around her little finger."

"I guess. I can't believe I fell for that. Maggie just warned me about picking on her, and when she started to cry, right away I thought I went too far. You don't think they set me up?"

"Smart kid. I doubt you have to worry much about that one."

"I'm taking her to the Keys with me to start on a case while Maggie gets certified for the new plane. We went with floats this time."

"What's the new case?"

"Ever hear of Roland Dunbar?"

"Lost his daughter in Hurricane Irma?"

"Lost is what we're hoping for. It's presumed she went down with her boat trying to outrun the storm. Roland hopes not. How is it you know him?"

"I don't know him personally, but he has a lot of money, and he gets his name in the paper all the time."

"I really need to read more," I admitted.

"Everybody does. But I'd heard the name somewhere else. His brother did some time years ago, and his DNA popped on a case I was working on down in Miami, the brother's, not Roland's. Turned out to be a dead end, but I suspect Ross Dunbar isn't the good guy his brother seems to be."

"Seems to be?"

"I shouldn't have put it that way." She shrugged. "All the evidence says he didn't kill his wife."

"It scares me what you're able to find out about people. What was the brother in for?"

"Statutory rape. They reduced the charge because the girl changed her story and said it was consensual. Didn't matter, she was underage and the State prosecuted with what they had."

"Considering what Maggie's Dad and Uncle were in to, I don't want anything to do with brothers like that again."

"Ross lives in Atlanta, and had an alibi for my case. But everything I've heard about Roland

Dunbar is all good. Can you even work? You look like your struggling."

"I tweaked it again last night, but it'll come around."

"Eric! Why aren't you sitting down?" I turned and saw Edith Templeton walking up, a present tucked under her arm. She had always treated me like a member of the family when I was her son's best friend, and even more so since his death. She gave Maggie and me full credit for finding Davey's killer, and she had expressed her gratitude with an abundance of cookies and concern while I mended on the couch.

"I'm supposed to start using it, and get some exercise. Thanks for coming, Edith."

"It's so nice and cool. I was going to walk over, but there's someone parked down the road between my driveway and the Fishers. I didn't like the looks of them, so I drove instead. They better not be traipsing around in our woods, or Eddy will shoot them."

"Maybe somebody having car trouble," I offered.

"Maybe, but I didn't recognize the van. I know most of the people living down your way. Could be a service truck, but it didn't have any signs on it."

"What color?"

"White. Too far away to make out the guy sitting in it."

"Did you get a plate number?" Susan asked.

"Eric is the Private Eye, not me." The old woman chuckled and held out her hand.

After the introductions, Edith made her way into the house. I eyed Susan, and without further explanation she opened her car door for me, and we drove out to the road to check on the white van. It was gone. It might have been someone stopped to use their phone so they wouldn't flatten a pedestrian, or it may have been the same van Maggie and I had chased through the streets of Jacksonville a few days before. Hard to know. We returned to the party in time for cake.

After we ate and Gabriela tore through her presents, Angela announced the pending adoption. While everyone cheered and gave teary-eyed speeches, I made my way over to Tommy Ackerman.

"Looks like you can tell your client that we'll take his case," I told him as we watched the festivities.

"Good! You two didn't hit it off, but he really is a good guy. He told you that I helped him before, but the thing with his wife got dicey. Isla swore up and down he was there, swimming in the pool with Caroline the night she died."

"And he said he was somewhere else."

"Now, I'm not divulging privileged information, since we both are working for him and it came out in open court." He looked at me from the corner of his eye.

"Okay, I'm not judging. I won't give you a hard time if you sell your client down the river."

"Funny. Roland was at another woman's house that night, here in Jacksonville. A married woman. It wasn't easy to get her to talk, since she's the wife of a state senator."

"No kidding? Which one?" It was worth a try.

He grinned. "Won't say, because lawyers have a code of ethics."

"Fine, you got me. Doesn't matter, unless she was lying. He did say that he wasn't getting along with his wife, not that that's any excuse."

"Again, because it's germane to the case, I think he strayed on a regular basis. He was kind of a hound. He told me Caroline knew, and that maybe she was straying too."

"I would think he'd be too old to be chasing around like that. Why the hell can't people just get married and be happy?"

"I am, Camille and I. If you're thinking about it, don't let people like Roland Dunbar change your mind." He cocked his head. "Are you thinking about it?"

"No. Maybe. Someday. Maggie's happy with the way it is, and I'm not going to rock the boat." I deflected. "Any chance Roland was fooling around with his current wife back then?"

"He says no, but if he's going to lie to his wife, why wouldn't he lie to you and me? Caroline spent a lot of her time down in the Keys while he was up here, so he had plenty of opportunity."

"It's going to be almost impossible to get anyone to open up to us, and it sure won't help if our client isn't telling the truth. One of us has to sit him down and explain that. If he's serious about finding out who sent that necklace, he can't be covering things up. Maybe it's someone he was fooling around with, a jilted lover just trying to make him miserable."

"That's why you and Maggie are perfect for this job. There's no hard evidence, but you're both good at reading people, and I'm betting Maggie can sweet talk Roland if it comes to that."

"There'll be no sweet talking. If he isn't straight with us, we'll walk. And you can tell him I said that. Is he all right? It seems like he's not all there sometimes, and he shakes a lot. Did he have a stroke? Maybe he's not a liar, maybe he just remembers things wrong."

"I'll call him before I leave and let you know how he wants to handle it. He said if you decide to take the case, he and his wife would go down and make the introductions. The caretaker and his wife were told that you and Maggie aren't really buying the place, but nothing beyond that. He trusts them, but the only person that knows the whole truth is his wife, Ginger, and she's not thrilled. She'll go along with whatever Roland wants as long as he pays her club membership and gives her expensive jewelry. I was surprised she complained about the idea. It's not like she wanted to go down there for the Labor Day party anyway, and she was never a big fan of Isla's. She would just as soon he forgot about the whole thing."

"Trophy wife?"

"I'd say, and maybe a gold-digger. She didn't want to sign the prenup, but I convinced Roland she had to for the good of his company. She'll have a share, but she'll never have complete control. She's about Maggie's age, and very easy on the eyes. Caroline wasn't dead a month and she'd already moved in. That's what made Isla so crazy. Crazy mad anyway. She called me to see if there was anything I could do about it."

"You knew Isla? This is news to me."

"Client privilege, remember." He grinned again. "She was an amazing kid, beautiful and smart as hell. Graduated from college at twenty. She was one of those people that took over a room when she walked in."

"Like her Dad?"

"I know you don't care for him, but he can do that. Charisma, I guess, and he has the Midas touch. He said Isla was doing drugs and acting crazy just before she died, but I never saw it."

"Do you think he knows more than he's telling us?"

"After seventeen years of doing this, Slater, I can tell you that the client always knows more than he's telling you, and Roland probably more than most. I like the guy, but he's always working

93

an angle. He may really think Isla's alive, or he may be just fishing for information. My guess is he's hoping you'll uncover something else while you're asking around about Isla, something he can't find out for himself. I don't think his neighbors trust him, after two deaths in four years."

"But you do?"

"The counsel-man's wife was very convincing. He didn't kill his wife, and he adored Isla. He says that she poisoned the neighbors against him, but I don't think she would have done that. I talked to her once about a year before the hurricane, and she said then that she wasn't convinced her father had killed her mother. She was back and forth on it."

"Did she have any theories?"

"It was ruled an accidental drowning, but Isla thought Ginger was involved somehow. That was the last time we talked. I texted her a couple times, but she never responded. I suspect she didn't trust me, since I work for her Dad."

"Think she tried to investigate on her own?"

"If she did, she was quiet about it."

"And she took the Caroline out of the marina just before the storm?"

"You know what I know about that, what Roland told us."

"I'll talk to the marina. I'm sure everybody in the Keys remembers what they were doing the day before Irma hit. The boat was hers to take, but I would have thought someone at the marina would call the Coast Guard if they knew what she had in mind. Of course, once the storm hit, they would have pulled their crews in, but it didn't sound like she waited until the last minute. Maybe they figured she could outrun the storm."

"Not much of a sailor myself, that's your forte." Tommy said.

"The boats I was on, we usually just dodged the big storms and rode out the squalls. But Irma was nothing to mess with, I don't care how big a boat you had."

"The Caroline was a forty-two-footer, I know that much. Is that big?"

"Fine for off-shore, day sailing, but I wouldn't want to go out in rough stuff with a boat that size, especially single-handed. Then again, people have sailed smaller boats around the world. Still, insanity to try to outrun that hurricane by herself. She must have been a very good sailor, but then she should have known better."

"She worshipped her mother, and it was like that boat was a part of her."

"Did she really buy into the ghost thing?"

"A lot of people believe in the unseen, Slater."

"Unseen and undead are very different things, Tommy. When people start talking about seeing ghosts, it's time to get the net out."

He laughed. "You're usually willing to accept other people's ideas, Slater."

"You can believe in the Butterfly, or not believe in the Butterfly, but dead is dead."

"You need to write a book, expound on your theory."

"I think that's been done. Let me know the details and I'll tell Jasmine to pack her bags."

"Think she's ready to be a detective?"

"I don't think Maggie wants to leave an eighteen-year old alone in her house for a week. Blue is pretty sensible, but that would just be asking for trouble. We told Maryanne we would keep an eye on her and keep her out of trouble, so she gets to go along."

"She's never going to want to go back to school, especially if you figure this thing out. How many people get to play detective when they're eighteen?"

"I'll be an extra mean, overbearing boss. By the time Maryanne gets back, Jasmine will be begging to go to college," I assured him.

"Sure you will Slater," He scoffed, then spun his wheelchair toward the festivities. "The day that happens is the day I'll start believing in ghosts. I'll call Roland before we leave."

Chapter Six

"We drive all the way to Marathon, pick up Roland and his wife, then go for another half hour? I'm sick of driving, and my butt hurts." Jasmine leaned back in the seat of Maggie's convertible and pushed harder on the accelerator.

"Yes, and we don't have to be there until nine, so you don't have to drive like the redhead. You both need to slow down."

"Do you think Maggie will make it down there with the new airplane?"

"Of course she will, she's a great pilot. She has to file a flight plan because of the Naval base, so if she does have trouble, at least we'll know where to look. But she's not going to have trouble, it's a routine flight." Over the Everglades and a hundred miles of open water, but I wasn't worried.

"Our cover is that she's a fifth cousin of Isla's?"

"Something like that, a distant cousin, because they never met. We don't want people who knew Isla quizzing Maggie."

"And what about me?"

"What about you?"

"What's my cover? Am I your daughter from a previous marriage, or just an incredibly attractive hitch-hiker that you're taking advantage of?"

"Good Lord, not that. And you're too old to be my daughter."

"Really? Okay, just so you don't have to admit your age, I'll say you're my uncle. My surprisingly young uncle that looks old enough to be my father."

"I guess we have to say something so people don't think…that other thing."

"Maggie's due in Thursday afternoon, right?"

"Worried I'm going to be too rough on you between now and then?"

"Not unless you want to walk home, and with that leg I wouldn't advise it."

"Maybe you'll see the ghost of Eli, and want to leave early."

"If I see a ghost, I'll stop smoking whatever it is the locals are growing."

"You can't get stoned, Jasmine." I tried to sound stern. "You're getting paid to be able to think straight and ask the right questions."

"I love messing with you. I won't inhale, okay? You know some of Isla's friends have to be stoners, and they'll want me to have a hit or two. It sounds like she was kind of wild, and a lot of people smoke pot these days."

"Not me." I said stubbornly. "A few beers, and maybe a bump of Scotch now and then."

"When I was with Cletus, I got stoned all the time. But I stayed away from the pills. All you had to do was look at him to know taking that crap was a bad idea."

"For what it's worth, Sidecar says Cletus is doing really well up north."

"Sidecar? Is that Brandon?"

"I told him you were staying with Maggie and me, and that you were doing great. No middle-aged bikers in your life these days."

"That relationship was a horrible idea, start to finish. Thanks again for getting me out of that mess, Slater. I hope Cletus is okay and everything, but if I never see him again, that would be fine by me."

"Is the white van still back there?"

She glanced in her mirror. "He's a long way back, but I caught a glimpse of him a few minutes ago."

"He probably knows where we're going, and he's hiding in traffic. Good thing, I'd hate to get into something when there's just the two of us."

"You should let me have a gun," Jasmine tried, then laughed. "You're right, I would be more likely to shoot myself or you, than whoever is tailing us."

"It's possible it's not even our guy."

"He's been behind us for five hours. We stopped for food and a bathroom break, and he's still back there. No way he's not following us."

"That was a test of your PI instincts."

She smiled vaguely and looked in the mirror again. "When we get off the Turnpike, I'll pull into the rest-stop, then we can see if he's waiting down the road when we head south again."

"I doubt he's going to do that. Just concrete, brush, and water from here south, so he'd be too easy to spot. I am curious to get a look at him, but he hasn't done anything to us."

"I wonder why he was chasing Roland?"

"Not sure, but there was definitely something going on."

"Bet our client knows. Are you going ask him?"

"Our client?" I grinned.

"Hey, you said I was on the team." Her bottom lip protruded impishly.

"Consider it a paid internship, until you go back to school."

"If I go back."

"Of course you'll go back, won't you? Maryanne is going to want you to run her company someday."

"So I can buy more oil wells and screw up the environment even worse than your generation has? No thanks." She motioned to the west. "By the time I'm Maryanne's age, all this will be under water if things don't change."

"Probably true, unless people like you do something to change it. Maybe you could help Maryanne transition out of fracking and go green. Of course, you'd need a few college degrees to do that."

"You're taking this uncle stuff pretty seriously, Slater." She gave me a smile. "Or is it that you just don't want me playing detective?"

"I get to do it, so you might as well too. But maybe you can do both."

We stopped at a rest area south of Florida City where the turnpike ended. While Jasmine went in to use the bathroom, I stretched my leg and watched the highway with my field glasses. The building stood off the road a bit, slightly higher than the road. I had just a second, and used it to look at the driver, not the license number. I couldn't see much. Dark glasses with bright yellow frames, a floral shirt, and a floppy hat that covered a good deal of his face from my angle. I caught just a glimpse of a smoky beard and a shock of grey hair that protruded from the back of the hat, possibly a ponytail. The hat shifted momentarily as its owner turned his gaze in my direction and I thought I caught a trace of a smile.

I kept the glasses trained on the van, but a grove of trees and an inopportune semi-truck made it impossible to pick up the license-plate number. Jasmine got in the car and we headed south, following the ribbon of concrete that split the miles of uninterrupted marsh east of the Everglades.

"Wow, not much out here." She commented.

"Once we get down around Key Largo the scenery gets better."

"I'm not easily impressed, Slater."

I shrugged. "We'll see."

"Okay, I'll admit it, this is awesome." Jasmine exclaimed as we neared the Marathon airport. "Why did I waste my time in North Dakota, when I could have been partying here?"

"Because you were too young, and still are. Did Maggie tell you anything about Roland?"

"She said he was good-looking for an old guy. We kind of had a meeting and she filled me in on what he said."

"Maybe, since I have the PI license, I should be at these meetings."

"We talked about you, better you missed it."

"If we ever need to hire another person, it's going to be a guy."

"Make it a cute one."

We turned into the airport parking lot and pulled up near the building. At Janet Hays' suggestion, I had picked up a temporary handicapped tag. I felt like I should prepare Jasmine for the meeting. "Roland is due in shortly, and he has his wife with him, so acting professional starts now."

"Yes boss," She deadpanned. "Are you going to be able to walk after sitting for so long?"

" A few days walking the beach, and I'll be good as new. Two weeks and I'll be ready to race Maggie." I winced when she stopped the car too quickly. "Maybe three weeks."

"I'm guessing that ship has sailed, Slater. You're not getting any younger."

"I think Roland's wife is closer to your age than his, or mine."

"Good. Maybe we can bond, and she'll volunteer some information."

"Tommy thinks she's a gold-digger, but nobody twisted Roland's arm to marry her."

"Most guys go for younger women. Look at me and Cletus."

"I'd prefer to forget that you ever dated someone thirty-four years old."

"I don't know if I'd call it dating, mostly it was just getting stoned and having sex."

"Stop talking! Let's go in and wait for them."

Despite her penchant for making me uncomfortable, Jasmine was good company. The eight-hour drive had passed quickly. I hadn't noticed a lot of pain in my leg, but it had stiffened up from the inactivity. Jasmine wasn't much help pulling me from the car, but I leaned on my hickory stick and managed to hobble into the terminal.

Roland Dunbar was there waiting. He picked up two small bags when he saw us, and started walking in our direction. A raven-haired young woman that might have just stepped out of a Victoria's Secret catalogue followed him and hoisted her stylish sunglasses to inspect us.

She glanced at me, then at Jasmine, then back at Roland. "How much are you paying these two, Darlin'?" She asked. Her drawl was exaggerated, syrupy.

"Three," I said, extending a hand. "My partner Maggie will be down in a couple of days with our airplane. Jasmine is our intern. She's very smart and capable and we need her to gain the confidences of Isla's younger friends."

"And I promised Slater I won't inhale." Jasmine laughed and extended a hand. So much for being professional. "I heard Isla's friends are stoners."

"I love your hair, Darlin'. It's so blue." Roland's underwear model giggled. "We're only staying a couple of days, but you and I will have so much fun! We can ditch the men and I'll take you to a couple of the local hangouts."

"Sounds great," Jasmine agreed quickly. "Can I get served?"

"No problem, Sweetness, I have my ways." More giggling.

"See what I have to put up with?" Roland chuckled. "You and I might have to just go out on the town ourselves, Slater, before your partner shows up. I have my ways too."

"Not much fun right now." I lifted my cane again. "Hoping to just walk the beach and get to know some of the locals, get a start on figuring this out."

"Plenty of time for that," He continued. "You and I got off on the wrong foot back home. One good drunk and we'll be the best of friends. Maybe we'll go down to Key West and do some sightseeing of our own." From his exaggerated wink, I concluded he was talking about going to a strip club. If his wife was aware of our conversation, or cared, she hid it well. She was still busy examining Jasmine's hair. She giggled happily and climbed into the back of Maggie's car with her husband.

"I have a car down at the house that you can use if you'd like, it's a little roomier than this," Roland mumbled as he tried to tuck himself into the back seat next to his wife. He seemed to be having more trouble than just his long legs. He grabbed at the headrest, missed it and nearly fell backwards, then lunged forward. "Isla hated it. She said it used too much gas and was going to wreck the planet. She bought a Hybrid that got about a thousand miles a gallon, then piled it into a road approach. I'm pretty sure she was stoned. By the time it came back from the body shop, she was gone."

"Didn't take you long to get rid of that car," Ginger said dryly. For a moment, she didn't sound like the displaced runway model from Georgia. There was a sharp edge in her voice, and the Southern Belle accent had disappeared. Then she caught herself, giggled loudly, and laid it on, "I told him, 'Darlin', it doesn't trouble me driving that, even though it reminded me of how poor Isla and I didn't always cotton to each other and she never even let me in it."

Roland's expression came back to me. Phony as a tent preacher.

"She says that now, but she really wanted a Caddy, so I got her the XLR. Business I'm in, I wouldn't be caught dead in one of those little windup electric jobs."

I shot Jasmine a look, before she could start something. As it turned out, I was glad I had. "What is it you do, Roland? It never really came up."

"We sell fracking equipment and oil rig supplies. I have a couple patents, and of course the industry really took off lately. That was just something more for Isla to hold against me. She liked the fancy houses and the sailboat, but she didn't want to admit to her tree-hugger friends where the money came from."

"You were very good to her, Sugar. She didn't appreciate you like she should've," Ginger put in. "You did everything you could for her."

"I wanted her to run the company someday," Roland said glumly. "A man works his whole life to build something, and it's your children you want to carry it on."

"Children, more than one?" I asked. I was turned in the seat as far as my bad leg would let me, and caught the quick look from Mrs. Tent-Preacher.

"Just Isla, though it wasn't from lack of trying. When we were young, Caroline and I wanted another, but the doctors say my boys don't swim so good."

"And I don't mind none. Just happy to have my Rollie." Ginger gushed.

"Maybe a son would have wanted the business as it is. Isla, she had plans to retool and build wind-generators. She had me thinking about it, but then the trouble started."

"I couldn't run a big company like that." Ginger stated the obvious, and threw in an extra giggle. "But Rollie isn't going anywhere for a very long time. Healthy as a horse, this man of mine."

Jasmine acknowledged the frown I sent her, but she couldn't help saying something. "How old are you, Ginger?"

"That's the beauty of being your age, Honey, you can't imagine the day you won't want to answer that question," Ginger said, then stared out at the bay.

"She's thirty-three," Roland put in and got a black look for his trouble. "It's not like you're ancient, Ginger. Tommy said we should tell them whatever they want to know, that every scrap of information might be important."

"Sorry Ginger." Jasmine glanced in the mirror. "I was just curious, not really important to the investigation."

"It's all right darlin'." She tried to plaster on the smile again. "Everybody thought because I was closer to Isla's age, we should be gal pals, or act like sisters. I tried to get along with her, I really did. She just hated me because I wasn't her mother." Her voice dropped and she looked out the window again. "Because her mother died, and I wasn't her."

"Like I said, Isla wasn't right in the head sometimes." Roland reached for his wife's hand. "It wasn't just you she didn't get along with, mostly it was me. Maybe if we had waited for a while longer to get married, she would have taken it better. But I fell in love, and I wanted to move on."

"And you're how old?" My blue-haired junior partner asked.

"Jasmine. Does it matter? Sorry Roland, she's always talking when she should be listening."

He laughed. "It's fine, people wonder all the time about our age difference, and they're afraid to ask. I've got twenty-five years on her, Jasmine."

"Hey, whatever works, I don't judge. Last year I was riding a Harley with a middle-aged speed freak, then there was the nut case that kidnapped me and kept me in his basement for two weeks. Just lately, I had a twenty-eight-year old body-guard that I couldn't keep my hands off of. Love is complicated." She looked at us curiously when we all started laughing.

"Honey, you don't know the half of it," Ginger said chuckling.

"The guys that hang out at our beach are going to love you," Roland added.

Jasmine grinned and winked at me. "Can't wait."

Roland's house was on the northwest corner of Big Pine Key, about as far from the main highway as the small plot of land would allow. It was tucked back from the road and sprawled across what amounted to several lots with a cobblestone circular driveway. There was a second smaller house at the head of the driveway that I presumed was the grounds-keeper's quarters. It, like the big house, was a light color stucco, pretty common in Florida. Working in construction, I noticed the steel roof and the heavy clad windows with the functional steel shutters. Hurricane proof, Roland had said.

An ancient wooden skiff sat beside a working fountain in the front yard, and the surplus water spilled into a small man-made pond. The skiff had a hole in the side and an old fishing net was thrown haphazardly across the bow in an attempt at authenticity. Flowers and vines filled the rear of the boat, and spilled out onto the ground and into a nearby garden with a small arch that was guarded by a life-sized statue of Poseidon.

The massive front door only opened on one side, and the stationary half held a huge anchor that looked like it might have been retrieved from a tug-boat or a small schooner. It too, was draped in fish-netting with a variety of shells caught up in the strings. It was obvious that whoever decorated the place loved the ocean and the maritime theme.

Roland fumbled with his keys, then handed them to Ginger, and we all followed her into the big front room. She tossed the keys on an end table and made a bee-line for the half bath that stood just to our left.

Jasmine looked awkwardly at Roland. "Damn, is there another bathroom handy?"

He motioned toward an open door at the opposite end of the Great-room. "Master bedroom is over there, bathroom is on the right."

"Thanks, long drive, and Slater wouldn't let me stop."

I nearly objected, then let that pass. I looked around the room. Whoever had decorated outside continued the same theme in the big living room and kitchen. Several oars and pieces of sail-rigging were scattered across the tops of the cupboards and hung at various locations on the walls. Pulleys and spools, sextants and compasses, shells of various shapes and sizes, filled every available shelf. On a set of hooks between the kitchen and the living room, two pairs of waders hung alongside an ancient looking canvas raincoat and three cane surf rods spooled with heavy cotton line.

The kitchen had an island sink with a butcher's block sitting next to it, the only area spared of maritime paraphernalia. To the right of those, and what I took to be the centerpiece of the room, stood a six-foot Captain's wheel. It looked too perfect to be authentic, but when I got close, I could see that it was made mostly of blackened Teak, with polished brass struts, and a copper colored centerplate that might have been functional at one point in time. It was situated so that the person standing behind it would have a view of the bay through the set of terrace doors on that side of the house. It was mounted on a heavy oak beam that was bolted to the floor with steel cleats. I limped over to it, leaned on my cane, and tried to turn it. It wouldn't budge.

Roland nodded his head at the collection of nautical paraphernalia. "Caroline always said she loved fishing, but mostly she just loved going to sales and buying every old piece of crap she could find that had ever been near the water. She loved all the old stories about the Keys, about the time before the roads, even before the railroad. That Captain's wheel came off a real Pirate's ship, if you're willing to believe the shyster that sold it to my wife for three times what it was worth. It made her happy to believe that it did, and that was good enough for me." His voice cracked a little and he looked wistfully around the room. "Ginger wanted to redecorate, but I wouldn't allow it. Caroline loved this house just the way it is."

"Seems like you're pretty fond of it too," I commented. "Maybe you should stick around for the party, spend the weekend. We could still say Maggie and I are relatives, and ask our questions."

"It was Caroline and Isla that made this place special. Truth is, Caroline was the love of my life. Once this business is done, I'll probably sell out. There are too many ghosts here."

Neither of us were aware of Ginger's return from the bathroom and we weren't sure how much of the conversation she had heard. She coughed uncomfortably and gave me a bleak look, then offered a weak smile to Roland. It surprised me when she spoke up. "I wouldn't mind if you sold this mausoleum. Caroline was your wife for a lot of years, but she was your wife then, and I'm your wife now."

"I didn't see you there, Baby." He extended an arm and she slid against him, offering the forgiveness that he hadn't asked for. "Sure, you're my girl now. Day after tomorrow we'll head back home and leave Slater and his partners to sort this all out."

"You said five bedrooms, the other four are upstairs?" I glanced apprehensively at the long spiral stairs that led to a second-floor walkway.

"Oh shoot, Mister Slater." Ginger's smile was genuine. "Why don't you take the Master, and Jasmine can have the bedroom right at the top of the steps. The east end is like a motel anyway, three bedrooms and two baths with connecting doors. Plenty of room for Rollie and me up there, especially since we'll only be here for a night or two."

"Nice house!" Jasmine said, returning from the bathroom. "Somebody's a fishing nut."

"We just covered that," Ginger said flatly. "I'll get our stuff out of the medicine cabinet, Slater, then it's all yours."

"I didn't mean to hurt her feelings like that." Roland said ruefully after his current wife left the room. "I'm always sticking my mouth in my foot."

He paused momentarily, then laughed. "Foot in my mouth, I meant. I'm tired, I can't talk when I'm tired. Jasmine, can I show you where your room is? Goodnight Mister Slater, tell Ginger I went up, would you?"

Jasmine picked up her bag, then turned to me. "Slater, don't go to bed right away, we have to talk. I'll be back down in a minute."

I had made it as far as the couch when Ginger reappeared with a small bag from the Master. She nodded toward the stairs. "Did he go up already?"

"I guess the plane ride tired him out. Is he all right? He was shaking a lot again."

"Tremors, the doctor said. I guess it's not a big deal, it just happens to some people when they get older."

"Okay. We're depending a lot on his memory to know what went on with Isla. I hope you can fill in the blanks if he forgets things."

"He's doing fine." She said emphatically, then bit her lip and backed up. "He has been stressed out ever since we got the necklace, and he gets confused when he's tired, but he's not a young man."

"Fifty-eight, that's not an old man. Early onset Alzheimer's?"

"No. I said he's fine, Mister Slater!"

"Slater, is good enough. Sorry, I'm just asking the questions that need to be asked."

"He doesn't have Alzheimer's, and he didn't kill his wife."

"I wasn't going to go there, but how can you be so sure of that?"

"I know him, he isn't capable of that." She had been angry, but now she looked petulant, wary.

"You knew him before she died, didn't you?" I tried, but she wasn't going to admit to anything that easily.

"Goodnight, Mister Slater, I hope you sleep well." She tossed her hair back and started climbing the staircase, then stopped and looked back down at me. "I really tried you know...to be Isla's friend. She never gave me a chance."

"I think that was her mistake," I conceded. She smiled at that, then turned and continued up the steps.

I pushed myself up from the couch and went to explore my quarters. Judging from the rest of the house, the Master bedroom was the only area that had seen some renovations. There were no Sailfish, stuffed and mounted on the walls, no oars or waders hanging from hooks, no nautical antiques.

The big bed had a canopy that was light blue and frilly. The walls were a soft white and there were several paintings of carefree little girls in lace dresses, a few posters of bands I'd never heard of, and a life-sized picture of Serena Williams, tennis racket in hand. The only thing that related to the ocean in the whole room, were a pair of shapely table lamps, maybe Mermaids, maybe not.

It was clear that Ginger had made a statement and drawn a line at the door of her bedroom; this is where the new wife lives, and she's only going to put up with so much. I suddenly found myself liking her a whole lot more.

There was a rap on the door, which was open, and Jasmine stepped in and closed it behind her. She grinned, pulled out her cell-phone and thumbed to a picture. She turned the phone toward me and scrolled through four pictures, all pill bottles.

I shook my head. "Let me guess, you said you had to pee, and right away you rifled through their medicine cabinet."

"Everybody does that anyway, now I have a good excuse."

"Why would you do that? Roland is our client. I'll admit, it seems like there's something wrong with him, but neither one of them will admit to it."

"Exactly. I'm an investigator now and that's what we do, we snoop. If he has Alzheimer's or some kind of dementia, we need to know that. He may be our client, but he may have killed his first wife. It's possible he killed his daughter too, and he's just covering his tracks."

I raised a brow. "This detective thing is going straight to your head. You're not Agatha Christie."

"I probably should know who that is, but I don't. You have to admit, he acts weird. He slurs his words and mixes them up. He almost fell over a couple of times, and what's up with the shaking?"

"I asked Ginger about it and she got defensive right away, said it's just age."

"I'm going on the internet and see what these pills are for. Maybe I'll call Janet Hays, see what she can tell me."

"You're on a first name basis with my doctor?"

"Contacts, Slater. Maggie says it's good to have contacts, experts we can ask about stuff like this. And she owes us."

"She does? All right, I guess that's reasonable. Just remember it's Roland that's paying for our services. Don't bite the hand that's buying us an airplane."

"Maggie says getting to the truth is always what's best for the client."

"You and Maggie seem to be talking shop a lot, considering I'm the one with his name on the door. You told me PIs just do the dirty jobs cops won't."

"I still say that's true, but it doesn't mean we can't be good at it. The cops would need a search warrant to look in Roland's medicine cabinet and a good reason to get one. We don't have to stick to the rules."

"Our obligation is to our client, that's the rule."

"I'm not breaking the rule, I'm just curious. That's a detective's job."

"Fine Agatha, just reign it in a little bit, okay? Which side of the house is your room on?"

"The beach side, why?"

I handed her the small carrying case that had been in my luggage. "It's a Nikon with a telephoto lens and a tripod. Set it up far enough back from the window so it won't be seen, and take it down at night so people can't spot it from outside. From the second floor you'll be able to watch the whole beach. I want pictures of everyone. The groundskeeper and his wife, the mailman, people walking their dog on the beach, everyone."

"People walk their dogs by here? Isn't the beach private?"

"There's a public beach down the shoreline, and you can't own the ocean. By law, anyplace that's covered by high tide is public. If the sand is wet, the state of Florida owns it and you can't stop people from using it. There must be twenty-five yards of sand between the dune in front of the houses and the water, and Roland says nobody worries much about it as long as people aren't littering. Plenty of room to play volleyball and throw a party."

"I have to stay in my room all day and take pictures of the perverts walking by?"

"That's what private investigators really do, Jasmine, mostly boring stuff. And you don't have to spend all day every day up there, just when I'm out front. I'm going to plop down at the picnic table, act like I'm enjoying the view from my new house, and see who wanders up. Maybe it'll be some old ladies from Michigan looking for shells, or maybe it'll be someone interesting."

"All right, I'll set it up in the morning. Are you going to call Maggie before you hit the sack?"

"I guess. I'd better talk to her before I take the new pills Doc Hays prescribed. She said they'll put me out for eight hours, which I could use."

"All right, tell her I'll call her tomorrow when I'm on camera duty." She walked to the door with the camera case and pulled the door open. "Goodnight, Slater. Love you."

"Night, love you too." It was so casual that I didn't think about it. Casual and obvious, but something we had never said to each other before. It was the kind of thing you said to a family member. It made me smile.

Chapter Seven

Sometime during the night, I woke up covered in sweat and in desperate need of a glass of water. I turned the bedside lamp on, dropped my feet to the floor, and stood up slowly. The room shifted, and I took a deep breath before moving forward. The good news was that there seemed to be very little pain in my leg. Actually, I felt pretty numb all over. I ignored my cane, and turned to the bathroom, then had a better thought.

My mouth tasted like a dirty sock, and my tongue could have been pulled from the same shoe. I needed ice water, and I had seen a dispenser on the refrigerator in the kitchen. I limped carefully across the tile floor, mildly curious that it didn't feel cold under my feet. Either it was heated, or the soles of my feet were as medicated as the rest of me.

The big room was dark, just a slight glow from the skylight overhead and an outline of the doors that faced the beach. A dense fog had moved in, telling me that it was later than I thought, probably getting close to dawn. I glanced down, searching for footing, but it was too dark to see, and I picked my way across the room, trying to remember where the nearest light switch was located.

When I glanced back in the direction of the beach, I froze in my tracks. My skin crawled, and the hair on my arms and the back of my neck stood up. I blinked, swallowed, and rubbed my eyes. The Captain's wheel near the front windows had moved, spun half a turn, then stopped and turned slowly back. It was dark, but I was very sure of what I'd seen. I stood transfixed, searching the darkness for the invisible helmsman that might have spun it. I waited. The wheel was framed in the lesser blackness of the windows and the shifting white fog. It moved again. A quarter of a turn to starboard, then back.

Then I saw him, or what I thought was a him. Against the deeper blackness of the room, not silhouetted against the windows, was the shape of a man; a fisherman, I was sure. I could barely see the outline of his body, his back hunched as he leaned forward to reach the old Pirate's wheel, steering his imaginary ship toward some great reckoning or tragedy that I could only wonder at. Such were the thoughts that went through my drug-addled brain.

I took one step forward, straining my bleary eyes against the darkness. I was sure I could make out shoulders and a head, a head covered by an old-style bucket hat that was popular anywhere the sun was unrelenting and the rains torrential. The head was suspended above the shoulders, unfettered by the convenience of a neck. Cold chills ran the length of my back, and I could taste the sweat on my upper lip when I bit down on it, fighting the impulse to call out. Though it was too dark to be certain, I thought that I saw the hat move, slowly turning a full 180 degrees as the soulless occupant looked in my direction. I couldn't see eyes, or any features, but in that moment, I was sure it must be Old Eli. He had returned, searching once more for his long dead mistress.

I have said I don't believe in ghosts, and maybe the hat didn't turn, and maybe I shouldn't have washed those pain pills down with two beers, but the big Captain's wheel spun again, guiding Old Eli's vessel through the foggy night. I had seen enough. I backed slowly toward my room. Tap water would have to do.

I continued to stare into the darkness, feeling my way back with my bare feet until I reached the entrance of the bedroom. My outstretched hand touched the wall, and then a light switch. I stood there, caressing the tiny plastic paddle for a long moment, undecided. Slater the Detective wanted to know, but another part of me wanted to be willing to accept the unexplainable, to believe in the unseen just this one time. I could turn the light on and be sure, or just lock the bedroom door and go back to sleep. Sometimes I hate how practical I am. I flipped the switch.

The sudden brilliance changed the scene. If Old Eli had been there, he was gone now. But someone had been there, that was a certainty. One of the raincoats that had been hanging near the entrance was draped over the back of a high-backed kitchen chair and an old canvas fishing hat was perched on the handle of a broom that leaned against the chair. In the darkness of the big room, the illusion had seemed very real. But to what end?

Feeling plenty foolish, and more than a little curious, I limped across the room and replaced the raincoat and hat on the hooks by the door. A bolt of lightning flashed from the coast, and the resulting thunder rattled the windows. I checked the locks, but everything seemed secure, so I went into the kitchen and drank my fill of ice water, hoping to clear my head and make sense of what I'd seen.

I was just ready to turn the light out and go back to bed when I had a thought, and returned to the Captain's wheel. I reached out, expecting it to spin easily, although I still had no idea why it had moved in the first place. I tugged on it once, then pulled harder, still nothing. By putting both my hands on the spires, and putting some weight into it, I could move the wheel, but barely. The bearings that supported it had long since dried out, and they squealed loudly in response to my efforts.

I was absolutely sure I had seen it move, but that seemed unlikely now. I turned the light out and returned to my bed. No more Vicodin for me.

"Sleep well Mister Slater?" Ginger asked me first thing when I walked into the kitchen that morning.

It aroused my suspicions, but I held my tongue. "Like a baby. Great bed, and even better pain medication. Still a little groggy, but my leg feels pretty good. I may try to get around without my cane today." I glanced around the room. Everything was as it had been, except the floppy canvas hat now hung from one of the spires of the Captain's wheel. I was sure I had hung it on the hook next to the coat, but the events of the previous evening didn't seem real in the light of day.

"We need to introduce you to Carlos and Teresa," Roland said from the top of the stairs. "They've been telling people you're buying the place. They know it's not true, but I didn't tell them what you're really doing here. They just think you're our guests, because Maggie is a shirt-tail relation. They don't need to know all the particulars. Teresa will be here at eight to make breakfast. Best damn pancakes you ever tasted. We usually fend for ourselves at lunch, and often as not, we go out in the evening."

"Careful on those steps, Darlin'," Ginger admonished.

"I've had a sore leg myself lately, Slater. Ginger acts like I'm a cripple."

"You will be if you fall down those damn steps. Use the railing." She stood quickly, and I thought she was going to run up to help him.

"Calm down! I'm fine, just a little stiff first thing in the morning."

"Generally speaking, you're in good health?" I took the opening.

123

"I told you, he's perfectly fine." Ginger growled, then switched to her Southern Belle act. "My Darlin' will be running marathons when he's eighty, right Sweetness?"

"I hope the hell not." He laughed as he limped down the steps. "Eighty is a long way off. You're an early riser Slater. Usually we wake up when we smell breakfast, but Ginger talked me into going back home sooner than we planned, so we have a lot to do today. First thing in the morning I'll have Carlos drive us back down to the airport. Sorry, but we won't be able to go out on the town."

"Jasmine and I can drive you to the airport," I volunteered. "My leg is still iffy, and I'm not sure I want her on her own down here. Maggie is coming in Thursday afternoon with our airplane, and by then we need to have the Labor Day party plans all figured out."

"We'll go up to the club at lunch, and I'll introduce you to some of the guys. Half of them won't talk to me anymore, but I still get along with Skip Jackson and Murphy. They're on either side of us. I called them and said you wanted to host all three days, and I'm having a big canopy tent set up. I have a local caterer coming in to roast a pig with all the fixings, bartenders and tons of booze, even a fireworks display. Going to be a hell of a party."

"Too bad you'll miss it, but I'll make it worth your while, Sugar." Ginger gave him a smile. "While you two go to the club I'll take Jasmine over to No Name, show her some of the sights."

"She's too young to drink." I reminded her.

"Sure she is." Ginger grinned at me. "Don't worry, we won't get in too much trouble."

Teresa and Carlos appeared at the door promptly at eight. After a quick introduction, Teresa, a quiet dark-haired woman of oriental descent, set about making breakfast. Roland insisted Carlos sit down, and he introduced us. Carlos looked a few years older than me. He was obviously Hispanic, but he talked like the man on the six o'clock news.

"The grounds look beautiful, Carlos. Roland tells me you help with his Jacksonville place too. Are you from Jacksonville originally?"

"Georgia boy, born and raised."

"Georgia?"

"I kind of lost my accent when I went up north for school. I have an engineering degree from MIT. Not everyone who looks like me is a gardener. I do it because I love it."

"Call me Slater. How long have you and your wife been with Roland?"

"What's it been Boss?" He glanced over at Roland. "Eight years for me, I guess, but Teresa has worked for Mister Dunbar since he started the company."

"Carlos had a lot of job offers when he tried to quit, Slater. He worked for me in research and development as an engineer and helped me and my brother come up with some new designs for our pumps. Now he works from his computer and comes to Jacksonville once a month or so and spends some time at the plant. Little less stressful down here, right Carlos?"

"I kind of burned out. Roland brought me down here for some R and R, and I didn't want to leave. Now, we have a beautiful place to live, and I pretty much work when I want to. Teresa and I are very happy here."

"Bit of a pay-cut, but you can't buy happiness." Roland chuckled.

"It was just time to go." Carlos added.

"Being an engineer, it's that stressful?" I asked.

"It wasn't the work." Roland spoke up. "Carlos couldn't get along with my brother. Nobody could. The shit hit the fan shortly after Carlos moved down here, and I finally gave my brother the boot. He had a share of the company and I had to buy him out. He didn't do a damn thing anyway. I came up with the designs and Carlos and a couple of the other geniuses at the company made them work. Ross took a good chunk of money and moved to Atlanta. He spends all his time chasing skirts and partying from what I hear. He's my brother, but I sure as hell don't care to be around him."

"So, Roland tells me he's going back to Jacksonville, and that you'll be staying on to entertain the guests?" Carlos asked.

"Maggie will be here tomorrow afternoon in our floatplane. She's much more entertaining than I am. Jasmine will be staying too. She's upstairs at the moment. She's my sister's kid, from up north. She's staying with us for the summer, and a three-day long party is right up her alley. She's a bit of a wild child, so if you see her doing anything illegal, let me know."

"Most of the neighbors show up, and half of Big Pine Key. It can get pretty crazy, but we don't go for people doing drugs," Roland said, then grinned. "Of course, a little pot never hurt anyone." He glanced at Carlos. "I mentioned Maggie, didn't I? She's a third cousin, or maybe fourth, I can't keep that straight. Daughter of Caroline's cousin, I think. Right Slater?"

"Something like that, fourth or fifth." Lies can trip you up, and I didn't want to commit to anything specific. "She always wanted to meet Isla, but never got the chance."

"Everyone loved Isla." Carlos smiled softly. "She was a very special girl."

It was where I hoped the conversation would go, but Roland put a stop to it with a sudden outburst. "Stupid, thinking she could outrun a hurricane. Ungrateful little bitch!" His expression changed to an empty stare.

Ginger turned from the kitchen where she had been helping Teresa with breakfast. "Rollie, Sweetness? It's okay, I'm right here. Would you like some coffee, or maybe some juice?"

He looked at her, or through her for fully half a minute, seemingly lost to his surroundings. Then, as suddenly as he had left, he was back. "Coffee would be great, how about you two, coffee?"

Carlos looked at me and shrugged. "I'd better get to work, Boss, a lot to do between now and Friday."

"The one thing you could do for me is help with the moorings for the airplane when you have time. The boat slip is too narrow." I stood and shook his hand again. "This leg is taking its sweet time healing, and I'm kind of useless for any kind of manual labor."

"No problem, I'll get some stakes lined up. Nice to meet you, and I'll talk to you later." He hesitated, then spoke to Roland. "I'll see you later, right, Boss?"

"I'll come find you after a bit and we can go over stuff, Carlos. Slater's a great guy and I'm sure you two will be fine without me, party-wise, I mean."

Ginger acted like nothing had happened and ignored my questioning glance. I could imagine him reacting to the frustration of losing a daughter, coupled with the hope that we might be able to shed some light on what had happened. It was probably on his mind a lot. But for a time, and I could see it on his face, he had been completely lost to his surroundings. Something was wrong

128

with Roland Dunbar, and he and his wife were hiding it from me, and probably from everyone.

The smell of bacon must have pulled Jasmine from her bed. She stumbled down the stairs, pajamaed, with blue hair pointing every direction but down and gave us a sheepish greeting. "I managed to brush my teeth, but breakfast smelled too good. I can shower after."

"Well Darlin', the chops and pancakes are ready." Ginger took a plate from Teresa and pulled a chair out. "You and Slater are our guests, so sit down and start eating."

I sat down at the table and picked up the cup of coffee Teresa put in front of me, sipping gratefully as I looked around the room again. The raincoat was hanging back on its hook, and the broom that I took for Eli's long neck was nowhere to be seen. Probably in the broom closet, where brooms belonged. The old hat was still clinging to the spire of the Captain's wheel, hanging slightly off to the right side. I studied it, then took another sip of the hot coffee. I was almost positive that when I walked into the kitchen that morning, the hat had been hanging to the left, and I hadn't seen anyone go near it.

The trek to the beach would have been tough had it not been for the boardwalk that extended over the four-foot dune, and sloped gradually down to the sand. I was okay on steps, but the beach sand pulled at my leg and I had to call Jasmine and ask her to bring me my cane. Roland had a couple of picnic tables with awnings set up closer to the water, and I limped over to them and settled onto a bench.

"I have the camera all set up and ready to go." Jasmine said when she delivered my cane. She looked in both directions. "Not many people, but it's early."

"I think you're right about Roland being sick. He had some sort of an episode this morning before breakfast. Did you find those drugs on-line?"

"Haven't had time yet," She mumbled, then looked down and kicked at the sand. "Okay, I did find something, but I hate to say anything yet. I'm waiting for Janet to get back to me."

"What is it, Jasmine? You look upset."

"The blue pill was obvious. He needs those to keep up with his hot young wife. The yellow one is dopamine for his tremors, or spasticity in his case, and there's a blood pressure pill. But his tremors aren't just from being old, Slater, they're just one of the symptoms he can't hide. He's dying."

"Based on what? What is it, Jasmine? What's the fourth pill?"

"The bottle says Riluzole, and it's only approved for one thing." I shrugged, and she continued. "I'm pretty sure he has Lou Gehrig's disease. I was up half the night reading about it. If he beats the odds, he might live five years, some

130

people even make it ten. Most people only last three."

"What about Hawkins? He lived for fifty years after he was diagnosed, didn't he?"

"Literally one chance in a million, maybe more. They're still trying to figure out what kept him going. But maybe the internet is wrong. Maybe that drug is used for other stuff. I sent my pictures to Janet and asked her about it. She should be able to tell us."

"There sure is something wrong with him."

"I guess the symptoms vary, but he has a lot of them. It seems odd that they left that prescription here, but there were only three pills left, so maybe they forgot them and then just blew it off. They're probably expensive, but that wouldn't matter to him."

"It might explain why he's clinging to the hope that his daughter is still alive. He's staring his mortality right in the face."

"I hope I'm wrong."

"Not a word to Ginger if you two go out today. She keeps saying he's fine, but I find it hard to believe she doesn't know."

"She seems pretty ditzy, maybe he hasn't told her what the pills are for."

"I don't think she's as empty-headed as she acts. Just be careful what you say around her. She knows we're investigating Isla's death, but I don't know if she's aware that Roland believes she might still be alive."

"Ginger is going to be a very rich widow in a couple years."

"Good point. I wonder how iron-clad that their prenup is, and I wonder who's in line to run the company. The company is privately held, which means Roland is worth almost a billion dollars." I smiled when she looked at me quizzically. "I have Google too."

"Is it okay if I hang out with you?"

I wanted her to go back to her room where the camera was, but her tone said she needed company. "Sure, sit. Did I tell you I saw Eli the ghost last night? Either that, or I took too many of those damn pills. Bring any beer?"

"It's ten o'clock in the morning, Slater, you don't get beer this time of day."

"My leg is starting to hurt again."

"Tough. I'm not going to let you turn into a junkie or a drunk just because you got shot."

"All right, Blue, I'll take a handful of Tylenol. Have you heard from Maryanne?"

"Before we left. She's not thrilled that I'm playing private eye. It's a good thing she likes you and Maggie or there would have been a fight. It's like the thing with Roland, she wants to leave a legacy, and I'm her only chance."

"I'd let you do whatever makes you happy, unless it was with a guy named Cletus."

She laughed. "Who names their kid Cletus? That's just horrible." We watched the water for a while, and she perked up. "Maybe I could take some classes, keep Maryanne happy, and still be a part-time detective."

"We have an opening for one of those," I assured her.

"I'm going up and finish unpacking. Text me if any nefarious types come walking down the beach."

"Nefarious? Take pictures of everyone, we'll sort out the nefarious ones later."

Chances are Deloris Morehouse and her husband Clarence weren't nefarious. They were a disheveled pair of senior citizens that were walking the beach in hopes of finding their lost Shih-tzu. He had bolted that morning before Clarence could attach his leash and Deloris spent fifteen minutes explaining his many failings to me; Clarence's, not the Shih-tzu. I wished them luck and assured them I would keep my eyes open. They left me a card, just in case.

The awning was directly above the picnic table, and the sun had started to roast my neck before anyone else appeared. Another dog walker wandered down the beach, and this one still had his canine secured to its leash. Not a Shih-tzu. It looked like an English Setter, but I'm no expert.

As I watched, he unleashed the dog and started throwing a tennis ball for it to chase, all the while coming closer and closer to where I sat. He was lean and bronze, not quite six feet tall in his bare feet, with a lined, leathery face that had seen too much sun. His yellow sun-glasses were propped on the top of his head and he had a greying pony-tail that extended onto his collar. He didn't look nefarious, but he did look familiar.

When the dog saw me, it picked up the tennis ball and came bounding up, throwing water and sand in every direction. It dropped the ball at my feet and danced back and forth on its toes, grinning, the way some dogs do. When I didn't look interested, the black and white put his head down and nosed the ball closer, rolling it up to my foot. A cute trick, and an excuse for the barefoot man to saunter up to my spot. "Sorry, he's hoping he can sucker you into playing catch. He wears me out, but he never gets tired of it."

"I know I'm going to regret this," I said, and tossed the ball as far as I could from my chair. The dog had the ball back at my feet before his owner had closed the distance between us.

"Will, Will Forester." He extended a hand, then nodded at the dog. "That's Jasper. Sore leg?"

"Yeah, another week, then I get the cast off. At least this one's a lot smaller than the first one. Eric Slater's my name, but everybody just calls me Slater."

"I fell off my roof a few years back and I had a cast just like that one. You fall off a roof?"

"More like I was pushed," I said. "You live on the beach?"

"Too rich for my blood. I'm back toward the main road. My son and I have a small place. I walk

134

out here most mornings with the dog, gives us both some exercise. I bartend nights, so I don't roll out until about ten in the morning. Is Roland going to throw the Labor Day party this year? Murphy was in and claimed Roland was going to spring for the whole works."

"He did say that, although my girlfriend and I might chip in if he lets us."

"Yeah? I heard Roland might have sold. You the new owner?"

"Maybe, not sure yet. Roland wants to keep it in the family. He doesn't get down here very often, but he can always visit. He's a busy guy, can't even stick around for his own party. Have you been to any of these Labor Day parties before?"

"Usually I get here late, work and all. But often as not they go most of the night. Murphy used to have the big tent in front of his place, and I stopped in there a time or two. Sorry, but the truth is, Dunbar and I don't always see eye to eye."

"Well, it's my party this year, so your welcome to join us. I know Roland kind of likes to run the show when he's around. He rubs me the wrong way sometimes too." I wasn't making that up.

"Isla, his daughter, worked for my son Jessie at the bar. Roland didn't care for Jessie, and he accused him of selling Isla dope, which didn't go over very good with me."

"That was something, her taking that boat out in the middle of Irma."

"Yeah, something all right. Roland managed to blame Jessie for that one too, claimed he should have stopped her. How was Jessie supposed to know she was going to do something that stupid?"

"Maggie, my girlfriend, is her cousin, third or fifth, something like that. Anyway, we never met her. From what I understand, she was normally a pretty smart kid."

"Crazy smart, and one hell of a sailor. That's what made it so hard to figure out."

"That had to be hard on your kid too, wasn't it?"

"No kidding. We all loved Isla, but that didn't stop Dunbar from ripping into Jessie. I lost it, and we had a little go around, cops and the whole nine yards. Kind of why I walked over here. I thought maybe you and I could start off on the right foot before Roland started talking shit about me. Usually Jasper and I stay out by the water so he can't accuse me of trespassing. I should just walk down the other way, but I'm too damn stubborn to give him that satisfaction."

"Lot of that going around these days. I think Roland is headed home tomorrow, so you two won't have to butt heads if you want to come to the party."

"Too bad, the way things went. When I first met them, I got along with him pretty well, even got invited over for supper from time to time. Of course, that was Caroline, she welcomed everyone." He glanced in the direction of the house, a wisp of a smile on his face. "Does the place still look like Davy Jones's locker, or did the new wife toss out all of Caroline's treasures?"

"Still there. Even Old Eli the ghost is hanging out. Not that I believe in that crap." He gave me a bemused look and I explained. "Don't mix Vicodin with beer, it makes you see all kinds of crazy things."

"Caroline swore Eli was real, mostly because she wanted him to be. It didn't take Roland long to replace her with a younger model."

There was no missing the edge in his voice. I was on the fence, but I defended Roland's young wife. "Ginger seems okay to me. No Rhodes scholar, but nice enough."

"She would come across that way." He said coldly, then painted on a smile. "I shouldn't bad mouth her. I've never met her, just heard things. Caroline would be hard to replace."

Jasper bumped against my leg suddenly. He had found a friend; a smelly bedraggled looking Shih-tzu that must have rolled in a dead fish. Reluctantly, I reached down and picked it up.

"I know a couple of people that are going to be very happy to see you, little dog."

Will nodded. "Jasper and I better get going. Slater, right?"

"Yeah, just Slater. Will." We shook hands again.

"That's it, but if I were you, I wouldn't mention my name around Roland."

"Like I said, you're welcome at my party any time."

He put Jasper back on his leash and they walked back the way they had come. Interesting, him coming to me. I was sure that he was the man in the white van.

I scratched the Shin-tzu's ears and it glowered at me, growling deep in its little throat. I dialed Deloris. "Come get your dog before he bites me."

Chapter Eight

Roland walked carefully across the hot sand and settled into a chair next to me.

"Nice view." I nodded at the pristine water.

"Yeah, it's great. I'll miss this...if I decide to sell."

"Is that what you started to say?"

"No, there's a lot of things I'll miss," he said soberly. "Wait until you see this beach tonight, when the sun falls into the ocean. It's incredible. Caroline and I spent a lot of nights out here, watching the sky turn colors that I didn't even know existed. That was back when we were still so God-dammed much in love that nothing else mattered. Red sky at night, sailors delight, you've heard that?"

"I have. I've spent a good part of my life on the water, and I still take the time to watch the sun go down whenever I can. Always makes me realize how insignificant we are."

"Surely does." He looked out at the horizon, and for a minute I didn't think he was going to tell me. Then he did. "I have to level with you about something, Slater, and I expect you'll have to tell your partner. But I need your word that it won't go any further than that. Your promise."

"Slater and partners, we're a team of three. Jasmine's a cut-up, but I trust her completely. I can say for sure it won't go further than the three of us."

"The first doctor said Parkinson's, but I didn't get that lucky. That's treatable, and he tried. Now the specialists all agree that it's late onset ALS. Lou Gehrig's disease. Three to five years is their best guess, which makes me one of the lucky ones. I'm told it's going to take its sweet time killing me."

"Does Ginger know?"

That surprised him, and he didn't like it. "Of course she knows, she's my wife!"

"Men lie to their wives all the time." My look said what I hadn't.

"You can be a real dick, Slater," He growled. "I just told you I'm dying, and you still have to bust my balls?"

"You didn't know you were dying four years ago. It's not my business, but it might tie into the necklace and the note you got. I'm normally open-minded, but for me, marriage is one of those things that's black and white."

He sighed. "For what it's worth, it was her that strayed first, years before. I know, that isn't the point. Really, the business was my mistress for a long time, and I guess she had just gotten so lonely that she couldn't stand it anymore. She begged me to come down here and spend more time with her and Isla, said she needed a husband that cared about her more than money. I wouldn't listen. I caught her red-handed.

"She said it was a one-time thing, but I couldn't put it behind me. After that, I made damn sure to hurt her as much as she had hurt me, with any woman that would have me. There was just too much of it, too much damage done. We might have fixed it, but I was too stubborn. After a while she gave up and started acting single, like I'd been doing. Had she lived, I doubt we would still be together."

"Could the man she was seeing when she died have killed her?"

"If it was who I think, no. He lives down here, and I checked it out. He was definitely down here the night it happened, and as you know, Jacksonville is a long drive. The police asked of course, when it came out that I was fooling around with someone else that night, but I swore that as far as I knew, Caroline was always faithful. Eventually they decided Isla was an unreliable witness and ruled it an accidental drowning."

"Did this man know Isla? Is it possible he would send you that necklace just to hurt you?"

"I don't think he would do that. Much as I hate the guy, he wouldn't sink that low. Actually, he's a decent person, it just turned out we were both in love with the same woman."

"And his name?"

He threw up a hand. "Let that go. We don't need to drag Caroline's name through the mud. She was gone two years when that hurricane hit. Nothing that happened back then made Isla do what she did, and my getting that necklace wasn't because of what went on with her mother." He put his head down and started to shake. He collected himself quickly and wiped his eyes. "God, I was such a fool. The company was in trouble, and I thought I had to be there night and day."

"And what about your brother? I haven't heard a lot as far as he's concerned. Tell me a about him."

"There's not much to tell, not a lot that's good. From the start, he was trouble. He wanted an equal share of the company, but he didn't bring anything to the table. I owned the patents, I found the money, and hired the best engineers. He didn't even want to work an eight-hour day. He does have the gift of gab, so I put him in charge of sales, and gave him a minority share of the company. I had to offer shares to some of the engineers to get them on board, but I always kept the controlling stock."

"His name came up through one of my contacts, trouble with a girl?"

"Lot of that. He was always getting in one mess or another with some woman, and usually it came back to cause me or the company trouble. I finally offered him a good chunk of money to go away. He took it and moved back to Atlanta."

"How long ago was that?"

"Five years, give or take. Right after Carlos threw in the towel, that was the start of it."

"The company wasn't worth as much back then, right?"

"It cost me more than it was worth to buy him out, and I know what you're getting at. As much as I think my brother is a bum, I don't think he would do anything to hurt me or my family."

"I may need to talk to him."

"If you have to, I can call him and set it up. But maybe you'll find something out over the weekend and we'll be done with it."

"Like I told you before, it's a long shot. You understand that Isla couldn't have survived that storm, right? It's a million to one shot that she's alive."

He grinned suddenly. "So, you're saying there's a chance?"

Lunch was late, at least that's what my stomach said. It was about two in the afternoon before Roland and I went to the bar that he considered his hangout to meet with Murphy and Skip Jackson. From what Roland said, eating there after four was nearly impossible because of happy hour and the early-birds looking to hit the sheets by eight o'clock in the evening. I wasn't quite there yet.

Murphy was a heavyset man with half a head of hair and a huge grin. He stood and shook my hand when the introductions were made. Skip was older, pushing seventy if I was going to guess, and considerably more reserved. He nodded, then gave Roland a dour look.

"Business must be good. Murph tells me you want to host all three days."

"A couple pigs and a bunch of beer, not a big investment. I just thought it would be nice not to have to move things around once everything is set up. Three years ago, you were bitching because your beach got trashed."

"That's why I think we should just cancel the whole thing this year." He said stone-faced. "It's always been the understanding that we all agree, or there's no party."

Roland looked stricken. "You can't be serious! It's practically an institution, and Slater is looking forward to meeting everyone. Everybody on the whole damn Key is going to be there."

"There were four people passed out right in front of my house last year, naked as jaybirds."

Roland laughed nervously. "That's the point, isn't it? It's a party. Slater, you might want to have a few extra blankets available. Skip's turned into a prude."

Skip gave me a sly look and winked. "Trash everywhere, and naked people. I'll bet they were out there fornicating on my sand."

Roland frowned, and seemed a little confused. "Skip, it wasn't that long ago you were out there fornicating on your sand."

"That was before I got married. I still say that girl wasn't a hooker, she just liked older men. The point is, I didn't leave any garbage lying around on your beach." He looked at me and put out his hand. "Slater, right? I'll tell you what, because I'm a nice guy and I want to be a good neighbor, you can have the party on your beach all three days. You have to keep the garbage and riff-raff in front of your house, but if there are any naked women, you send 'em my way."

It took him a minute to sort it out, but Roland laughed the loudest. "You're an asshole, Skip. You really had me going."

"I'm glad we have some new blood, but what the hell, Roland, you aren't going to be here?"

"Work is kicking my ass. They don't know it's Labor Day in the middle east, and Ginger has a big tennis tournament. I have to be around for that."

"Yeah, you need to take care of her. At our age, women that look like Ginger are hard to come by." Murphy nodded. Odd that I found that sexist. "Come to think of it, they're hard to come by no matter how old you are. How about you, Slater? Is there a Ginger in your life?"

I grinned. "She is a ginger, but her name's Maggie."

"Pretty woman, gorgeous woman," Roland volunteered. "She's flying in Thursday, right Slater? These two will be over at the house all day helping you set up for the party once they get a look at her."

"She is easy on the eyes," I acknowledge. "Smart too, I'm a lucky guy."

"What'd you do to your foot?" Skip asked, inspecting my cast.

"Fell off a roof."

We spent an hour shooting the bull, talking about the party, politics, and women; not necessarily in that order. Both Murphy and Skip were great guys, a little spoiled by their wealth but not pretentious or self-entitled. It was obvious they both liked Roland, but when he forgot what he was talking about they exchanged a look. After a couple of beers, he headed to the bathroom, and they started quizzing me.

"Your wife, she's related to Caroline's side of the family?"

"Distant cousins, but we're not married, yet. I know Roland because of a mutual friend that has a few oil wells." The easiest lies are the ones that contain some truth. I was hoping they wouldn't want a lot of information, but it seemed logical that Maryanne might use Roland's products.

"Is it me, or is Dunbar getting really forgetful?" Murphy asked. "He hasn't been around much since Caroline died, but he doesn't seem to be as sharp as he used to."

"Yeah? I haven't noticed." I shrugged. "Caroline must have been quite a gal, he mentions her a lot."

"That's an understatement." Skip nodded. "She was about the most amazing woman I've ever met."

"Every one of us was secretly in love with her." Murphy shook his head. "But Roland just kept chasing around and he finally lost her. She gave up, and started fooling around, too."

"You don't know that for sure," Skip interjected. "But nobody would blame her if she did. There's people down here still think Roland killed her."

I nodded, watching the bathroom door. "Yeah, I've heard that rumor. But there was a full investigation and he was cleared."

"Even if he was capable of something like that, which I doubt, he was so in love with that woman it was painful to watch. But he just kept screwing up, sleeping with other women. It was sad." Murphy concluded as Roland came back to the table.

He settled into his chair, oblivious to the fact that he was being talked about. "All right, let's get down to the particulars of the party. You two need to make sure Slater here has a good time and gets to meet everyone. I wish I could stick around, but it's not going to happen."

When we got back to the beach house Roland said something about a nap and disappeared up the stairs. I settled into an armchair with a book and managed to doze off myself.

Even though I was pretty much out, I heard the hysterical laughter before they opened the front door and practically fell through it. Drunk, the both of them.

They were hanging onto each other, laughing about something that made no sense to me, which wasn't surprising, because it wouldn't have made sense to anyone. Since I have been known to tip a few more than I should from time to time, I don't usually get too worked up about someone else doing it. But this time the someone else was Jasmine, and despite her worldly ways, she was only eighteen, and on the clock.

I hobbled around the riotous pair and stuck my head out the door. A van was just pulling out of the driveway, a sober-cab. I shut the door and turned back to them. "Ginger, you know Jasmine isn't old enough to drink."

"Looked like she was doing a pretty good job of it to me," Ginger stated. I guess that was funny too, because they started cackling again and fell on the couch.

"Slater, lighten up." Jasmine finally managed. "We didn't drink that much, we're just being silly." I was pretty sure they did drink that much. Her eyes widened suddenly. "We saw two Key deer, coolest thing ever! We made the driver stop so we could get out and pet them. They didn't go for that. Poof. A couple of jumps and they were gone. Still, it was the closet I've ever been to a real live deer."

A few months earlier, when she was with Cletus, I had treated the then seventeen-year old

148

girl as an adult without much thought about it. But back then, the concern was getting her away from her middle-aged boyfriend, and the couple beers she had or the joint I saw her smoke, hadn't troubled me overly much. Then she had just been a job, a spoiled runaway that I had to get back to her grandmother. Now, I was invested. I might have overreacted.

"Jasmine, you had no business drinking in a bar, or drinking at all. What if a cop had walked in and caught you?"

"Come on Slater, it's no big deal." She continued laughing, which didn't sit well with me.

"You're on a job. We agreed, no inhaling."

"I kind of inhaled that third drink, but it tasted just like peaches." I guess that was funny too, because they both started in again.

"Come on Mister Slater, she was with me, and I know everybody at that bar." Ginger snickered, then tried to look serious. "We played darts and had some fun. I introduced Jasmine to some of the locals. Two of them fell in love with her, so I'm pretty sure they'll be at the party."

Jasmine was having no part of it. "I'm eighteen Slater, and you aren't the boss of me."

I bristled at that. "I literally am the boss of you."

"Maybe I should quit. Or maybe you should just fire me!"

"You're drunk. Maybe you should go to your room and sleep it off."

"Go to my room! Am I eight? I knew this would happen. I told you we'd butt heads. Why do men always think they can tell us what to do?" This was directed at Ginger, who shrugged. "I'm sitting on the couch with Ginger, and if you don't like it, go to your own God-damn room."

"I'm going to the beach." My room would have worked, but I didn't want to give her the satisfaction. Also, I didn't want to argue anymore. I grabbed a bottle of water and my cane and followed the walkway out onto the beach.

I sat at the picnic table brooding for half an hour until she came and sat down across from me. She didn't look at me. "Ginger's making food, and Roland is awake."

"No doubt, all that yelling."

"You made me mad." She stated the obvious.

"I wasn't very happy either. I am kind of responsible for you."

"Maryanne knows better than to tell me what to do."

"She has a lot more experience dealing with teenage girls. I worry about you, you know that."

"You're not my Dad, Slater." She looked at me and relented. "Okay, you're like a big brother."

"A big brother that you might listen to?"

"If I had a big brother, I doubt I'd listen to him either. But you are kind of my boss. Truce?" She held out her tiny hand. "And I didn't get that drunk. As my boss, you'll be happy to hear that I learned a thing or two from Ginger."

"Really? Like what?"

"Like the fact that Isla didn't leave the day of the evacuation, she left the house two days before, after a major blow-up with her dad."

"She took the Caroline north the day before the evacuation order?"

"She might have, I don't know. Ginger said she left the house around noon the day before they were told to, and she told them then that she wasn't going to evacuate. Roland must be remembering it wrong."

I stood and we started back to the house. "How'd you get that out of Ginger?"

"She was going on about how she always tried to get along with Isla, so I started asking questions."

"It makes more sense if she was planning to take the boat out of here. She probably wasn't the only one trying to get their boat to the mainland. But why didn't she make it? She would have had plenty of time."

"Maybe she didn't go right away. Maybe she was a stoner, and she put it off too long."

"Tomorrow we have to go to the marina, and see if they have records, or if someone remembers something. We can't just take Gingers word for it." I peered closely at her. "Are you still drunk?"

"No...a little maybe, why?"

"Did you get good pictures of my visitor this morning, the guy with the dog?"

"Sure, who is he? I got two or three closeups."

"I'm not sure, but I'm guessing he drives a white van. I need to send those to Susan Foster. She can run his picture through the database, find out if his parking tickets are all paid, or if he's secretly an axe murderer."

"I can send those right to her if you want, I have her number."

"I just introduced you? First Janet, now Susan, are you stealing all my contacts?"

"Just doing my job, Boss."

"I talked to Roland, and you were right. He does have ALS. But you can't tell a soul that, okay?" She nodded, and I continued. "The internet must have been right about that medication."

"I haven't heard back from Janet, but that really sucks. I guess I wouldn't want to know my expiration date. Ginger didn't say anything about it, just that she's been worried about his memory. She seems to really love the guy."

"Tommy says that the prenup keeps her from getting the company. I don't think he's a big Ginger fan."

"I don't get it."

"Get what?"

"What big case are we trying to solve? Somebody sent Roland a necklace his daughter always wore and called him a murderer. Big deal. I get that he has a lot of money, but why is this important enough to hire three PI's?" I raised a brow. "Okay, two and a half."

"Considering you're still fairly inebriated, that's a pretty good observation. I think he's really holding onto the hope that Isla might actually be alive."

"If she were, why wouldn't she just show up?"

"He has a theory that she might have survived, then ended up dead recently."

"Because of the necklace? He thinks someone murdered her just lately?"

"I guess, I don't know. Maybe the disease is affecting his thinking. Maybe we shouldn't even be taking his money. I've been wondering about that key, the one on the chain."

"Key to her stash?" Jasmine snickered. "If it was me, I'd hide my dope on that sailboat."

"Bad example, but a good point. At some point, we're going to have to check that boat out."

Jasmine objected loudly, "I can't even swim."

"Not you, Blue, I meant me. I was a SEAL, remember? And Maggie's been diving before."

"I'll be glad when she gets here."

"Sick of me already?"

"She never yells at me."

Chapter Nine

"If you have any questions about the house, just ask Carlos or Teresa. She said she plans on making you breakfast every morning, so be prepared to be spoiled. I trust them both, but neither one of them knows the whole deal."

We were just pulling into Marathon with Roland's car, and he was giving us last minute instructions. "How often do they go up to Jacksonville?" I asked.

"Once a month, for a week, sometimes longer. Carlos comes in to the plant to troubleshoot and help out. He's too valuable to have him cleaning gutters and cutting grass when he's up there. But it's nice, because Teresa gives the house a good shaking out while she's there, and of course there's the pancakes. I'm glad I got those two together."

"Rollie is quite the matchmaker." Ginger was back to acting the part of ditzy wife.

"Teresa's been with me for years," Roland said. "After Caroline died, I moved her down here so Isla would have some company. Then when Carlos and my brother had all that trouble, he came down and lived in the guest house, and we moved Teresa into the big house. Actually, into the room Jasmine is in now." He paused, smiling at the memory. "But her and Isla didn't always see eye to eye, and it wasn't long before Teresa and Carlos

154

were sneaking back and forth. She finally just packed up and moved into the guest house with Carlos. They've been together ever since."

I treaded cautiously. "Teresa, she seems easy going. Was Isla difficult?"

"Like her mother, hot headed, more than difficult. I don't know what their problem was, but it seemed like Isla had it out for Teresa, and Teresa got sick of it. Pretty sure, if it wasn't for Carlos, she would have moved back to Jacksonville."

"If I can ask, Roland, why have you kept the place? It's a lot of expense, and you said yourself, you hardly ever come down here anymore."

"I've asked him that more than once." Ginger said quickly.

Roland shifted in his seat uncomfortably, eyeing his young wife. "Those sunsets, Slater, and the memories. Can't have too many of either one."

"He's so damn sad," Jasmine commented, waving to them as they boarded. "Why don't you like him?"

"Who says I don't like him? We didn't hit it off at first, but he's growing on me."

"That's the way I feel about Ginger."

"Then you're a good actress, I thought you took to her right away," I admitted.

"Part of the job, Boss. How about you?"

I watched the pair as they stood in the boarding line. Ginger leaned over and gave Roland a small kiss on the cheek, then smiled and took his hand. "I like her more than I did at first. There's more to her than meets the eye. But she's one of the people on my list."

"You have a list?"

"There's always a list."

We drove back to Big Pine, and instead of going back to the house, went straight to the marina Roland had mentioned. It was a small Mom and Pop operation that sold and rented boats, as well as providing slips for a few bigger craft. There were spots for a dozen boats, a bait store, and a gas pump. They were located in a channel that wrapped around on the back side of a bay, about as far as you could get from open water on Big Pine Key. But from the videos I'd seen, there was no safe place on the island when Irma hit. Isla must have seen that coming and decided that her boat wouldn't be safe at the marina.

We didn't see anyone outside, so we walked into the dimly lit boat shack. It smelled of oil and exhaust fumes, and I could see through an open door that there was a mechanic in the back, sitting in a boat, with his head tucked under the raised cowling of an inboard. When he heard us, he lifted his head and wiped his hands quickly on a towel.

"Nobody out there?" He asked. When I shrugged, he tossed his towel down and shook his head, mumbled an expletive that I missed, and climbed down from the boat. He might have been forty-five, looked fit, and a little frazzled. "My wife is sick today, but Jack's around here somewhere. What can I do for you?"

"We're just looking for some information. Do you keep records of the boats that come in and out of here?"

"You mean, storage receipts, tax records?"

"No, more like if someone takes their boat out and doesn't come back for a few days. Would you be aware of that?"

"I don't have a log or anything. What are you saying?" He looked at me like I'd lost my mind. "Do I look like a babysitter? People take their boats out, then they come back. As long as their fees are paid up, I could care less."

"No record of any kind then?"

"Does it look like I have time for that? Who the hell would keep records like that?"

I backed off. "The Navy. Sorry, stupid of me, but I thought it wouldn't hurt to ask."

"You're a Navy guy? Did four years, myself. You a lifer?"

"Twenty years, and he was a SEAL." Jasmine sniffed, and lifted her chin like she was a proud daughter.

"Well thanks for that. Whose boat are we talking about?"

"Isla Dunbar's, the Caroline? She went out a couple days before Irma came in."

"Horrible damn deal. If I'd thought she was going to make a run, I would have tried to stop her.

She told us she was taking the boat back around to their slip at the house, and that they were going to tie it off to some trees and hope for the best. She said she was worried about it battering against the other boats if she left it here." The door creaked open and a sandy-haired teenager in a floral shirt and sandals walked in. The owner scowled in his direction. "Where've you been, Jack?"

"I dunno', around. I was out by the pumps and didn't see them come in."

"Fooling with your guitar, or did you fall asleep?" He nodded at the blue-eyed miscreant. "Not a care in the world, this one. Thinks he's going to be a rock star when he flunks out of college. You were here the day Isla took the Caroline out, weren't you? That was right when you were starting your freshman year."

"Go Hurricanes." He gave us a half-hearted fist-pump and smiled shyly at Jasmine. "Yeah, I was still here. That sucked, her going down like that."

"Do either of you remember what day that was?" I asked.

"It was Friday, because I was home and classes were already canceled for the first part of the next week. Go Hurricanes." He grinned at Jasmine and did the fist-pump thing again. She blushed and giggled appreciatively.

"Friday? We were told it was Wednesday or Thursday. Are you sure?" I asked, glancing back and forth between the pair.

His father agreed. "Yeah, it was Friday afternoon, because I remember thinking that she'd be all right getting it back to her dad's place before things went to hell. It didn't get bad here until Saturday afternoon. We had already decided to ride it out. Let me tell you, don't ever try that."

"I was scared shitless," Jack muttered, peering at Jasmine through the blond curl that had fallen over one eye.

"Do you remember if she left her car, or did someone drop her off?"

"Her car wasn't here, so I'm guessing someone dropped her off. Jack?"

"Yeah, I saw a guy drop her off, then I got busy." He glanced at me, then looked at the floor. Considering he hadn't taken his eyes off Jasmine up until that point, it made me wonder.

"Anything else you remember? Do you remember the car, or the guy in it?"

"Same guy she was with when they brought the boat in for service," Jack offered. "I'd seen him before."

"Jessie Forester?"

"No, I know Jessie. He lets me play my guitar at his place once in a while. It wasn't him."

"Anything else?"

"Nope, nothing I can think of."

"Was the boat in good shape, mechanically? Hurricanes don't move that fast, I would have thought she could make it to Marcos Island before

Irma caught up with her. What size inboard did it have?"

"The smaller option, a twenty-horse diesel. Still, a good sailor like she was said to have been, she should have made it with no problem," the older man said, then scratched his head. "You being Navy and all, I don't mind being helpful, but it seems like you're asking an awful lot of questions considering I don't really know who you are."

I stuck out my hand. "Slater, and this is Jasmine."

"Jeremy Belmont, and Jack." We exchanged handshakes.

"Jasmine's my niece, and my girlfriend is a shoestring relative of Roland's. We're buying his property, so I'm going around and inviting everyone to the Labor Day party we're having this weekend. And maybe I'm sticking my nose in where it's not wanted, sorry."

"I always wondered about that deal myself." Jeremy acknowledged. "The whole thing seemed weird. She always struck me as being smarter than to get caught that far from land. Roland's had more than his share of bad luck, first his wife, then his daughter."

"He's still torn up about it. I'm just trying to make sense of it, maybe give him some closure. Sounded like she just made a terrible choice, but I think he wonders."

Jack spoke up. "She told me she was just taking the boat around to her house, I swear."

"Not your fault, Jack." I assured him.

"She was really worried about that boat, and maybe I should have known, but she said she was just taking it around."

Jasmine poked me with an elbow. "Let's get going, Slater. Tell them what time the party starts."

"Sure, okay. Friday at five. Volleyball, pop, beer, and a pig roast. Stop by any time after five. We'll get out of here and let you get back to work. Nice to meet you."

"You're going to stop by, right?" That was Jasmine. She and Jack were having a moment.

"Yeah, for sure. We always go to Roland's parties. I have a gig, but I'll come by for a while. Cool."

"What's the deal?" I quizzed my diminutive partner as we got in the car. "The kid knows more than he's saying."

"Probably, but he wasn't going to tell you, not when his Dad was standing right there. When he comes to the party, I'll get it out of him. Mata Harry, that's me."

"Mata Hari, and you're not her. But you might be right, he did seem to take a shine to you. Kind of looked like the feeling was mutual."

"We're on a job, Slater." She mocked me. "But he was kind of cute." Her phone buzzed and she glanced at it, then handed it to me.

I read the contact, Susan Foster, then opened the message. *'William Forester, aka*

"Woody" No known arrests. Two hitches in the Army, ten years with Miami police department, twelve as a licensed private investigator in Florida, licensed lapsed, not suspended, widower, two sons, Jessie and Jonathan. That's all I've got.'

"Anything else in here I should look at?"

"No. Hand it over." She snatched the phone from my hand. "Now what?"

"I guess I'll go sit on the beach again. Carlos is going to help me get set up for the plane, but Maggie won't be here until tomorrow."

"We could go back to the bar. Two of Isla's friends were there yesterday. They seemed kind of sleezy to me."

"Did they bring her up, or did you?"

"I don't know, we were drinking and playing darts."

"That's why it pays to be sober, Jasmine. If you started talking about her, of course they would claim to know her, because you're cute, and you're in a bar."

"But they did know her."

"You should have mentioned her to Ginger, see if they took the bait."

"I guess there are times when that might matter. Okay, I'll try to stay sober the rest of the trip, okay, Boss?" She looked over and gave me a big grin.

"Not like you're going to lose your low paying job," I admitted.

Chapter Ten

Time and the tides, to quote a wise old friend of mine, waits for no man. That saying applies to people, and also anything man-made that's exposed to the elements and the comings and goings of wind, water, and hurricanes.

Roland Dunbar and his neighbor to the east, shared a small channel that had been dug before the existence of ordinances prohibiting homeowners from doing that sort of thing. There was a dock on either side of the channel, and treated railroad ties had been driven into the muck to prevent the sides from caving and eventually refilling the canal. Time and the constant battering of water and wind had depreciated the railroad ties, and the sides were in danger of collapsing. The whole channel wasn't a hundred feet long, and probably forty feet wide, but there were a couple of large trees back from the shoreline, substantial enough to have kept even a sizable boat like the Caroline from being blown away by a hurricane.

I stood as close to the edge as I dared, wondering why Isla had risked her life rather than trust the huge Bayan trees. George Murphy appeared on the far side of the canal, also standing perilously close to the edge, and waved a greeting.

"I talked to Dunbar about fixing this up, but we haven't gotten around to it. Maybe you can light a fire under him. We're going to need a permit, and finding someone to do any work these days is tough," He lamented.

"These old timbers are irreplaceable," I said, pointing to some of the worst. "Probably salvaged from the old railroad, or surplus, that somebody scavenged." Murphy struck me as the more affable of the two neighbors, and the most likely to divulge information. "I've got a beer if you want one. The outfit that's going to set up the big tent is supposed to show up pretty soon. We can have a cold one and pretend like we're helping."

"Pretty early, but you talked me into it," he said. "I'll be over in a few minutes."

There must have been a trail through the brush just on the back side of the dune, because I had no more than settled into my spot at the picnic table when he came stumbling out onto the beach. He swatted at the air, then shuffled through the sand to where I was sitting.

"Plenty of mosquitoes when you get in the brush. Where's your little friend?"

"You mean Jasmine? She's my niece, and I think she's had enough of me for a while." Actually, she had returned to her room to be ready with the camera.

"Your girlfriend, she's coming in tomorrow?"

I grinned. "Yeah, tomorrow afternoon. Why, what else did Roland say about her?"

"You said she's easy on the eyes," George grinned. "Dunbar said she was all that and then some."

"The old hound." I chuckled, and handed George a cold one. "Look, but don't touch. Likely as not she'd break something for you. Roland better tend to his own wife, she's a good-looking woman herself."

"He's always liked the ladies, that's for sure. Him and that brother of his."

"Shirt-tail relation to my girlfriend, but I've never met the guy." The conversation was steering itself right where I hoped it would go.

"He used to come down here now and again when Roland was around, and then, sometimes when he wasn't."

"Yeah? What was that about?"

"I'm not one to gossip," Murphy claimed, then proceeded to do so. "Ross is a charmer, just like his older brother. Good looking guy too. A younger version of Roland. Seemed to me, he and Caroline got along pretty well." He raised an eyebrow to make sure I wouldn't miss the innuendo.

"That's cold, fooling around with your brother's wife."

"You didn't hear that from me," Murphy shook his head sadly. "All I know, is Roland would be up north, Isla would be working at the bar, and Ross's car would show up for a few hours."

"What about Carlos and Teresa? Didn't they say anything to Roland?"

"Don't know, not really my business."

"She killed herself, didn't she?" He seemed to know a lot about things that weren't his business.

"Accident, or accidental suicide, I guess you could say. She was taking something for anxiety, and took too much, or something. That's what the police thought." He paused and gave me an odd look. "Ross hadn't been around here for a year or so, so I never mentioned that part to the cops. They sent a local investigator out here to quiz me and Jackson both, because they thought maybe Roland had done it. Good thing he was banging that woman up north, so he had an alibi."

"Nice family I'm hooked up with," I said dryly.

"Roland's settled down some since he's gotten older. I don't think he fools around on Ginger. Caroline and him, that was a mess at the end. She got to where she didn't care. I think she was ready to walk out and go live with Woody."

"Woody?" I acted like I'd never heard the name.

"Yeah, he's a bartender at the Saltwater. I'll take you down there. Music some nights, and it's more of a locals' hangout. He and Caroline did a piss poor job of sneaking around. Pretty much everybody knew they had something going on."

"What's his real name?"

"Bill, or Will, I think. Forester's his last name. That's why everybody calls him Woody."

"I met him. He's got a dog, right?" Murphy nodded. "He was out walking the beach, and he came up and introduced himself."

"Good thing Roland didn't see him." Murphy shook his head. "No love lost between those two."

"He said something about that. They actually got in a fight, didn't they?"

"Not much of a fight. Roland started swinging and Woody threw him down and sat on him, that was about it. Woody was a cop in Miami. I wouldn't want to mess with him."

"Roland is getting too old to be fighting anybody."

"He got wind of what was going on between Woody and Caroline. Roland's no angel, but it killed him that she'd cheat on him. Well, look at that." Murphy motioned toward the water. "Speak of the Devil."

Will Forester was out walking Jasper. Today, he kept throwing the ball into the water so the dog wouldn't have any reason to come in our direction. He spotted us watching him and waved briefly, then kept walking down the beach until he disappeared around a corner.

Murphy wasn't done gossiping. "Woody took it really hard, Caroline dying like she did."

"I imagine he would. He said his son Jessie and Isla were close too, then she drowns two years after Caroline. Hell of a streak of bad luck."

"I don't think Jessie and Isla had anything going, they were just hanging out, because she worked at the bar."

"Were Woody and Caroline carrying on right in front of Isla?"

"As I remember, she came back from grad school the year before Caroline died. But she worked at the Saltwater all that summer, so she had to know what was happening."

"This place is like one big soap opera. I'm going to have to keep an eye on Maggie."

"The stories I could tell," Murphy said as he reached for another beer.

Mercifully, Jasmine rescued me from Murphy after another hour of stories about the misadventures of everyone that lived on Big Pine Key. She sat down and introduced herself.

"Slater calls me Blue, but I don't encourage it. He's a mean uncle."

"Looking forward to the party?" Murphy asked. "There are a lot of young people that show up. Most of them sneak beers, then go sit on the dune and smoke weed. We pretend we don't see them."

"Sounds about right. I'm always sneaking beers, and Slater's always trying to stop me."

Murphy polished off his fourth one and stood up. "Well, I'd better get home, or I'll be in trouble. Time for lunch anyway. Nice to meet you, Jasmine."

"Thank God," I said as he disappeared over the dune. "What took you so long?"

"I was busy. Teresa's nice, but she kept talking and talking and wouldn't leave me alone. She finally left and went back to the guest house."

"I forgot to invite Carlos for breakfast. It's ridiculous that he wouldn't just eat in the house with us."

"She went home to feed him, I guess. As soon as she left, I started digging through stuff, investigating some more."

"Super. Now what did you do?"

"I made a big discovery, thank you very much."

"You snooped in Roland and Ginger's room, didn't you?"

"Of course. They left all those pill bottles in the upstairs bathroom, so I looked at them again. I'm not sure if I like Ginger anymore."

"You'll have to explain that."

"Janet got back to me. She said that as far as she knew, Riluzole is only used for ALS. She had to look it up, because that isn't something she ever sees. But she also said that as far as she could tell, there is only one manufacturer. The pills should be either round or oblong, and white, stamped with the dosage, usually fifty milligrams. She said that

169

from the pictures I sent her, the pills in that prescription bottle aren't Riluzole. The pills aren't white, they're reddish brown."

"What are they, do we know?"

"I sent Janet another picture, just the pills laying on the counter. She just texted me back." Jasmine looked at her phone and read the text. "LOL, that's Omeprazole, OTC."

"Sorry, but I don't know what that is," I admitted.

"Lucky you, you never get heartburn. It's Prilosec, Slater. You can buy it off the rack at Wal-Mart."

"You think Ginger is giving him fake pills?"

"Obviously. She's trying to kill him off."

"Well, I have to admit it does seem odd, but it doesn't mean you're right. Maybe they just threw some Prilosec in an empty pill bottle, for convenience."

"That's weak, Slater, but it is possible I guess," she said, deflated.

"But it was a good thought, following up on the medication thing, good job." I tried to sound encouraging.

"Next time you talk to Roland, try to ask him if he has trouble with heartburn."

"I don't know how that's going to come up in casual conversation. Bottom line, he's going to die, and that drug isn't going to change that. I read about Riluzole too, and it isn't that effective."

"Still," Jasmine muttered, "Ginger's on my list."

Women, to one degree or another, have always been a mystery to me. Early on, I decided to accept the conventional wisdom that men and women were from different planets, and let it go at that. Every time I thought I had cracked the code, something unexpected happened and I was left wondering how I had managed to screw up, again.

Maggie Jeffries was the exception to that rule. I always had a sense of what she was thinking, but I didn't plan to ever admit that to her. As she had pointed out recently, unrealistic expectations were a good way to ruin a relationship. But when she climbed out of our new airplane and surveyed the beach, I could see she wasn't pleased. I pretended not to notice.

"Good flight? How'd the new plane handle?"

"Never missed a beat. We got a great deal. Is all this for the party, or is the circus coming to town?"

The rental shop had put up two tents, one a canopy style, and one that could have housed half a dozen Elephants, a Lion tamer, and several clowns. I suspected that at some point it probably had. The big tent was tucked back close to the dune, and was intended for backup in case of rain. I suggested that they didn't even bother putting it up, but according to the man with the clipboard,

171

Roland had insisted. They had also installed two volleyball nets, set up two large gas grills, and four guys had carried a portable rotisserie down from the road, with the promise of a whole hog and a chef to follow.

"I agree, it does seem like a lot. But Murphy said it's not unusual to get a couple hundred people, sometimes more."

"This whole idea seems ridiculous, Slater."

I knew better than to remind her that I had voiced that opinion early on. "Actually, we have made some progress by being here. Jasmine and I talked to the marina, and Isla didn't take the boat out until Friday afternoon. I met the guy that may have been seeing Caroline when she died, found out that she might have been fooling around with Roland's brother at one point, and what else, Jasmine?"

"Did you tell her that Roland is dying from Lou Gehrig's?" Jasmine asked.

"Okay," she admitted, "that's a lot. I'm impressed. But what are we going to learn from a couple hundred drunks?"

"Hopefully, more than we know now. How're things in Jacksonville?"

"I knew there was a reason Stacey Lane was suddenly taking all those classes. I followed her last night, after she finished Pilates."

"Of course you did. Nobody listens to me."

"Good thing I did, Slater. She didn't leave alone. She followed Margret Henderson to her house, hung around for most of the evening, then snuck home."

"Stacey loves to hear herself talk, were they swapping recipes, or does Margret like women too?"

"Married and divorced, and I don't know her very well, but I'm pretty sure she likes Stacey. After about half an hour, the only light on was the one in the bedroom. I don't think Stacey has any intention of leaving her husband, it's just another con."

"Sounds like it. Wow, Stacey sure gets around. Is that why you're upset?"

"I'm the one that's going to have to tell Janet and convince her that she's being conned. She needs to get her lawyer involved, or hire Tommy. Margaret has some money, but not so much that she can afford to lose a couple hundred grand like Janet has, or will, if she doesn't wise up. But it's time somebody put a stop to it."

"I'll talk to her," Jasmine volunteered, "and tell her what you found out."

"Thanks, but it probably should come from me or Slater," Maggie said. "It's part of the investigation."

"Am I part of this team or not?" Jasmine asked.

"Okay, I'm sorry." Maggie put her bag down. "I didn't mean to imply you're not a part of the team, but I didn't realize you knew Janet that well."

"I didn't, but she's been helping us with this case. She called me last night, and a couple of other times."

"Called you?" I asked.

"Yeah, to cry on my shoulder. For some reason we hit it off, and she's all tore up about Stacey. She's figured out she's being used."

"Yeah, that's probably it."

"For crying out loud, Slater, she knows I'm straight. She just needed someone to talk to." Jasmine crossed her arms and gave Maggie and I a defiant look. "Am I a part of Slater and Partners or not?"

I exchanged a grin with Maggie. "As the Slater of Slater and Partners, I can say that you're definitely part of the team. But you are still going to college, young lady."

"I'll tell her what Maggie said, but I won't name names. I think I can talk her into taking legal action against Stacey and Derrick."

"And how do you plan to do that?" I asked.

"Girl talk, Slater. You just let me handle it." She grinned. "If I really am on the team, you have to trust me."

"And you have to share information with your superiors." I folded my arms, mimicking the blue-haired girl. "And that would be me…and Maggie."

"I'll fill you in, but not until I know my plan is going to work."

Maggie chuckled and picked up her bag. "Let it go, Slater. Learn to pick your battles. Where am I sleeping?"

Chapter Eleven

"Morning." I woke up to a pair of blue eyes inches from my own, and a very warm, very feminine body pressing up against me. The previous three nights were the first time that Maggie and I hadn't slept in the same bed since we moved in together, and I had missed her. Judging by her enthusiasm the night before, and this early morning encounter, she had missed me as well. Surprisingly, my leg didn't hurt the whole time, and that's all I'm going to say about that.

After, she tucked her head against my shoulder, and started to doze. "Can't we go back to sleep?"

"I was sleeping nicely before you woke me up. Breakfast is at eight around here. Teresa comes over every morning and cooks, and I invited Carlos to join us so you can meet them both."

"And what do we know about Carlos and Teresa? Seems like an odd arrangement, Roland letting them live here."

"Teresa's been with Roland forever, and Carlos worked at Roland's factory in research and development, until he got into it with Roland's brother. They know we're not really buying the place, but not that we're investigators. Oh, and Jasmine is my niece. We decided that would be a good cover story. She came up with it on the drive down. Makes sense."

"She's really getting invested in this PI stuff," Maggie said cautiously.

"You make that sound like a bad thing."

"She's not going to want to stop and go to college, not if she can keep playing detective. That won't make Maryanne very happy."

"She still needs to go to college, I pointed that out to her yesterday."

"I heard you, just don't let her forget it. If we have to, we can make it a contingency of her employment. It's that, or have Maryanne Thatcher mad at us."

"Jasmine needs a degree, but she does have some good instincts."

"You just like having her around." Maggie laughed as she dropped her feet to the floor and reached for her robe.

"I will admit, having my own personal Smurf is kind of nice."

"You have to share her with me. It's already seven forty-five. Shower?"

"I'm not sure that will save any time, but you talked me into it."

"You two almost missed breakfast," Jasmine said around a smirk. "Carlos already went down to the beach to check on the moorings for the airplane."

"Good morning," Maggie said cheerfully, and extended a hand to Teresa. "I've heard wonderful things about you and your pancakes, Teresa."

"I've had a lot of practice making them for Mister Dunbar over the years. Mister Dunbar told me you looked a good deal like Caroline, and he's right. You're very pretty, Miss Jeffries."

"Thank you. And Roland told me plenty of nice things about you, besides the pancakes."

"I've worked for him for a long time. I used to clean the offices when he first started his business, and then his house. I even watched Isla when she was little, when Caroline was busy helping Mister Dunbar do the books."

"I am sorry I never met Isla, or her mother. Tragic, that they both died the way they did."

"Caroline, she was so beautiful, and it was better when she was still working with Roland. Once the business took off, and there was all the money, I think she got bored. It was better, back in the old days, before all the trouble."

Maggie didn't ask what the trouble was, and I trusted her instincts. "When did Roland build this place?" I asked, then turned to Maggie. "Old Eli is wandering around here somewhere."

"Silly old story," Teresa said, handing us plates of food. "Caroline loved to tell everyone that Eli came and talked to her. Sometimes I wondered if she actually believed it. Isla carried it on, mostly to terrorize her father and his new wife. But, to answer your question, they bought this property ten or eleven years ago, right when the economy went in the toilet. Roland has a knack for getting good deals and making money."

"Slater said you go up to Jacksonville with Carlos once a month, for a week or so." Maggie said, smiling around a large bite. "You're going to have to show me how to make these pancakes."

"It will be good to have people in this big house again, at least for the weekend. It sits empty a lot of the time, and I have trouble staying busy. Carlos works on the computer a lot, helping with the business, but I struggle to find enough to do."

"Good of Roland to let Carlos split his time like he does," I said. "I'm sure keeping this house is quite an expense."

"Not like he can't afford it," Teresa said dryly. She back-tracked quickly. "Forgive me, that was inappropriate. He has always been very generous, and a good friend."

"Great breakfast." Maggie said quickly. "I'm not as keen on having this party as Slater is. Do you join in?"

"Not if I can help it. It would be too much for me to cook, so Mister Dunbar always hires a caterer. Carlos doesn't drink, and I don't care for all the noise. Mostly, it's just a lot of privileged, rich people, with nothing better to do."

"That's my opinion too," Maggie said. "But I do like to play volleyball. Slater is going to have to sit on the sidelines and watch this year."

"You're getting too old to play volleyball, Uncle Slater."

Jasmine giggled when I narrowed my eyes, then Maggie joined in. "Still planning on racing me, Slater?"

"When I get this cast off, it's on." I assured them both. Even Teresa thought that was funny.

"Can I take some time off, or do I have to stay up there and take pictures all day?"

Maggie and I were sitting at the picnic table on the beach. Other than the unexpected appearance of Will Forester, my idea of chatting with the locals didn't seem to be working. I wasn't really worried. I knew the lure of free food, free beer, and Maggie Jeffries in a bikini, would guarantee that the locals would start showing up by late afternoon. None of them knew about Maggie yet, but I appreciated the bikini.

"Might as well not bother." I told Jasmine. "Party starts at five, but it's too hot to sit out here all day. We should go over to the Saltwater for lunch."

"What's the Saltwater?" Maggie asked.

"It's a bar and restaurant, and it's where Woody Forester works. His son Jessie owns the place, and Isla waitressed there before she decided to go for that boat ride. Also, I'm pretty sure Woody drives a white van. Ex-cop, and he was a PI for quite a few years."

"What's his deal? You said he and Caroline might have been close. The plot thickens."

"You might want to put some clothes on, I'm not capable of defending your honor in my present condition."

"I doubt I'd need you to, but I planned to change."

"I'm probably going to pass, if that's all right," Jasmine said. "I might go for a little boat ride instead, see some of the sights."

"Let me guess," I snorted. "The kid at the boat yard."

"He packed a picnic lunch and he's going to pick me up on the beach. Should be here pretty soon."

"You're incorrigible."

"I try. Look at that, he's early."

The Saltwater wasn't on Big Pine Key, so we took Maggie's car and made the short drive down Highway One. It gave us a chance to talk.

"What are you thinking, Slater? Is this all a wild goose chase?"

"Probably. Chances are pretty good that Isla got swept off her sailboat and drowned. But we're back to where we started as far as the necklace goes. If Roland is right about Isla refusing to ever take it off, how is it that it showed up at all, much-less on the anniversary of his wife's death. And what is the key for?"

"Nothing in her room? I presume Roland and Ginger cleaned it out."

"Roland said there wasn't any kind of storage box, or anything in her room with a lock on it. I'm guessing she mostly lived at beach house, because Roland and Ginger were hardly ever there. She must have burned through her mother's insurance money, because she insisted on working so she didn't have to take money from Roland. It could be she locked something up on the boat, but it must be important for her to have the key on that chain. At some point, if Roland wants us to keep digging, we'll have to go out there. Are you a good diver?"

"I'm good to sixty feet, but it's been a few years. One thing, I hate sharks, a lot."

I laughed. "I didn't think you were afraid of anything."

"I wouldn't call it fear, just a very, very, healthy respect."

"I'm wondering if Ginger isn't right, that Isla's boyfriend had the necklace and sent it just to mess with Roland. That would be a shitty thing to do, but I don't think there's much love lost between those two families."

"The father and son both work at this bar?"

"I Googled it. Jessie Forester is listed as the owner. Looked like a fairly good-sized place from the pictures on the website. Odd, if they're doing well, that a thirty something kid would be living with his father."

"He has two boys, right? Jessie and Jonathan?"

"Were you and Jasmine trading notes?"

"Technology, Slater, she sent me Susan's text."

"I thought maybe Isla and Jessie were together, but Murphy says not. Woody never said that she was going out with Jessie, just that Roland didn't like him."

Maggie chuckled. "Woody? Are you two friends now?"

"He doesn't seem like a bad guy. I'm not sure what he was doing in Jacksonville, chasing Roland, and at some point, we're going to have to ask him about that. Murphy likes them both, but I'm sure that's just because he's always in their bar, and they probably give him free drinks."

The Saltwater was tucked back off the highway half a block, but you could still see the Atlantic from the spacious parking lot. It wasn't a new building, and it looked like it had been added on to several times. There were a dozen cars and three motorcycles in the parking lot, and a big sign stood beside the main entrance promising that a jazz band was coming all the way from Atlanta to play on Saturday and Sunday night. This was the off-season in the Keys, too hot for all but the most diehard Floridians, and the Saltwater was only a third full.

The front room looked like a thousand other hometown bars: two pool tables, a long shuffle board table, and half-a-dozen grizzled barflies that glanced at us when we walked in, then swiveled their necks for a second look at my girlfriend. The welcoming smell of steamed shrimp assaulted my nostrils, reminding me that Teresa's pancakes had been five hours ago. I could see a small dining room in the back, but the bartender looked familiar, and I wanted to talk.

"Gentleman." I nodded to the other patrons, and offered Maggie a stool a couple of seats over from the nearest, then sat on the end. Will Forester glanced at us, tossed his towel over his shoulder, and came down.

"Good to see you again, Slater." He reached across the bar and shook my hand. "I see you brought your better-looking other half."

"Will Forester, Maggie Jeffries."

"Slater tells me you have a very nice dog," Maggie offered.

"Jasper loves Slater. You throw his ball one time and you have a friend for life."

"You said you were a bartender, and here you are," I said looking around. "I Googled good food, and this place came up, even had a picture of you and your son."

"So Woody," Maggie inspected the free chips in the bowl in front of her, then pushed them aside. "You have the early-shift, you could come to our party tonight."

"Busy weekend, but I might be able to slip away. You two hungry, or did you just come for a second look at my van? It's parked around back if you're interested."

"Both actually." Maggie gave him a bemused smile.

"I never told Slater my name was Woody, so I figure you've been asking around about me. Of course, there's Murphy, he has all kinds of stories."

"I take everything he says with a grain of salt." I slid the chips over and tried a couple. "Curious, you being in Jacksonville on the same day we had a meeting with Roland."

"Just driving down the street minding my own business when some crazy person in a convertible started chasing me. Good thing the police managed to get her stopped." He grinned, stole a chip, and popped it into his mouth, then opened two beers and slid them in front of us. "On the house. How much was that ticket?"

"Two hundred and twelve dollars, thank you very much." Maggie smiled around the neck of the beer bottle, then put it down. "Who's your client?"

"I'm a bartender. I gave up chasing perps a long time ago."

"Be nice if we don't have to butt heads," I commented. "And a plate full of steamed shrimp wouldn't hurt a thing." Maggie shot me a look. "What? I'm hungry."

Woody handed us each a menu, then leaned in close and spoke quietly, "No reason we can't get along. Caroline's dead, and I'd like to know who's responsible, and why Isla would take that boat out in a hurricane. I know you're an ex-

SEAL and a licensed PI, and that the two of you managed to take down one of the biggest child-traffickers this side of Perdition, so I'd like to think we're playing for the same team. I just don't know if that's Roland's team."

"You checked us out?" I asked. "Do you still think Roland killed Caroline?"

"This isn't the time or place." He nodded at the other customers. "I'll come by tonight and tell you what I can. It isn't just about Caroline. The shrimp is good, but the Flounder is on special, and we just brought it in yesterday."

We sat nursing our beers until the food came. Woody had disappeared, and we had a new bartender. Two of the men seated at the bar greeted him, but I would have known who he was anyway. Same hair as his father, sans the grey, and the same slim face and lean frame. There was a large framed photo of him with Isla over the bar with an inscription that said '*In Loving Memory*'. Jessie spotted us and brought our food over.

"Two specials, on the house. My Dad said you're privileged customers. Something about a speeding ticket."

"Finally," Maggie said, "a little justice."

"He tells me your looking into Isla's death."

"How about we keep that between us?" I looked down the bar to see if anyone was listening. "Far as everyone knows, we're relatives of Roland's, and we're buying the house. I'm hoping your dad won't tell anyone anything different."

"No worries, he's careful about what he says in here, and nobody wants to figure out what happened more than he does. He was a mess when Caroline died, and he was sure Roland had something to do with it. The thing with Isla, that was just unbelievable."

"In what way, because she waited until the last minute?"

"She knew better. It's funny, Roland hiring you to look into her death."

"I don't recall saying that he did," I pointed out, biting into my fish.

"Okay, maybe you can't tell me that, but who else? And why now? It's been two years."

"She worked for you, right?" I nodded at the picture. "Or was there more to it?"

"We were really good friends, and she was a great waitress. Waste of her real talents. She was a damn genius, but her dad wouldn't let her get involved with the company. She was a tree-hugger, and she wanted him to stop making fracking equipment, go green."

"You don't like tree-huggers?" Maggie asked. I knew that tone.

"Just an expression." He held up his hands and took a step back, laughing. "I'm as green as anybody. That water only needs to come up about five feet and it'll be running in my front door."

"Good answer." She acknowledged. "Coming to the party tonight, or do you have to work?"

"Storms coming, if the forecast is right. I own a bar, so I don't need to stand out in the rain and drink. Plus, we have that band coming Saturday and Sunday night, so I doubt I'll make it."

"You have a brother, right? Does he work here too? The whole family's invited," I said.

"Jon's a damn hermit," Jessie said with a wry smile. "He has a little greenhouse on Big Pine and he doesn't drink. He's trying to break into the medical marijuana business, but I think he smokes more than as he sells. My Dad's not thrilled."

"Would it be okay if we come back sometime when you can talk, privately?" The locals were taking too much interest in our conversation.

"If it would help, but my Dad and I have been over it a hundred times." He paused and looked into the dining room. "Look, I don't feel comfortable talking about the trouble Isla had there at the end. It got pretty bad, but you need to talk to Dad about that. He's the professional."

"He says he's just a bartender these days."

Jessie chuckled. "He'll never stop being a cop, not in his head. And he's not going to let this go until he knows what happened to Caroline, and Isla. Sorry, but I have customers to tend to."

Chapter Twelve

"The party starts at five, where is Jasmine?" I asked my red-haired partner.

"I'd guess she's investigating something, but probably nothing you want to know about."

"Okay, she could do worse than this Jack kid. Go Hurricanes! But she's on the clock."

"Was that a fist-pump?"

"I never got to go to college, so I adopted Miami as my team. My Mom had a cat, and I named it Sebastian."

"I have absolutely no idea what that means."

"Sebastian the Ibis, the Hurricanes' mascot?"

"Still drawing a blank. How's your leg?"

"Great. Couple more beers and I won't feel a thing."

"After this fiasco, you and I are both going on the wagon."

"Looks like our junior partner made it back."

Jack Belmont ran his small boat up onto the beach and jumped out, then helped Jasmine. Hand in hand, they walked up to where we sat, and Jasmine introduced Jack to Maggie.

"Jack has something to tell you, Slater." Jasmine said, and motioned to her reluctant accomplice.

He looked at her sheepishly, then shrugged and talked. "I kind of remembered something else about the day Isla picked up her boat."

"You remembered, or finally decided to tell us?" I asked. "Okay, it doesn't matter. What do you know?"

"Isla wasn't alone that day when she took the boat. There was another girl, and she got on the boat with her."

"Jesus!" I stood up too quickly and nearly fell on my face. "And I was just starting to like you."

"They swore they were just going around to Isla's house," he said quickly. "I went to Miami right after the hurricane blew through to get moved into the dorm. Our marina was trashed, but my Dad made me go to school anyway. My parents didn't tell me about what had happened to Isla. They were busy trying to rebuild, and must have forgotten to mention it. I was just starting college, worried about them losing the marina, and partying. College kids don't read the news, and I didn't hear about what Isla did until I came home for Thanksgiving."

"And then, you still didn't tell anyone?"

Jack kicked at the sand and his face fell. "It was stupid, I know. But everybody said it was just her on that boat. I read all the news, and they never said anything about another girl."

"Of course not," I ranted, "they wouldn't have known about her." The kid looked like he might cry.

190

Jasmine pulled him closer and glared at me. "Okay, Slater, he should have told someone once he realized what had happened, but it wasn't intentional. You never screwed up?"

"Nothing will change what happened, but you need to talk to the cops about it," Maggie said, standing and handing me my cane. "What about the guy that dropped them off? He would have known if the second girl stayed on that boat, and he would have reported it. Any idea who he was?" Jack shrugged and shook his head. "It's likely the other girl wasn't on the Caroline when it went down. Isla probably dropped her off before she left the island. But it's still a possibility, and you have to tell the authorities."

"Dozens of girls go missing in Florida every year, Maggie." I pointed out, then relented. "Sorry, Jack, I know you didn't intend to hurt anyone."

"How do I figure out who to tell? Just go to the police station?"

"I can't believe I'm saying this, but don't do that, not yet," I said.

Maggie looked at me. "You sure that's a good idea, Slater? Someone might be out there wondering what happened to their daughter."

"And they still wouldn't know for sure. Roland said that divers scoured the boat and there were no bodies, Isla's or otherwise. We need to go down there ourselves as soon as I get this damn cast off, and see if we can find something, anything they might have missed. If we get the police involved, they might blow it off, or they might reopen the case. That would just complicate everything. We're starting to make progress, and a couple weeks won't change anything."

"You're the one with the PI license. You lose it, and we're out of business," Maggie pointed out.

I shrugged. "Are you okay with waiting, Jack?"

"Whatever you say, Mister Slater."

"Just call me Slater." I reached for his hand. "Something tells me I'm going to be seeing a lot of you."

Not judging, but if drinking were an Olympic sport, the people of the Keys would qualify for a Silver, some of them Gold. They started showing up at four-thirty in the afternoon, earlier than we had planned. They were all ages, shapes, sizes, and colors, all happy to meet the new owners, and all thirsty.

Mostly, they were locals that had been to the Labor Day parties in past years. They told stories about previous debauchery and said they hoped, with a smile and a wink, that nothing like that was going to happen this year. It was an interesting assemblage. There were lot of older people, some with grandkids in tow that had no business being there, a pair of very attractive twins that were both dating the same guy, and a giant, loud mouthed Shrek look-alike that everyone just called Wild Bill. It didn't take long to find out why.

Those that could started playing volleyball, and those that couldn't stood around to watch. I sat down at a picnic table. Maggie, not surprisingly was a fan favorite, and not just because she could spike the ball. It was scorching hot and the bikini was back.

Not all of our guests were to my liking. Two lanky twenty-somethings wandered in and grabbed a beer, stood in front of Murphy and me, and started watching the match.

"Hey," I spoke up. "Slide over, can you? We're trying to see too."

"Yeah, sorry, Dude." The taller of the two glanced back at me and moved over. When his friend didn't move, he reached out and tugged him over by the shirt sleeve. "Better?" The first one asked, staring at me through his two hundred-dollar sunglasses.

I don't like to be called, Dude, and I don't care for people that wear mirrored sunglasses. You can't see where they're looking when you talk to them, and it always makes me wonder if I have something hanging out of my nose. Petty prejudices, but we all them.

"I'm Slater, the new owner."

"You talking to me?" He turned back toward me slowly.

"Slater. I just wanted to introduce myself. Welcome to my party."

"Yeah, cool." He turned back around, then poked his friend. "Hey, Mick, there's the girl with the blue hair, the one we saw at the bar the other day."

"Wonder where her friend is," Mick asked.

"That's my niece," I volunteered loudly. They both finally turned around and gave me their attention. "And she's eighteen."

"Nice girl. I figured she wasn't old enough to drink," Sunglasses commented.

"Legal though." Mick said. That didn't help me like them.

"My friend's a dick sometimes," The tall one said. "Thinks he's funny. I'm Markus." He flipped his hand. He glanced at his friend. "Introduce yourself, Dumbass."

"Yeah, Mick. My Dad's Senator Nelson. He's going to run for governor in a few years."

"As if," Marcus snorted, then turned to me again. "Your niece is cool. Too bad, but it looks like she found herself a boyfriend already." Jack was sitting on a log and Jasmine was molded to his side, whispering in his ear.

"How old are you, Marcus?" I asked.

"Twenty-nine, why?"

"You're welcome to some roast pig and all the beer you want, but stay the hell away from my niece, Dude."

"Wow, harsh." Mick snickered. "I guess he told you, Marcus."

Marcus's eyes may have narrowed, I couldn't tell because of those fucking sunglasses.

"Yeah, no problem. It's your party. Later, Dude." He and Mick walked away, apparently in need of a refill.

"That wasn't very neighborly of me, was it?" I asked, when Murphy started snickering.

"Self-entitled little pricks," he said. "They cause trouble everywhere they go. Mick's dad is always bailing them out of one scrape or another, drugs mostly."

"That's the trouble with a party like this, hard to keep the riff-raff out."

"Nice airplane." He looked out at the Cessna. "You going to keep that here, or up north?"

"We'll fly back and forth with it, pick up a car to leave here, or use Roland's." I was beginning to feel a little guilty about lying to Murphy. Other than the fact that he couldn't keep a secret, he was a great guy. It would have been easier to explain that I had been hired to be there, but loose lips sink ships, as Roland had said. I wanted to know more about Caroline and Roland's brother.

"Roland tells me Caroline was a great hostess."

"She had her moments," he chuckled. "Most of the time she was a lot of fun, and she never lost it at the party, but she had some head issues. I knew her for a long time, and she was always up and down a lot. The last couple of years before she died, it seemed like it was mostly down. I don't know if her drowning was an accident."

"Maggie's sister is bi-polar, but she's on medication. Seems to work pretty well."

"Maybe Caroline wasn't taking the right stuff. Roland said she honestly believed that Old Eli was real, and that she actually thought he was talking to her sometimes. But she told me one time that she was always hearing voices, voices in her head. Scared the shit out of me, but Roland said she was just making it up, to sound glamorous."

"Sounds schizophrenic, is what it sounds."

"Whatever. They must not have had her medicated right. She told me that her mother killed herself when she was only seventeen. Makes me wonder about Isla, too."

"Just sail away and forget your troubles, permanently?"

"Wouldn't be the first person to do that. Isla was so gifted." He choked up a little and wiped quickly at his eyes. "I knew her since she was a little girl and my wife was teaching her to play the piano. Ten years old, and she was already Glenda's best student. Genius at math too, I'm told. What a horrible damn thing."

Hard not to really like a guy like that, even if he did talk too much, and I told him that. "You're a hell of a good guy, Murphy. I'm glad we're neighbors."

After another ten minutes, he sighed deeply and emptied the remains of his beer into the sand. "Much as I appreciate all these young ladies jumping around, I think I'll go home to the wife.

Maybe she'd be willing to snuggle with a tired old man."

"Take her something to eat, Buddy. There are some sandwiches already made up. I'm told a woman can't turn down a man when he's got a ham sandwich in his hand."

"Worth a try. Thanks Slater, and good luck."

After about twenty minutes, Maggie joined me at the picnic table. "How's it going, Slater? Volleyball is fun, but I can't say I'm learning a lot about the case."

"Murphy enlightened me a little, again. He said Caroline was hearing voices."

"I'm going to run in and change, then circulate and talk to people."

"Okay, I'm not moving for a while, the drunks can come to me. There aren't many people here that are Isla's age, so I don't know where to begin anyway. I'm starting to think that you might have been right about this whole party business."

"You're learning, Slater." She laughed and leaned against me to kiss my cheek. "Look at it as a paid vacation. But we have until Monday. By then it will just be the diehards, and they're the ones most likely to know something. Back in a minute."

The volleyball players had taken a break, and everyone was lining up for food so the noise level had dropped considerably. I was thinking about a ham sandwich of my own when Woody Forester sat down across from me. He had two plates, and he pushed one in my direction.

"Figured I'd save you the effort, with that cast and all."

"Thanks, I was just about to stumble up there. Good thing people are eating, maybe they won't get quite so drunk."

"The hostess left, so they all gave up on volleyball. That girl of yours is a looker."

"I'm aware. How about you, any women in your life?"

"If that's your subtle way of getting me to reminisce about Caroline, don't bother. I'll tell you anything you want to know."

"Do you have a client?"

"Okay, not everything. Does it matter?"

"Not really, unless your client is Ross Dunbar." He'd been a cop and a PI, so I really wasn't expecting an obvious reaction; maybe just a pause, or a hitch in his breath, some small tell that it bothered him. It bothered him, and he let me know about it.

"Don't go there, Slater," he growled. "That's a bull-shit move. Half the time, I think Caroline thought he was Roland, come to her from the past, or whatever hocus-pocus her diseased mind managed to fabricate. He was just using her to get at Roland."

"Just how sick was she?"

"She was diagnosed with paranoid-schizophrenia shortly after they built this house. It came and went, but it was getting worse. She would be fine for a while, then be completely irrational. She refused shock therapy, so they kept changing the drugs to try to stay ahead of it."

"Murphy did say she acted odd from time to time."

"No one else knew. Isla told me once Caroline and I started getting close. Roland hated that no amount of money could fix her, and he couldn't stand that she was so sick. Isla said that's why he stayed away, that he loved her too much, and couldn't stand to see her like that. I thought it was just plain cowardice."

"What about Isla? Is something like that hereditary?"

"Not a guarantee, but it does run in families, I guess. Early on it's hard to know. Isla was always a little out there. She believed in Astrology, the spirit world, even Old Eli; things that make you a flake in my book, but not crazy. She did seem to be getting awfully paranoid at the end. She claimed people were driving by the bar, wanting to shoot her. One time she got food poisoning, and she said it was someone trying to kill her. Somebody did run her off the road one day, but that sounded like road rage to me. She liked the Ganja, and she drove about twenty miles an hour."

I chuckled, then apologized. "Sorry, but that's funny."

"It was," he agreed. "I thought it sounded funny at the time. But someone pushed her into a bridge abutment and totaled her car, that wasn't cute. Could have been the channel, and then she might not have walked away from it."

"Maybe it was just the smoke making her paranoid, not schizophrenia."

"Maybe. She agreed to see a doctor about it, but she died before the appointment."

Every bit of logic told me to keep my mouth shut, but all my instincts told me I could trust this man. This time, I ignored my practical side.

"What about the necklace?" I asked.

"What about it? Caroline gave her that when she was little, she never took it off."

"Was she wearing it when she took the Caroline out that last time?"

"She never took it off. I have no way of knowing for sure if she had it on her that day, but I never saw her when she wasn't wearing it."

"Roland got that necklace in the mail on the twelfth of August," I explained. He sat there studying my face. I guess he had a practical side too. "That's why Roland hired us," I added.

"Someone that knew what day Caroline died, and more importantly, had the necklace?"

"Any thoughts?"

He studied my face again. "That there's an outside chance she's alive? I hadn't even considered that possibility until now. Why now, after two years?"

"How long does it take to be considered legally dead?" I'd already asked Tommy that question, but I was curious if Woody knew.

"Five years in this state, if you just disappear. But there's a presumption that Isla was on the Caroline when it went down, so Roland could petition to have her declared legally dead just about any time."

"Except now he's like you, he's not sure."

"Maybe that was the idea, to keep him from filing." I could hear the excitement in his voice, and I knew what he was thinking, because I had been thinking it too. Was it possible that Isla Dunbar really was alive?

Chapter Thirteen

Once the sun went down everyone lost interest in volleyball, but the party was just getting a good start. Woody went back to his son's bar to help out, and I sat watching the mob. The idea was to get people talking about Caroline and Isla, but that seemed impossible given the din of the music and the condition of most of the people at the party.

I could see Maggie, wandering from table to table, meeting people, and undoubtedly picking their brain. Jasmine and Jack found me just as Skip Jackson sat down.

"Different crowd this year," he observed. "Everybody must know it's going to rain, they're not pacing themselves. Most of them are already drunk."

"Maybe the problem is that we're not. But if they all go home by midnight, it wouldn't hurt my feelings. I'm all for meeting the locals, but half of them can't even talk. If it starts raining, I'm calling it."

"Slater." Jasmine called loudly, to be heard over the music. "I'm going to take Jack home to get his ride. He has to play guitar tonight at the Saltwater. You need me here, right?" There were a few people her age and younger, and several that I guessed to be Isla's age. I wanted her talking to them.

"Yeah, really I do."

"He's opening for the jazz band tomorrow night, maybe I can go then?"

A compromise. I jumped on it. "Absolutely. But if you can run him home and come right back, that would be good. You haven't been drinking?"

"No Dad, no drinking."

Skip watched them go. "I thought she was your niece?"

"She is, she's just a smartass."

Skip either knew less than Murphy, or just wasn't as willing to share it. We watched the partiers for twenty or thirty minutes while I talked around Caroline's issues and waited for him to tell me something I didn't know. He never did. Finally, I stood and stretched.

"I'm supposed to be walking around and talking to people or I'll get busted for being a bad host. Want to come?"

"Couple of people I could introduce you to, I guess. Randolph and his wife are over on the far side, sitting with a couple other friends of mine. We're all in the Save Our Key Deer Association. They'll probably hit you up for a donation."

It was bound to happen. You mix pretty girls, testosterone, and a bunch of beer together, and you'll wind up with a fist fight nine out of ten times. I was minding my own business, just trying to cross the tent without banging my leg against something, when the fists and bodies started flying. I managed to be right in the middle of it.

203

Two well intentioned, college age guys were holding Wild Bill back from trying to pummel another behemoth, and he wasn't happy about it. He was yelling, and pushing and shoving, and they were pushing back. Bill must have slipped, because all of a sudden, the two smaller guys managed to throw him over backwards. The problem was that he landed right on top of me, then stomped on my cast as he lunged forward to take another shot at the two heroes. And that hurt.

They got it all sorted out and everybody shook hands, then carried me back to my table and returned my cane. Maggie came over, and helped me stand and try walking. It was plenty sore, but I was reasonably sure I hadn't refractured anything. Correction, Wild Bill hadn't refractured anything for me.

"Just sit for a while, Slater," Maggie advised. "Does it hurt?"

"A little," I lied, because it hurt like hell. "I'm going to walk up to the house and use the bathroom. Moving around will do me some good."

"Need help, or can you make it?"

"I'll be fine," I assured her. "But if Wild Bill starts another fight, shoot him for me, would you?"

I hobbled up to the house and went into the bathroom. I didn't want to go back to the party, but I didn't want to leave Maggie on her own. My leg was throbbing, but it seemed usable. I made a few laps around the living room with my cane, then sat down to rest.

I hadn't had much beer, and I had eaten. Maybe just one pain pill to take the edge off? I lost the argument with myself and went to the medicine cabinet, then drank a big glass of water, and sat down on the couch again. I would close my eyes for just a second.

I wasn't sure when or why I woke up, but then I heard the distant rumble of thunder and caught the flash of far off lightning. Rain had been predicted, I remembered that. I fought through the fog between my ears, grabbed my cane, and stood up cautiously. My leg felt better, and I took a tentative step. Not bad at all. Maybe I could go back to the party.

The bathroom light was on, but the rest of the house was dark. I had started toward the terrace doors when the lightning flashed again and the bathroom light winked out. I waited, hoping for another flash to guide me. When it came, I happened to have my eyes on the Captain's wheel. I was a little loopy, but I was pretty sure of what I saw. The next flash confirmed it. The big wheel was turning again, spinning wildly this time.

"Bullshit." I said aloud. "Don't pull this crap, Eli, I know better." Confidently, I hobbled over to the wheel. When the lightning lit the room again, I gave it a substantial tug. I couldn't budge it. I stood there in the dark for another long moment, waiting. The storm was moving closer. A series of flashes lit the sky and the yard in front of the terrace windows. What I saw illuminated there terrified me, and sent me stumbling toward the front door.

Old Eli was forgotten, and I hurried across the kitchen and out into the garden. I skirted the fountain and pond, circled around the side of the house, and hobbled behind the garage as fast as I could. There, I stopped for a moment, and listened. I heard a whimper, a curse, then what could have been a slap. I did my best to run.

There was just enough light shining through the brush from Murphy's yard for me to see them. I remember wondering why his lights were on, when all of Roland's power had gone down. They had her pinned to the ground behind the garage, Marcus on top of her, holding his hand over her mouth and pulling at her shorts, while Mick tried to grab her flailing legs.

"Hold her feet, Asshole, so I can get her shorts off. God-dammit, she bit me." Marcus cursed and raised a hand to hit Jasmine again.

I moved as fast as I could. I could have called out, but I didn't. Despite struggling to hold Jasmine's legs, and his altered state of mind, Mick sensed my presence as I got closer to them. He stood and turned to face me. Realization and fear crossed his face as I lashed out with my cane.

Jasmine had teased me about that piece of hickory, and I had actually weighed it. Just an ounce under four pounds. I laid it across Mick's nose with every ounce of strength I could muster.

Other than the hideous crack of cartilage and bone collapsing, Mick didn't make a sound. He crumpled to the ground. I remember wondering if I might have killed him, and not caring.

Marcus pushed himself away from Jasmine and started to get to his feet. I lunged at him, and before he could turn on me, I wrapped my arm around his neck from behind. Five weeks on the Bow-flex hadn't done a thing for my aerobic fitness, but once I got ahold of Sunglasses, he didn't have a chance of breaking free. I locked my right arm under his chin and pulled on my wrist with my left.

I like to think it was because of the drugs, because stopping them should have been enough for me; but in that moment, there was nothing I wanted more than to squeeze the life out of Marcus. All I could feel was a blinding rage, and all I could think of was what he had almost done; that, and the fact that I couldn't let him get away. He kicked back against me and we both went to the ground.

Vaguely, I heard Jasmine screaming, and the strangled gasps as Marcus tried to draw a breath. He flailed and kicked at me, but like my leg, I was numb to the pain. I squeezed harder. I didn't care that I had been in time to stop him, I wanted him dead for what he had almost done.

Then suddenly there were people everywhere, yelling and swearing, and trying to pull me away from Marcus. I held on stubbornly, sure he would get away somehow if I loosened my grip. Finally, mixed with all the chaos, I heard Maggie's voice in my ear. "Slater, stop, you have to let him go. You're going to kill him."

Several pairs of hands pulled me away and I heard someone calling for an ambulance, then the cops. Mick came to first. He was covered in blood, disoriented at first, then furious. He started screaming, telling everyone I was a lunatic and that I'd attacked them for no reason. One of the bystanders was a first responder, and he worked on Marcus until he was breathing normally. They propped him up against the wall, and we all waited for the ambulance.

The thing about Opioids...you feel numb all over. They take the pain away, but they also rob you of your other senses. Somehow, somewhere, my walking cast had disintegrated. I pushed at the broken pieces with my other foot until it fell away, revealing a pasty white appendage that glowed eerily in the dim light. Lightning split the sky again, and the thunder sounded an ocean away, even though the two were nearly simultaneous. I could see giant drops of rain ricocheting off my bare legs as the storm moved in and I knew that they must be cold; but they didn't feel cold, they didn't feel anything. I didn't care that somehow I had broken my cane, and I didn't care that I had nearly killed two men.

I watched as Maggie held Jasmine, rocking her slightly as she cried, and as someone wrapped her in a blanket because her shirt was torn, but by then it was difficult to remember why she was crying. I was numb. I closed my eyes and drifted away.

I wasn't surprised when I woke up in a jail cell. My foot felt odd, and I raised my leg high enough to examine it. The walking cast had been replaced with an argyle sock and an oversized tennis shoe. I tried to remember what had happened after I came to. The ambulance had taken Marcus and Mick away after the EMTs had decided that I was just drunk, and left me in the care of the police. The cops had talked to Jasmine while Maggie and Wild Bill tended to my leg. I looked again. I was pretty sure it was Bill's oversized sneaker that still clung to my foot. I dimly remembered having a conversation with him, then they'd loaded me in the squad and transported me to lockup.

One of the cops had rambled on about knowing how something like this would happen one day, because the Labor Day parties were out of control and the Senator's kid and his buddy were dangerous little pricks. He said the Senator wouldn't be happy, and that I was in a lot of trouble. I couldn't tell you if he was on my side or not.

A key rattled in the door and I realized it was that noise that had roused me. A dour-looking officer nodded his head. "You made bail, Asshole, time to go."

"Where's my cane?" I stood up and flexed my leg. It didn't feel bad at all.

"Kindling mostly, and now it's evidence. Assault with a deadly weapon, I'd call it. You're lucky you get to go home."

"Yeah, I stopped two punks from raping a little girl, I'm a dangerous criminal."

"You're a smart-ass, is what you are. We'll see how smart you are when Senator Nelson gets done with you."

That didn't deserve an answer. I walked out into the lobby and Maggie and Jasmine both rushed up. Jasmine buried her head against my chest and sobbed. "I'm sorry, Slater. I'm so sorry."

I was flummoxed. "What are you sorry about? Marcus and his buddy are the ones who should be sorry."

"They're pressing charges."

"Marcus hit you, tried to rape you, and they're pressing charges?"

"Assault, Mister Slater."

I recognized the small man with the horn-rimmed glasses. "Davis. Did Maryanne send you all the way down here to spring me?"

"Indeed she did," he said. "Shouldn't be much to it. Jasmine made a statement last night, so your actions were justified, to a degree. Not totally. All the physical violence probably wasn't necessary."

"It sure made me feel better." No one laughed, and Maggie just shook her head. "Tough luck," I said stubbornly, "they had it coming."

"Undoubtedly. They're only filing charges so they can work an exchange."

"What do you mean, an exchange?"

"They'll want Jasmine to recant her story in exchange for dropping the assault charges against you."

"Then we might as well not leave here, because that isn't going to happen," I said.

"Slater, it's okay," Jasmine insisted. "They didn't hurt me, I was just scared."

"Jasmine, we can't let them get away with this." I looked at Maggie and she shrugged. "No! I say no deal. I saw what I saw. I'll make a statement if you won't. It's attempted rape unless you say it was consensual, and you're not going to do that."

"But, you could go to jail."

"Maggie, say something. I'll sit in jail for as long as I have to, but we can't let those bastards get away with this."

"Maggie? What should I do?" Jasmine turned to her with tears starting to trickle down her cheek.

"It's got to be your decision, Jaz. But remember what I told you about my Dad? It kills me that he kept hurting Angela. If I had told someone when he tried to touch me that time, it might have stopped him from hurting her again."

211

"Don't worry about me," I said quickly. "I was heavily medicated, right, Davis? I wasn't responsible for my actions. Davis will get the whole thing tossed. Even if those assholes don't get jail time, it'll be on their record. Maybe they'll think twice before they try it again."

She looked back and forth between us. "Okay. No deals then. Is that okay, Mister Davis?"

"I love a good fight, Miss Thatcher. I will do my best to put those reprobates in jail."

I put my arms around Maggie and Jasmine, and they helped me down the steps of the police station.

"Now what, Slater?" Maggie asked.

"First thing, I'm going to tear into that Captain's Wheel and see what the hell is going on there. Then, no more parties. The tents come down. Tonight, we'll go to the Saltwater and watch Jasmine's new boyfriend play his guitar and listen to some Blues music. Maybe by Sunday morning we can come up with a new plan, or maybe Roland will fire us. At the moment, I couldn't care less."

It was a good day, all things considered. Good food, good music, and good people to enjoy it with. Maggie and I went home early, made love, and I started to drift off.

"Slater, are you awake?"

"Hmm, kind of, what's wrong?" There was no mistaking the worry in her voice.

"You would have killed him if we hadn't heard Jasmine screaming and stopped you."

"Too bad the music wasn't louder," I mumbled, still half asleep.

"I'm serious. You were out of control, completely homicidal."

I opened my eyes and faced her. "It was Jasmine, Maggie. If they had done what they wanted to, no one could have stopped me from choking the life out of that pig, and the world would be a better place for it."

"You don't get to decide that." She searched my face. "What if you had killed him, then what? Then Jasmine and I would lose you, for God knows how many years. How could that be a good thing?"

"I know, but I wanted them to hurt, like they were trying to hurt her. I'm a guy, remember? Justice is great, but revenge feels better. Those two don't care about anything or anyone, so why should I care about them?"

"Because...you have to be better than they are, even when it's hard. We both do. I love you and I don't want to lose you. You stopped them, thank God, and no one died. But what if you had killed him? How would Jasmine deal with you being in prison for twenty years? She would blame herself. She already does. She's afraid that you're going to lose your PI license because of this, and maybe spend time in jail."

"None of that is her fault. They made it sound like they knew something about Isla, and lured her away from the party. They got what they deserved."

"I know how much you love her, but we have to be on the right side of things, or we're no better than they are. I killed Dinar because I had to, only because I had to. You beat those two idiots half to death because you lost your temper, and because you wanted to."

I knew she was right. The beer and the pain pills might have sent me over the edge, but that was just an excuse. There had been too many moments in the last year–the moment an assassin had used a child as a shield, the time I watched Rashad Dinar pistol-whip Angela Jeffries, and the afternoon that I learned what atrocities Maggie's father had committed; moments when I knew with absolute certainty that each of those people didn't deserve to draw another breath. I had made peace with their passing, and I didn't have any second thoughts. I knew it shouldn't be that easy for me, but evolution doesn't happen overnight, and I wasn't quite there yet.

Intellectually, I was aware that I didn't have the right to choose who would live or die, no matter how foul or loathsome they were. But thinking back to that night years later, I still wonder if the world might not be a better place if I had just squeezed a little harder. I blame it on the Butterfly.

Chapter Fourteen

"We'll be home in a couple days. Say Hi to Maryanne for us."

Jasmine's grandmother had called her home, and it didn't sound good. We were all afraid that Slater and Partner's might be losing our newest investigator. But Maryanne Thatcher had done so much for us all that Jasmine decided to swallow her pride, put aside her stubborn streak, and return to Jacksonville ahead of Maggie and me. And, as she reminded us, she missed her horse.

"Long drive by herself," I said as she disappeared down the driveway.

Maggie smiled. "I doubt she's going all the way today. Jack is headed back to school this morning, and he's not living in the dorms this year."

"I'm not worried about Jack. He seems like a good guy."

"I didn't tell her we have a meeting with Woody today. She would have wanted to stay."

"I didn't tell Roland either. He wouldn't be happy if he knew his dead wife's lover was helping us with the case."

"What else are we supposed to do? You need to see Janet and have that leg checked out, and we need someone down here we can trust. We do trust him, right?"

"He wants to know what happened to Isla as much as we do."

"And prove Roland killed Caroline," she pointed out.

"Hopefully that's enough incentive for him to take Roland's money and give us a hand. We'll call it miscellaneous expenses."

Carlos and Teresa had been conspicuously absent during the party. Word of the assault on Jasmine and my subsequent meltdown had traveled fast, and there were very few would-be party-goers that showed up the next night. By then, all the tents, the grills and even the volleyball net had disappeared and we sent them on their way. Roland grumbled, but agreed that there was no point continuing with the party. But he didn't want us to give up completely, we would continue to play the role of new homeowners and stay on the case.

"Is Jasmine doing alright?" Carlos asked over pork chops. "Strong girl, to go through that and then be able to drive off alone, all the way to Jacksonville."

"She's a tough kid," I said, as I took my plate from Teresa. "Her new friend is going as far as Miami, and I'm guessing she'll stop for a break there. She's young. Kids heal faster than us old guys. No pancakes? Those are my favorite."

"Sorry, I'm completely out of syrup." Teresa shrugged. She didn't sound very sorry.

"Maggie said you're going north tomorrow to have your leg looked at. I hope you haven't given up on the Keys," Carlos said. "Most people down here aren't like the Senator's kid and Marcus."

"Roland says we can come and stay anytime we want, so I'm sure you'll see more of us."

"Ginger doesn't like it here," Teresa volunteered, deboning a pork chop with a chef's knife and a competent flip of her wrist. "She wants to be in Jacksonville where she can keep an eye on things."

"And play tennis?" Maggie asked.

"And stick her big nose in where it doesn't belong," Teresa replied.

"Teresa! Ginger comes to the plant to help Roland, not to spy on us." Carlos frowned and rolled his eyes when she walked back to the stove to spear another pork chop. "My wife doesn't care for Ginger. She thinks she's plotting to take over the company."

"Roland doesn't seem well to me." The dark-haired woman said casually, as she brought her own food to the table. "If something happens to him, he should have you and Bishop running the company, not that empty-headed bimbo."

"Roland is still a fairly young man," I pointed out.

"Still," she said shrugging, "he will not live forever, and there are several hundred employees to consider."

"Is Ross out of the picture all together?" I asked.

"No one is sure," Carlos spoke up. "Roland said he bought him out, but the rumors are that he still has an interest, that Roland couldn't afford to buy him out completely. I thought about going back full-time, but if there's any chance Ross will be back, I want no part of it."

"So, go to Roland, you and the other engineers, push for ownership, a bigger share." Teresa was suddenly very earnest.

"And be stuck there if Ross does manage to weasel his way back in? I'd rather trim hedges for a living.

"Careful what you wish for," Teresa said. "Ross isn't likely to want to work with you either."

"We're not going down that rabbit hole again, are we?" Carlos asked. Maggie looked as uncomfortable as I felt, but we both held our tongues.

"Heaven forbid you would let that go!" Teresa snapped. She stood and grabbed his plate and half-eaten breakfast. "Fine, be a gardener and waste your talents. Go find your clippers, Carlos, those hedges won't trim themselves."

"That got weird," Maggie stated the obvious as we drove south to meet Will Forester. My leg was feeling significantly better, and Maggie had suggested I drive.

"Maybe the cops keeping my cane as evidence was a good thing." I suggested. "My leg feels a lot better today."

Maggie gave me a sour look, and pulled out her phone. "I'm going to enroll you in anger management classes." She started punching buttons and scrolling through what could have been a search.

"Are you serious, is that what you're doing right now?"

She chuckled, and continued scrolling. "No, Dummy, but I will if you ever pull something like that again. I'm looking for something on Facebook."

"Now? Not a fan." But my curiosity was piqued. "What are you trying to find?"

"Pictures. Sometimes people don't delete things they should."

"You mean, like celebrities that post inappropriate stuff?"

This time she laughed out loud. "Yeah Slater, I'm looking for naked pictures of my favorite movie star. Do you men ever think of anything other than sex?" She went back to her search and I went back to driving. After a couple of minutes, she handed me her phone. "Take a quick look, I'll steer."

I enlarged the picture. A younger version of Woody, his son Jessie, and another boy all stood on a dock holding a nice catch of Yellowtail. I handed the phone back. "You're thinking that's Jonathan?"

219

"I'm going to send this to Jasmine and have Jack take a look. It must have been a long time ago, but maybe Jack can tell if Jon was the guy that dropped Isla and the other girl off at the marina that day."

"Seems feasible. It sounded like Isla got along with Woody and Jessie better than her own family, and according to Roland, she was always stoned."

"I don't think Roland is leveling with us completely, do you?"

"Never did, and I believe I mentioned that." Saying I told you so is seldom helpful, and it got me a nasty look. "Tommy warned me about him, and clients in general. If he doesn't tell his lawyer everything, he's not likely to tell us either. Roland claims he bought Ross out, but if he still has some ownership, that raises a lot of questions."

"Maybe, but it still doesn't explain why someone sent Roland that necklace," Maggie pointed out.

"It takes five years for a person to be declared legally dead in Florida unless there's an obvious cause for presumption, like going down in your boat during a hurricane. There's no body, but a court would go along with the obvious and rule Isla deceased if someone petitioned for it. It's been two years, maybe Roland was starting to think it was time to give up on the idea of an heir."

"Sell the company, or just turn it over to Ross and live out his days?" Maggie asked.

"It scares me how much we're starting to think alike." I admitted. "And?"

"And someone saw that coming. They sent him the necklace, hoping that he would do exactly what he has done, think that Isla might still be alive, and start digging."

"There's a very small group of people privy to that information that might also have had access to that necklace if Isla wasn't wearing it."

"Ginger," Maggie stated.

"Tommy said Roland cut her out of the will as far as the business goes. Maybe she wanted to buy some time. She might think she can get Roland to change his mind and give her control of the company when he gets too weak to run it, then leave it to her when he dies."

"But then she'd have to deal with Ross."

"Or partner up with him. Jasmine told you about the pills, right?"

"And the fact that you shot down her theory."

"I said it was weak, but she might have been right. Ginger could be switching the pills, hoping it will make Roland sicker, and more dependent on her. We need to find out more about who owns what, and what's in that will."

"And more about Ginger," Maggie said.

"I hope I'm wrong, but it fits."

"There's another possibility," Maggie suggested.

"A couple," I admitted. "What are you thinking."

"That Isla really is still alive."

"Woody and I arrived at the same conclusion the other night, but it seems unlikely."

"Are you going to tell him everything we know?"

"I'm going to leave out the second girl. Jack might want to play at the Saltwater again if he flunks out of school, and that would make him look bad."

"Jasmine says he's a straight A student."

"We need to talk to Jonathan, and if Jack thinks it was him at the marina that day, he has a lot of explaining to do. But we'll need Woody to get anything out of him. A hermit pot-farmer might be a little difficult to deal with."

"If it was Jon who took the two girls to the marina, and they both were on that boat when it went down, wouldn't he have told someone, Woody, at the very least?"

"You'd think. But we don't know if it was Jon, and we don't know that the second girl stayed on the boat. We can't even be sure they left that day. Irma didn't show up until the next afternoon. A good sailor would have been able to outrun it easily if they left Friday."

"I wonder how much of this Woody knows?" Maggie asked.

"We were hired to find out who sent the necklace. Why would Woody send it? Just to make Roland feel bad? Same for either of his kids."

"I thought we agreed it was probably Ginger?"

"She's on the top of my list, but it could be Jessie, or the guy that brought Isla and her friend to the marina that day. That could be Jonathan, or somebody else entirely."

"The list again?"

"There's always a list."

We had a table in the small dining area of the Saltwater. Midday, and it was quiet. Woody and his son were both working, but after we were seated, Woody sat down with us.

"Hogfish today, I already ordered for you."

"Are we still working on my speeding ticket?" Maggie tried.

Woody chuckled. "Time to spend some of Roland's money, isn't it?"

"That's what we're trying to do," I said. "Are you going to help us with this case?"

"I've been at it for four years. I'm not sure what else I can come up with."

"You've been operating under the assumption that Roland killed Caroline. I get that it's hard to let that go, but maybe you should put that aside, at least for now. I really don't think he did, too many witnesses saying otherwise."

"Witnesses can be bought," he said, stubbornly. "Okay, I talked to the woman Roland was sleeping with, and she was pretty convincing. But maybe he had help."

"Ginger? How would she manage to drown Caroline? Besides, she wasn't even in the picture yet."

"You believe that? Roland knew her before Caroline died. I don't know if he was sleeping with her, but he knew her."

"Okay, I'll go along with that." I wanted to give him something. "Ginger told me as much. Doesn't mean they killed Caroline."

"Doesn't tell us what's going on now, either." Maggie said. "We're trying to figure out who sent Isla's necklace to Roland, and why. Help us with that. Maybe we'll uncover something that will help you with what happened to Caroline."

"She wasn't well, Woody. Is it possible that she just fell in the pool? She had taken sleeping pills. After my little episode, I can tell you, any kind of barbiturates and alcohol are a bad combination."

"There was a time I liked Roland," he admitted.

"And Ross? What was that all about?"

"He's a bastard." Woody said coldly. "Back in the day, when I was a cop in north Miami, we would have bagged a guy like that, and put him away."

"Bagged?" Maggie asked.

"Pulled him in, and planted drugs on him. Sometimes you do what you have to."

"Charming," Maggie said. "But Slater tells me there might have been a relationship between Ross and Caroline."

"Thanks Slater," he said dryly, then waved a hand when I started to object. "She's your partner, of course you would tell her. Caroline was spiraling down, and despite the fact that she cared about me, she still loved Roland, desperately. I really think she mixed them up in her head sometimes, and Ross knew that. He's a bastard, plain and simple. But I already checked it out, he was in Miami when Caroline drowned."

"Other than being a bastard, why would Ross seduce his brother's wife?"

"Roland forced him out of the company and I'm told it got very ugly. Simple revenge, I guess."

"What if I told you he still has an interest in the company?"

"I'd say you need to check your facts. Any chance your buddy the lawyer will tell you?"

That made Maggie and I both laugh. "You did your homework," I said. "I'm impressed. If Tommy won't, or can't tell me that, I'll go straight to Roland and get it out of him."

"Okay, so what is it I can do for you?"

"Isla trusted you, and Jessie. Straight out, did she give one of you the necklace, and was it either of you that sent it to Roland?"

"Absolutely not. I'll swear it on Caroline's grave if necessary."

"Were Jessie and Isla together, romantically?"

"No, they were very close, but just friends."

"You sure? Kids don't tell their parents everything."

A smile flickered across Woody's face.

Maggie spoke up. "Crap, Jessie is gay, isn't he?"

"How could you possibly know that?" I asked when Woody nodded.

"Woman's intuition, Slater. A lot of stuff goes over your head."

Our food came and we spent the next few minutes digging into it. Usually, I would heed the advice I had given Jasmine, and try to bait Woody into telling me what I wanted to know, but I really liked the guy and I wanted to be straight with him. When you're in the Navy, you're used to eating on the run, and I finished my food long before Maggie and Woody. I used the time to explain to Woody everything we knew up to this point, almost.

"Bottom line," I concluded, "there aren't many people who might have had access to that necklace, and most of them are in your family."

"Ginger seems like the more obvious choice to me," he said. "I never have trusted that woman."

"That's why we're going north, to talk to her again, and see my doctor. But let's say it's not her.

Then who? Not you or Jessie. You swear you didn't do it, and I presume you're saying Jessie didn't either. What about your other son? Did he know Isla?"

"Yeah he did, and if I was going to guess, Isla might have been getting her pot from him."

"I'm no doctor, but pot makes me plenty paranoid without having any psychological problems," Maggie said.

"That we know of." I grinned at her. When your significant other throws you a softball, you have to take a swing. "I didn't know you ever smoked pot."

"Not much. I tried it a few times in college. There are still a lot of things you don't know about me, Slater, I'd be careful."

I turned back to Woody, and the case. "What about Isla and Jon, any chance they were more than pot buddies?"

"I really doubt that. Jon would have said something to Jessie if they had anything going on. Jon's not likely to be someone Isla would have been attracted to. She seemed to like smart guys, and guys that showered once in a while." He rolled his eyes. "He's my kid, but most of the time I wonder what he's thinking. Jon is...very different. He's part entrepreneur, part hippie, and part drug-dealer. Full-time burnout, I'm afraid."

"Any other people in her life that she trusted? Good friends from college, or high school?" I decided to stick with a part of my plan.

Knowing about the second girl might prove to be important.

"No one I can think of, but she was my kids age, we didn't socialize outside of work."

"But she knew you were spending time with her mother, right?"

"She wanted what was best for Caroline. She would have done anything for her mother. She thought that I could make her mother happy, or at least end the suffering, and talk her into divorcing Roland."

"Still, he was her father."

"And Isla loved him, but she blamed him for her mother's misery, and that would have been enough to drive a wedge between them. After her mother died, she was truly afraid of Roland. She told me she was sure she saw him in the pool that night, even after the police proved that he couldn't have been there."

"And you're one hundred percent sure that it couldn't have been Roland's brother? I'm told they look a lot alike."

Woody pulled his phone out, found a picture, and handed it to me. Roland and Ross stood side by side, smiling for the camera. They might have been twins but for the thinning of Roland's hair. "I called someone in my old precinct and they did some checking. He was in jail for beating up a hooker, bailed out the day after Caroline died. By Roland's attorney, no less."

"Hallucinations?" Maggie asked. "Didn't she claim later that Old Eli had told her about it?"

"She knew people made fun of her for believing the ghost stories, but she swore she and her mother had both seen him, and that Caroline had even talked to him."

"Nobody can see God, but a hell of a lot of people think he's up there," I said, as much to myself as to either one of them. "Look, Woody, we really need to talk to Jonathan. Can you make that happen?"

"That's really what this is all about, isn't it?" He eyed me and chuckled.

"Mostly," I admitted and shrugged. "But we really do want you to keep asking questions while we're up north. Jackson knows more than he's saying, and maybe Murphy, although Murphy isn't shy about talking. There have to be other people that came into the bar and talked to Isla. I know it was two years ago, but maybe someone remembers something about the necklace. Did you ever notice if there was a key hanging on it?"

"No, can't say that I did, but she was careful to keep that necklace tucked in her shirt so some drunk wouldn't grab it, just horsing around."

"There's a key on it now, and we have no idea what it fits. Could be a lock box on the Caroline. Once the doctor gives me the go ahead, we're going to go down there and see what we can see. Are you a diver?"

"Are you kidding? There are sharks out there. I like to eat fish, not the other way around."

"You're not helping," Maggie said. "I don't like sharks either, but it looks like I'll be the one going down there with him."

"No more dangerous than going to see my boy. Pot farmers don't like people they don't know coming around and asking a lot of questions, and Jon always carries his gun. I'll take you out there. He doesn't care much for me coming around either, but at least he won't start shooting. He's a piece of work, but he's my kid, so what do you do?"

"Maggie's already been shot once," I shared, "and so was I. I think I complained a lot more than she did."

"I know you did," Maggie said quickly. Another softball, and the score was tied.

Chapter Fifteen

Big Pine Key isn't a very big island, but it is surprisingly woodsy. It took us ten minutes of back streets and backroads, and another five on a bumpy dirt trail that turned into more of a path before we burst into a small clearing on the north side of the island that backed up to the shoreline of a tiny bay. A small rowboat had been pulled up on the shore and was tied to a tree. An old casting rod pointed at the sky, unused and stuck in one of the oar locks. We pulled up beside an aging Bronco and got out.

"Nice piece of property," I said to Woody, "but he sure didn't spend much on his truck."

"The house and bar both belonged to my wife's folks and the boys split them down the middle. Jon couldn't have been happier, but I think Jessie got the better end of the stick."

The climate being what it is in the Keys, vehicles tend to last a long time and seldom rust, but the Bronco was ancient, and had started to go. There were a couple pieces of aluminum fixed to the sidewall with sheet-metal screws, as well as a pair of patches made of duct tape. I ran my finger across one piece, and could see the outline of what had to be a bullet-hole. The tape over the second hole had started to disintegrate, and clung to the door by one corner. I bent down and saw that there was steel plating underneath.

"Told you, Slater, pot farming is dangerous business," Woody said when he saw what I was doing.

"You're not worried about your kid getting shot at?" I asked.

"He claims he saw a wolf chasing a Key deer through the yard, and tried to shoot it. A dog, maybe, but it sure as hell wasn't any wolf. I talk a lot, but he doesn't listen."

"I know the feeling," I admitted, "reminds me of Blue."

"You mean Jasmine, your niece?"

"I meant Jasmine, but she's not really my niece."

He shrugged. "I never thought she was."

The house was a small two story, and looked a lot like the Bronco, old and worse for wear. The fact that it had survived Irma seemed remarkable, but it still bore the scars. The shutters that remained were broken, half the porch was gone, and a thirty-foot palm was nestled up to the peak. The house looked like it might be leaning into the tree, each holding the other from toppling over.

An ancient air conditioner rumbled from the back, and all the windows were shaded, either to keep out the searing heat of the midday sun, or the prying eyes of unwanted guests.

I glanced at Woody. "Does your son live alone?"

"He had a girlfriend at one time, but what woman in her right mind would live here? I think he has running water, but you couldn't prove it by the looks of him."

We walked around the corner to the greenhouse. It too was backed against a tree, although I suspected the location was by design. A huge Gumbo Limbo spread its branches over the entire structure, sheltering it from prying eyes from above. Woody had said that his son was a licensed grower, so the attempts at secrecy seemed overblown. The amount of pot he could grow was tightly controlled by the state, but we were a long way from Tallahassee, and I guessed he might have a few more plants than he was allowed.

"You can't go in there!" Jonathan Forester came walking around the corner with a small spade in his hand just as his Dad was about to knock on the tiny door of the greenhouse.

"Hi Jon." Woody nodded, then pointed at us. "No worries, these two aren't Revenuers."

"Very funny." The stocky young man said. "You know I don't like anyone snooping around in there."

"Eric Slater and Maggie Jeffries." Woody introduced us.

A father and son couldn't look much different. Jonathan was disheveled looking, bearded, and half a head shorter than his father, with a dew rag that held his unkempt hair out of his eyes. I didn't bother trying to shake his muddied hand. He stood back a couple yards and didn't make any attempt to close the distance. He was carrying a revolver in a western holster that was tied to his leg, quick draw style. Clint Eastwood had pulled that off, but on a twenty-five-year old pot farmer in desperate need of a shower, it just looked silly. The pearl handled Colt was probably good at killing Broncos, but it wouldn't stop any Revenuers.

Maggie cocked her head, peered at the greenhouse, and used her girly charms. "I tried growing pot in my college dorm room, and I killed it in a week. I can kill anything that's green. Show me your secrets?"

"We're not from the government, I promise," I added with a grin.

"Temperature and humidity control." He relented and led us to the door of the greenhouse. Undoubtedly it had been rebuilt after the hurricane. It was all glass and plastic, with crank out windows and fans hanging from the steel supports to keep the air moving. Maggie started talking about fertilizer and the right amount of shade, and things that I didn't care about. Jonathan was excited to explain everything to her and show her around. Could be he just liked the way she smelled.

"I grow tomatoes and sweet corn, beans and cucumbers, and some peppers that will light you up. That's where I make most of my money."

He made a face and decided to trust us. "The extra pot, I sell for cash."

I wasn't expecting a tour of a professional cannabis operation, but Maggie kept quizzing him, and he kept volunteering more information. I wasn't sure if she was playing him or not, she seemed genuinely interested in the whole operation.

"You're not going to start growing pot in the basement of our house, are you?" I finally asked.

"It's good for all kinds of things, Slater, right Jon?" He started listing off all of the benefits of CBD oil and pot in general, and it was starting to look like we'd never get around to talking about Isla.

Finally, I brought her up. "Your Dad told you why we're here, right?"

"Sure, but I doubt I can help you much. Isla was good people. She stopped out here from time to time to buy sweet corn and some herb. We knew each other when we were kids, fooling around on the beach and stuff, but then she went off to college and I didn't see a lot of her."

"Fooling around?"

"Not like that." He picked up a pair of clippers and grinned as he started pruning a tomato plant. "I wish! She was always so beautiful. She had a ton of guys chasing after her, but she never got into the parties and stuff. She was super serious about school, and really smart. She was all about running her Dad's business someday."

"I heard she wanted to start building wind-turbines," I said.

"Sounds like her, she always talked about saving the planet. She was cool, too bad what happened."

"Did you know any of the people she was hanging around with before she died, a boyfriend, or any of her girlfriends?"

"Jessie would know that sort of thing better than me. She and I didn't hang out, she just came out here once in a while for pot, and the sweet-corn."

He clipped away at the tomatoes, then reached back and trimmed one of the huge Marijuana plants that surrounded the perimeter. I noticed two more pair of trimmers, and picked one of them up. It didn't feel right.

"What's the deal with this one? It looks bent."

He glanced at it, then took it out of my hand. "I don't care for the electric jobs, I'd rather do it the hard way. These are special, for getting at hard to reach spots down low, see?" He reached out as far as he could and awkwardly clipped a plant in the back, then dropped it back on the table. "Can I interest you two in a fresh tomato, on the house?"

We left the greenhouse and walked to the broken-down porch. There was a hose reel hanging from the wall and he turned the tap on so we could all wash our tomatoes before we ate them, then disappeared in the house and came out with some herbal tea that tasted like vinegar.

"Did Isla ever come out here with another girl, shorter, with dark hair? Maybe had a guy with them?" I asked, emptying the last of the foul-tasting tea on the ground.

"Nope," Jon said quickly. "I'm pretty careful about who I let on the property. It's usually only two people at a time, so I can keep an eye on everyone."

"I hate to ask," Maggie spoke up, "but do you think I could use your bathroom?"

"I don't think you'd want to. It's broken, and I couldn't get a plumber until tomorrow. I should have done that instead of trying to break into the pot business. Those guys charge a fortune, and they're always too busy to show up."

"Man, I really have to go," Maggie complained.

"You can use it, I guess." Jonathan shrugged. "Just don't flush, because nothing goes down."

Maggie shuddered visibly, and reconsidered. "Yeah, I can wait."

"We'd better go then," Woody volunteered. "Not likely you want to run out in the brush."

"Nothing else you can tell us?" I tried one last time.

"Stop back in a week or so," he said, and nodded to Maggie. "I'll start a couple of trimmings for you, the good stuff."

"That was a bust." I complained after we had dropped Woody off at the house he shared with his other son.

Maggie's phone buzzed and she glanced at it. "Jack said he has no idea if the guy he saw was Jon. He was too far away and wearing a hat. He remembers he had a beard, but that doesn't prove much."

"I doubt Jon would have the ambition to send Roland that necklace, even if he had a reason to. Did you need to stop for a bathroom break?"

"I didn't really have to go, I just wanted to take a look around in the house. Paranoid as he is, I was afraid he'd follow me in, and I sure as hell wasn't going to go into that bathroom."

"I'll bet the whole place is full of pot plants. Sooner or later, that guy is going to get busted."

"I thought there might be something around to tie him to Isla, if he was the person that dropped her off that morning."

"Maybe Woody can find something out while we're gone."

"How's the foot?"

"I'm going to have to send Wild Bill a thank-you card, I think he tweaked it just right when he fell on me."

"You better let Janet decide that."

"I can walk on it without much pain, and I'll bet I can swim just fine."

"Crap. Does that mean what I think it means?"

"I'll buy you a magnetic wristband, sharks hate those."

The next morning, we loaded what little luggage we had into the Cessna. We did the preflight and Maggie started us out into the bay, taxiing downwind to give us plenty of room for takeoff. We reached the downwind leg and she turned into the wind just as the engine started to sputter.

"That's not good," I shared the obvious.

"Oil pressure is dropping, and it's heating up. What the hell?"

Before Maggie could shut the engine down, it stopped on its own. It made a series of grinding and screeching noises, a clatter that I knew wasn't normal, and belched out a substantial amount of smoke. Before I had even unbuckled my seat belt, I could see flames licking at the cowling.

"Fuel pumps off. I've got the extinguisher." Maggie shouted, opened her door, and stepped out onto the float. The Cessna had two doors, and I wasted no time sliding out of my seat and onto the other pontoon. That was the intent, but my leg picked that moment to betray me, and before I could grab the strut, I was in the water. I swam to the front of the airplane, hoping to help Maggie put the fire out, but that wasn't going well. Aviation fuel burns hot, and by the time I got around, she had given up. She dropped the extinguisher and dove into the water, surfacing thirty feet from me.

"Nice day for a swim," I said as I paddled over to her. "We'd better back off, in case it blows."

"We really don't have much luck with airplanes," Maggie stated, as we tread water at a safe distance. The fire was growing, consuming the cabin and feeding off the upholstery. I knew the tanks were half full, and that sooner or later they would ignite.

"This one's on you, I didn't even get to fly it. I'd race you to shore, but my leg still hurts."

"Excuses, excuses." She laughed. We stayed there for a minute, watching the fire grow.

"We have insurance for this, right?" I asked.

"Of course, Slater, the planes covered. I don't know about sabotage."

That was the question. Given that we might have made it into the air and stalled at an inopportune moment, the consequences of losing the engine might have been a lot worse. I heard the churn of an inboard and turned toward shore.

"Good day for a boat ride," Murphy said as he pulled up fifty feet away in his old Mastercraft and killed the motor. "The wife called the fire department, but by the time they get here, there won't be anything left. Never a dull moment with you around, Slater."

"It wasn't me this time," I said as I followed Maggie up the small ladder into the back of the boat. "It's almost like someone doesn't like us."

He tossed us each a towel, and appeared to consider that for a moment. "Just so you know, rumor is that you aren't what you say you are, that maybe Roland sent you down here to ask people questions."

"People sure like to gossip," I agreed.

"Doesn't matter to me." He turned the key and fired up the boat. "I like you, the beer was good and cold, and I sure as hell haven't done anything wrong. Guessing, once you get things figured out with the wreckage, you'll be needing a ride to the airport?"

"Looks that way," I said as Maggie leaned into me and flames consumed the Cessna. "I think we've done enough damage for one weekend."

Chapter Sixteen

It was a nearly half a mile down the wooded lane that led to Maryanne Thatcher's estate, and it was getting to be a familiar drive. Every time we made the trip, I watched through the breaks in the perfectly groomed hedges, waiting for the welcoming committee. Invariably, the half a dozen horses that Maryanne kept as 'show ponies' would spot us, and canter alongside until they ran out of real estate and fence. As often as we had been there, I wondered if they recognized Maggie's car and looked forward to our visits. The reality, I was sure, was that they were extremely bored and chased anything that moved.

Today, they were more motivated. The lead horse, a particularly difficult mare that had finally accepted me, had a rider. It was an idyllic scene, flashes of the mare with the small herd following after her, while the blue-haired jockey urged the horse to keep pace with us. Maggie grinned at me and slowed the car, then drove across the grass and pulled up in front of the small barn, the closet spot available to the pasture fence.

"Hi guys," Jasmine called from the saddle. "Dolly is rambunctious today, she wants to run. Maryanne is waiting for you. Private meeting, I'm told. Try not to talk about me." Without invitation or direction, the horse spun and started back across the field at a full gallop.

"Stupid horse is going to kill her," I admonished.

"You're ridiculous, Slater." Maggie laughed and backed onto the driveway. "Don't be a mother hen, you can't protect her every minute."

"My little chick may have wings," I went with the metaphor, "but she still needs help learning to fly."

"Remember this is Jasmine we're talking about. You have some points in the bank for keeping those two idiots off her, but that doesn't mean she won't fight you the first time you try to tell her what to do."

"I may not have to worry about that. Maryanne probably won't let her work with us anymore."

"I doubt that, but let's go find out why we're here."

Edgar, Maryanne's long serving butler answered the door and greeted us formally, then announced us to Maryanne like we were the Duke and Duchess of York, not the frequent casual guests we had become. Maryanne stood by the window, chuckling at the equestrian antics of her granddaughter. She motioned us into the two chairs that were always in front of her massive mahogany desk.

"That damn mare will be the death of her, or me."

"Exactly what I just told Maggie," I nodded, feeling vindicated. "That horse has a mind of its own."

"Undoubtedly why she loves it so much, they're kindred spirits. I'm not worried, she's become a wonderful rider, and that horse loves her as much as she loves it." She turned and settled into her chair. "The world can be a very dangerous place, and her falling off that horse is the least of my worries."

"I'm really sorry about what happened in the Keys," I volunteered. "Jasmine wasn't to blame for any of that. I hope you'll still let her work with us, at least part-time."

"Of course." Maryanne shrugged. "It was a good lesson for her. Following two men she barely knew into a secluded setting was very poor judgement. She thinks she can control any situation. Self-confidence is great, but so is common sense."

"And you're not mad?" I asked.

"Is that why you thought I called?"

"We really weren't sure," Maggie spoke up. "Jasmine did nearly get hurt because she was on a case with us."

"Perhaps, but the experience lit a fire under her. Actually, I should thank you. She's been dragging her feet about going to school, finishing her GED and going on to college. Now it's all she can talk about. She's thinking about Criminal

Justice, maybe a Law degree, because she likes working with you two so much."

"Let me guess, the University of Miami." I said. Maggie and I exchanged a look.

Maryanne laughed. "She told me all about Jack, and yes, undoubtedly that has everything to do with her wanting to get back to school, but I don't care. She insists she still wants to help you two as much as she can, and she won't start until after Christmas. I'll have her for a while yet. Jack may not last, but I'm guessing you two will always be a part of her life."

"He is a pretty good kid," I said. "And he's a 'Caner', so how could she go wrong?"

"That happens to be my Alma Mater." Maryanne said.

It seemed worth a try. "Maggie, would it be okay if I go back to college while you run the agency?"

"Animal House for the middle-aged? That ship sailed, Slater, you're stuck with me."

"Worse things could happen," I allowed. "Thanks for sending Davis down to get me out of jail, Maryanne."

"No problem. He's a little concerned that Senator Nelson will push for assault charges."

"Let him. I can get Tommy in on this if you want, you shouldn't have to foot the bill. We were on a case when it happened."

She waved a hand. "You were defending Jasmine, and Davis has experience with this kind of thing. They're still trying to leverage a deal and get Jasmine to withdraw her statement."

"She was the one that was assaulted, I just stopped it. Senator Nelson and I will be drinking ice water in hell together before I ever agree to a deal." The idea that you could try to rape a girl and get off without any consequences made me a little crazy.

"Jasmine is okay with just letting it go." Maryanne said again, and shrugged.

I didn't mean to raise my voice, but I couldn't not. "And another rich kid walks away unscathed? How in the hell is that okay? Maybe that's how Dinar became the monster he was. Maybe his rich Daddy told him the rules didn't apply to him. We all know how that worked out."

"Slater, it isn't Maryanne's fault, sit down." Maggie said sharply.

I didn't remember standing. I sat down and apologized. "I didn't mean to get worked up, but those bastards should be in jail."

Maryanne waved a hand and smiled. "If I got upset every time someone raised their voice, I wouldn't have gotten far in the oil business. I'm glad your passionate about what you're doing, Slater, and that you care so much about my grand-daughter. But be aware, those two will probably plead out, pay a fine, and get a year's probation. That's just the way the world works."

"Well, it shouldn't," I said stubbornly.

"The world has an annoying habit of being what it is, not what we want it to be," Maggie said. "It was you that told me that."

"Thanks for reminding me." Her smile broke my mood. "If they can cop a plea, so can I. But no deals, I'll take my chances."

"Didn't expect anything else." Maryanne tipped her chair back and studied us for what seemed like a full minute. "None of this has anything to do with why I wanted to talk to you. I wanted to discuss the case you're on."

"We figured you might know Roland," Maggie said, "being in the same business."

"Nothing I tell you can go beyond this room." She leaned forward, looking back and forth between us. "You can't tell anyone, including Jasmine. Especially Jasmine."

"You and Roland?" Maggie asked. I have to admit, that hadn't occurred to me.

"It was five, five and a half years ago. His wife was staying in the Keys a lot, and he said they were talking divorce. I was widowed and weak, and because of business we spent a lot of time together. One thing led to another. It went on for quite a while, six months or so. By then I could see he didn't ever plan to divorce Caroline, and that he was so in love with her that he never would. Jasmine didn't tell me details, just that you were working for Roland. Maybe what I know doesn't matter, but I thought I'd better talk to you."

"We can't tell you why he hired us," I cautioned. "Even you."

"Doesn't matter. I know how much he loved both his wife and daughter. He did tell me that he's sick, dying."

"You spoke to him recently?"

"Yes, but he's known for quite a while. He's beaten the odds for well over two years."

"About the same time Isla disappeared," I said.

"Disappeared? Is that what you're calling it?" Maryanne studied me again.

"I'm not saying anything more. You're supposed to be the one volunteering information."

She nodded and laughed. "You said enough. When I was seeing Roland, he shared some inside information with me, nothing illegal, just the fact that his company was going to eventually get out of the fracking business and diversify. He urged me to start considering other suppliers, and diversify myself."

"When's the last time you spoke?" Maggie asked.

"Not for a few months. Back when we were spending time together, he had just pushed Ross out of the company, and it wasn't pretty. The changeover from fracking equipment was supposed to be gradual, five or ten years. Roland wanted Isla to take over the company, and she had been working on him to go green. He was starting the process, but he didn't want the industry at large to know about it. Ross was furious about being pushed out, and demanded more money. He threatened to spread the word that Roland was getting ready to retool and stop selling fracking equipment, just leave everyone high and dry. No pun intended."

"There have to be other companies selling the same products."

"Not the same, exactly. Roland holds the patent on some important products. But even he couldn't afford to lose half his customers overnight. Isla had him looking to the future, developing and manufacturing products that would be important when fracking becomes too expensive or too regulated. I've been investing in new technologies myself, because I know the oil boom in this country can't last forever. But Ross was always after the quick buck."

"If he was out of the company, why did his opinions matter?"

"Ross was in charge of sales, at least that's what his office door said, and he had the ear of a lot of clients. If he went to them and told them that Roland was planning to pull the plug, he would have lost their business, overnight. That would have bankrupted the company. Roland and Isla had a long-range transition in mind, but they still needed the income the fracking equipment sales brought in."

"Ross left the company several years ago," Maggie said. "How old was Isla?"

"She graduated from high school early and fast tracked through college. She was incredibly bright. Roland was already grooming her to run the company, but then her mother died. Everything went to hell after that. Roland and I stayed friends, and we talked. He was devasted. The marriage was about over anyway, but you can't divorce your children," she smiled, "or your grandchildren. More than anything, he wanted to leave the company to Isla, and any children she might have someday."

"And now there's Ginger."

"Yes, Ginger. Have you met her?"

"I have, and Jasmine, but not Maggie," I said.

"Young and beautiful, I'm told." Maryanne crossed her arms and frowned.

"Speaking as Roland's ex-lover?" Maggie dared.

"Yes and no. I moved on from Roland Dunbar, but I care about him. Tommy says trophy wife, what do you say?" She raised a brow and looked at me.

"There's some of that, but she really seems to care about him, or she's a very good actress. Jasmine likes her, but she's on our list."

"As she should be, I would think. She's from Atlanta, you know."

"No crime in that."

"Did she mention the fact that Ross is the one that introduced her to Roland? She was working at a club and he was a frequent customer.

Not a strip club, just so we're clear, but kind of a seedy nightclub."

"Doesn't make her a bad person," I said.

"Considering my daughter's history, of course not. I was just pointing out the fact that she knew Ross before she knew Roland. And if I haven't made it clear up to this point, I think Ross Dunbar is a lowlife snake."

"I haven't found anyone that would argue with that. Teresa, Roland's housekeeper, seems to think Ginger is after the company. Tommy said that Roland's will prevents that, although I'm beginning to see that a good lawyer can find his way around any problem."

"You're the investigators, I'm just sharing what I know. I know Ross is a bastard, and Ginger isn't everything she claims to be. They have the most to lose, if it turns out Isla is alive."

"And what would make you think she is?" I turned to Maggie. "Sounds to me like we need to explain the finer point of confidentiality to our junior partner."

Maryanne shrugged. "I may have implied that I already knew what was going on, and tricked her into telling me things she shouldn't have. My granddaughter is very smart, but I've been around the block a few times too."

I cringed. "I really hate that expression, especially when we're talking about Jasmine."

"What's your take on Ginger." Maggie asked as we drove across town to meet with Roland and his young wife.

"She's all southern belle, the simple country girl act, until she gets mad. Then she doesn't seem so brainless. She watches out for Roland like a mama bear protecting her cubs, and I get the idea she really cares about him. That said, she still may have designs on the company."

"Her own designs, or her and Ross together? Seems that's what Maryanne was suggesting."

"Between them, they have the best claim on the company, no matter what Roland's will says. I'm going to have to get that out of Tommy."

"If Isla hadn't died, the company would be hers. She's on my list."

"Now you have a list? Isla is dead, how can she be on your list?"

"We were hired to figure out who sent that necklace, and until I see some evidence that Isla really did drown, she's a candidate."

"Only one place we're going to find that." I reminded her.

"Bring on the sharks, Slater. If that's what it takes to figure this out, I'm ready."

Roland Dunbar's Jacksonville house was considerably more modest than the beach-house in the Keys. It did have a cobblestone circular drive and when we approached the front door, I could see the corner post and chain link of a private tennis court. I pushed the doorbell and Roland's voice resonated from a speaker somewhere, telling us to come in. We walked into the front room and he called again, this time without aid of electronics, instructing us to join him.

We walked across the main room to the office, which was nearly as big as the great room, without the high ceiling. Roland sat in front of a desk with two computer screens and several piles of paperwork scattered about. On the end wall there was a table with more papers and a couple stacks of books. He sat in a conventional desk chair with rollers, and by the scratches in the hardwood floor, I could see it got plenty of use. Beside the desk, within arms-reach, stood an aluminum framed walker. He caught me looking at it.

"You're walking pretty damn good, Slater, considering Wild Bill McConnell landed on top of you. Skip Jackson said you took the worst of it, then all but killed two of the local boys." He chuckled and directed us to a pair of chairs. "You're walking a lot better, and I'm going the other way. There's no healing what's wrong with my legs, I'm afraid. I can still get around, but all of a sudden, it's getting tougher. They tell me I've already outlived what's normal, so I guess I have to be grateful for that."

"Damn, and I was just starting to like you." I wasn't sure levity was called for, but he appreciated it.

"I knew you'd come around. And I still owe you a good drunk. We'll get that done one of these days. I'm not quite ready to give it all up. Sorry you missed Ginger. She ran over to the office to grab a few things for me. I fell down yesterday morning and she had a royal fit, talked me into working from home. Probably for the best. I don't want the whole crew seeing me stumble around like a drunken sailor. No offense to sailors."

"None taken. I know we were kidding about it before, but does Ginger know much about the workings of the factory?"

"Ginger knows a lot about everything," he said. "I couldn't have managed this long without her."

"Roland, this is tough, but you agreed we could be open about things."

He shrugged and nodded. "You want to know if I trust Ginger? Completely, why?"

"She was one of the few people with access to the necklace. Are you going to let her run the company when you're not able to? I presume she's your sole heir and will end up with it, eventually." I knew better, but I had to cover for Tommy.

"She's young and beautiful, Slater. Why would I saddle her with that kind of responsibility? I've taken care of her. She'll have this house and enough money to last her a lifetime is she isn't foolish with it."

"She's taken a bigger interest in the company lately, so I've been told."

He waved a hand. "Not too hard to guess where that's coming from. Ginger and Teresa have issues going back a long while. Teresa's had her share of bad breaks, and there's a bit of jealousy there. Not because of me, but Ginger is Ginger, and she's not always nice to Teresa."

"And the company?" Maggie asked. "Are you the sole owner?"

He paused, considering a lie. "The upper level employees have shares, and Ross still has a substantial block. I couldn't afford to buy him out completely. If I turn the company over to Carlos and the other engineers, Ross would still have enough ownership to raise hell and tie the whole thing up in court for years. By the time they get that all sorted out there wouldn't be anything left."

"Ginger would have the most legitimate claim. Has she said she doesn't want to be involved?"

"She'll have some shares, but not a controlling interest. It's too much to expect of her, Slater, and I won't have her banging heads with Ross. I want my company to continue, but I can't saddle Ginger with a giant mess after I'm gone. I'd rather just turn the whole thing over to Ross than put her through that."

"And the ALS, you're being treated for that?" I knew I was on shaky ground, but I had to ask.

"Yeah, for what good it's doing."

"Ginger, she takes care of those drugs for you?"

His eyes narrowed. "Dammit, she's my wife and that's the end of it. You are supposed to be finding out who sent me Isla's necklace, not investigating Ginger. She has no reason to hurt me, or see me dead any quicker than is already going to happen."

"Alright, but didn't Ross introduce you two?"

"Please Roland," Maggie said. "We have to consider all the possibilities."

"Alright." He sighed. "Yes, he introduced us. They knew each other in Atlanta. And I'll admit, that was before Caroline died."

"And Maryanne Thatcher?" I asked.

He glowered at us. "Maryanne and I were together before I met Ginger. She's a wonderful woman. If the world were a simpler place, we would have been good together." He looked up at me, knowing I would understand. "There were just too many of those sunsets."

"We need that key, right Slater?" Maggie spoke up, and pulled me back to the moment. "Slater and I are going to go down to the boat and have a good look around, Roland. We need the key that's on Isla's necklace. Maybe it fits something on that boat."

He was happy to change the subject. "The divers I sent didn't find anything, but they were mostly just looking for...any remains. They were bonded, and highly recommended, so they wouldn't have removed anything they shouldn't have. The GPS coordinates are in my phone, I'll text them to you."

"I have to get a release from my doctor, but I'm seeing her tomorrow," I said as he pulled a drawer open. "I have an old friend from the SEALS that owns a dive service in Marco Island, and he has a boat lined up for us."

Roland lifted the gold chain with his left hand and grabbed the locket with his right, setting the necklace on the desk in front of him. The clasp was intact and the chain was unharmed, but there was no key.

"The key was there, I know it was." He rubbed at his eyes. "I brought the necklace to our first meeting, then I put it in this drawer."

"Would Ginger have put it somewhere, for safe keeping?" I asked.

"Ginger again?" He bristled. "I don't know where it is, but I'm sure she didn't take it. If your worried about it, I'll ask her when she gets back."

"Alright," Maggie said diplomatically. "Odds are if there's a lock down there, the key wouldn't work anyway. If we have to, we'll break something."

"The insurance company talked about salvaging the Caroline, but I told them to go to hell and to keep their money. I wouldn't want anyone else to ever sail that boat, and I sure wouldn't. The boat is like the house, just a reminder of how badly

I failed Caroline and Isla. I'm tired of this whole damn business." He sighed, sat back in his chair, and looked at the tiny pictures in the locket, then up at us, and asked the question he had asked at our first meeting. "Why would someone send me this?"

"Would you like me to guess?" I asked. He nodded solemnly, and I tried to give him some hope. "No matter what's become of Isla, someone doesn't want you to give up."

"Sooner or later, this disease will decide things for me, Slater. Pretty soon I have to make some hard decisions about the company, while I still can. You can't do that for me, but I hope, before it's too late, you can tell me what happened to my daughter."

"We'll do our best, Roland." Shaking his big hand seemed like a hollow gesture, given that I was still reasonably sure his daughter had been swept from existence by hurricane Irma. But I hoped it made him feel better, because it helped me. I glanced back at him as we left. He had the locket open, and was smiling down at the picture of his young wife and child.

It struck me how wrong I had been about Roland Dunbar. He wasn't the shallow, arrogant person I had imagined at our first meeting. In my head I saw one of those sunsets long ago, a younger Roland, his beautiful red-haired bride and their young child, staring out at the sunset and looking forward to the life they had planned together. But the Butterfly had different plans. It had all been swept away, by stubbornness, pride, and the unrelenting power of a hurricane.

"You okay Slater?" Maggie asked as we pulled out of his driveway.

"Don't let me screw up like Roland did, okay?"

"Not likely that you would." She said, then grinned. "Keep in mind, I have a gun."

"Your leg is looking great, Slater." Janet walked into the room the next morning and showed me an x-ray. I could see a couple of pins and the shadow of a bone, all of which meant absolutely nothing to me, but I nodded. She chuckled. "Okay, what I can see, is that you're making great progress. No marathons yet, but you're definitely cleared to swim. That is what you wanted to know, right?"

"We're doing a dive tomorrow, if the wind lets up. Nothing tough, thirty-five or forty feet. I'm guessing dive fins will stress it a little, but I'll take it easy."

"You're walking well. Another month and you'll be good as new. I hear there's a big race coming up, but I'd wait a couple months for that. I can't imagine why you'd want to race Maggie anyway."

"You women talk a lot amongst yourselves," I observed. "I still think I can beat her in a mile, once I get back in shape."

"There are people putting money on it, just so you know."

"Great. No pressure there." I started pulling my shoes on. "Since you and Maggie have been talking, have you resolved your issues with Stacey and her husband?"

"I believe so. I have a meeting with them this weekend, and I'm bringing a friend."

"A lawyer friend?"

"Not quite, but close. I'll let you know how it turns out. Stacey had me completely fooled, but it sounds like they were trying to pull the same scam with other people. Maggie told me she made a pass at you."

"Pass is a polite way to put it. I've had hernia exams in the Navy that were less invasive."

"Too much information, Slater." Janet laughed and opened the exam room door. "We'll see what she has to say for herself this weekend."

Chapter Seventeen

Captain Tom Fisher was my dive instructor in the SEALS. I made it four years in the elite unit, a good portion of which was training. After four years, I had the option to reup for a substantial bonus, get out, or transition into another specialty. By then, the memory of the Two Towers falling wasn't as fresh in my head, and I was starting to lose my enthusiasm. I had toughed it out the first four years, fueled mostly by testosterone and bravado, but the idea of continuing after that was too much for me.

Up until then, I hadn't been put in the position where I had to kill anyone, either in self-defense, or in the completion of a mission. It was a difficult time, both in the Navy, and in the country. It seemed likely, that sooner or later I might be called upon to do things that I wouldn't be comfortable with. Certainly, defending our country was a high calling, and I knew going in that it was what SEALS did. But I could see the time was coming when I might doubt the mission, and start thinking that the target might have a political purpose, rather than one of self-preservation.

A SEAL couldn't do his job with those kind of doubts in his head. Tom Fisher told me that, and it was the best advice I ever got. He finished his twenty then returned to his home town and continued to do what he was good at, teach people to dive. We stayed in touch over the years, and I still had his number in my phone. One phone call, and we had a boat.

"What if the boat goes down, Slater? I told you, I can't swim." Jasmine said from the back seat.

"We're going fifteen miles out, Blue, too far to swim. There was a time I could do it, but I wouldn't want to try it now. Besides, the sharks would eat you before you got very far." I winked at the redhead.

"He's joking, Jasmine," Maggie said. "But that's not funny, Slater. I told you, I hate sharks."

"You have the magnetic bands," I reasoned. "The odds of you killing us on the road are better than getting attacked by a shark, especially as fast as you drive."

"It would be quicker," Jasmine said. "I'd much rather be road kill than shark bait."

"The dive boat has an inflatable, but there's no reason to think we'll need it. The wind has died down, so there won't be much of a chop, if any. If you're really not comfortable, we can hire one of Captain Tom's guys to run the boat, and a diver for that matter."

"Leave the women in the boat where it's safe? Fat chance of that, Slater." My girlfriend said immediately.

"Okay, but don't say I didn't offer."

Jasmine piped up again. "And if I sink the boat while you two are down there, don't say I didn't warn you."

Tom Fisher was on the long side of fifty, but only a few flecks of grey in his short beard would have given that away. He stood looking down at us from the deck of one of the bigger dive boats. He was shirtless, lean and well-muscled, an inch taller than me, and baked by the sun to a golden bronze. Jasmine stared up at him, then poked me with an elbow. "I'd like one of those, please," she whispered.

Captain Tom jumped down from the boat and threw his arms around me, then started pumping my hand. "It's been too long, Slater! Looks like you're walking just fine. Takes more than a nine-millimeter to put one of us down, right?"

"It put me down for a while, Cap, but I'm almost back to full strength." I turned to the redhead. "This is Maggie, my girlfriend, and partner in the PI thing. And this," I turned to Jasmine and couldn't help myself. "This is Jasmine. She gets mad when I call her my Smurf, but just look at her."

"Cutest Smurf I've ever seen." He wrapped one arm around Jasmine and the other around Maggie, then looked at me. "You can go now Slater, your boat's at the end of the dock. I'll take care of these two for you."

"You're married, Tom, behave." I extracted Maggie from his grasp, but Jasmine continued to cling to his arm. "Blue has a thing for older men," I explained. He laughed and politely eased away from her.

"You should be all set. Regulators and masks, fins, plenty of tanks. The Caroline isn't listed on any of the dive sites, so I'm guessing not too many people know she's there. Waters a little murky from all the wind the last couple of days, but there's plenty of hi-res line and buoys on board. I put in the co-ordinates you gave me, so the GPS will take you right over the top of her."

"Any big sharks out there?" That was Maggie.

"It's a big ocean, and there are no fences," Tom pointed out. "But we don't see many Whites over here. Hammerheads and Bulls, but nothing real big."

"That's reassuring," she mumbled.

"There's a powerhead in the cabin, if you're really worried. Homemade. I designed it myself. You twist the head, which cocks it. It's hard on sharks, but don't use it unless you absolutely have to. It's hard on eardrums too."

Maggie looked at me and I explained. "A bang-stick. It'll kill all but the biggest ones. Maggie, I've literally spent a thousand hours under water, and I've never seen a shark attack. You have two bands, wear one on your wrist and one on your ankle."

"What about you?"

"I'll stay close to you. It'll be fine."

"I'd go, if you can wait until tomorrow." Captain Tom volunteered.

"No," Maggie grumbled. "I know, it's not rational. I'm not going to let a stupid fish stop me from checking out that boat, no matter how big it is."

"That's the spirit," Jasmine said. "I'll be up top, working on my tan."

Tom chuckled and turned toward the end of the long dock. "I'm giving you the Whaler. It's only thirty-four feet, but it has plenty of freeboard, not that you'll need it. It should be flat calm out there today, and the forecast is clear. It's got a diving deck, and the ladder's easy to get on and off of, so it should work for that bum leg."

"How long to get to the Caroline?" I asked.

"It's down south a bit, and fifteen miles out. Not more than an hour, tops."

"Buy you a beer when we get back?"

"Evelyn would love to have you all over for supper, if you have time."

"The Caroline's not a big boat, but we're going to give it a good look. You don't happen to have a set of bolt cutters, do you?"

Captain Tom laughed. "What self-respecting, part-time treasure hunter wouldn't have bolt cutters? I'll grab them for you."

"Better than a key," I said, when Maggie gave me her look.

"You can have the bolt-cutters, I'm bringing the stick that kills sharks."

It took me fifteen minutes to get through the channel and out into open water. Riding around on an aircraft carrier didn't qualify me to operate an oversized speedboat in tight quarters. Once we made it out into open water, I pushed the throttles forward and the twin outboards came to life. There was no chop, just some small swells that we climbed over easily and outran as we headed south.

I glanced over at Jasmine. She looked a little green. "How fast are we going?" she asked.

"Thirty, thirty-five knots."

"What's that in English?"

"About forty miles an hour. Have you ever been out on the ocean?" I asked, over the roar of the outboards.

"No, but it's cool." Her smile was half-hearted at best.

"Here, take the wheel." She blanched, but I waved her up, and showed her the GPS screen. "Just keep us on that heading, and watch the horizon. You're less likely to get sick if you're looking at something farther away. Just don't make any sudden turns."

I settled into a seat beside Maggie. She tossed her head and let the wind carry her hair back, laughing carelessly. "I love this. We should forget about replacing the airplane and buy one of these."

"After that last fiasco, I'm inclined to agree."

"I still say somebody messed with it. Skip had all the maintenance records, and there just weren't that many hours on that engine. All those drunks around, somebody watered the fuel, or something."

"It was embarrassing, having Murphy rescue us. The insurance company will probably have the engine checked over, if there's enough left."

"I know you didn't really want to buy it."

"Not at first, but I do miss the Piper," I admitted.

We reached the Caroline shortly after ten in the morning, or at least the spot where the GPS said she was. Tom's equipment was top-notch, and I knew that the system was tried and true, because he took divers to ship-wrecks on a daily basis. There was just a breath of wind, and I put us upwind of the spot where I knew the Caroline should be, then showed Jasmine how to operate the electric winch that lowered the anchor, and let out some slack.

She turned in every direction, searching for the shoreline. "Which way is land?"

I pointed straight east. "Fifteen miles that way. If there were mountains, you could see them, but the Everglades aren't high enough. If it was dark, we would see the lights from Marcos Island."

"This is really creepy."

"Turn on the radio, it'll distract you."

"That's it? You just want me to sit up here and listen to the radio?"

"No, you need to do something else. I'm going to throw out some buoys, and your job is to keep an eye on them. If they disappear, get on the radio and call Captain Tom. He'll know what to do. The radio is already set to his frequency."

Absolutely none of that was true. I couldn't imagine any reason we would tug on the buoy lines, and Captain Tom was a long way off, too far to help us if we did get into trouble. Mostly, I just wanted to give her something to do to keep her mind off the endless miles of ocean that surrounded us. But the buoy lines were bright yellow and I knew they would help us stay oriented if it was darker than I thought at thirty-five feet.

A storm front had moved through the day before, and the water wasn't as clear as I had hoped. I put my face in the water, and I could just make out the shape of a mast, and possibly the ghostly silhouette of the hull.

"She's straight below us," I told Maggie. She had slipped her tanks on and we checked each other's equipment, weights, and ran through some rudimentary hand signals. She had the bang-stick, and I had my bolt cutters. We both had mini-lights on our masks and hand-held lanterns. I gave Jasmine the thumbs up and slipped over the side.

Once we were a few feet from the surface, the clarity of the water improved, and we could see the Caroline clearly. We hung there, thirty feet above the stricken sailboat which was outlined against the crystalline white sand of the Florida shelf, allowing the combined weight of our equipment pull us slowly to the bottom. A few groupers and a couple of eels moved away to the darker side of the boat, and we circled it slowly, inspecting what damage we could find.

The Caroline lay tipped at a forty-five-degree angle, held somewhat upright by the shattered mast that had twisted off six feet from its base. There were fragments of the jib sail, still tethered to the halyard, but the main sail was gone, either torn off in the storm or swept away by a subtle current. The bottom of the broken mast was pushed against the cabin door, blocking our entrance. We circled the boat looking for another way in.

Most of the plexiglass was gone, and we could see inside with our lights, but even a person Jasmine's size couldn't have fit through those openings. The previous divers must have peered in the same way and concluded that there were no bodies in the aft cabin, but it wasn't possible to see into the forward area where more bunks were, or all the way under the deck, where the aft cabin bunks were located.

The cabin door was partially shattered, held in place by the base of the mast, which in turn, was lying on top of the boom. Given the right equipment and a couple of my shipmates, we could have cut our way in, but from what I could see, it didn't seem worth the effort. The previous divers couldn't have gained entry into the cabin, but they might have sent a drone in to look in the spots they couldn't get to. They had guaranteed Roland that there were no bodies aboard, but that didn't mean there was nothing to find, if we could get in.

I didn't know a lot about sailboats. Growing up in Florida, I had been on a few small single sail crafts, and knew the difference between a jib, a mainsail, and a lanyard. That was about it. Just because you're in the Navy, doesn't mean you're automatically an expert on anything that floats.

The boom was intact, but was twisted under the broken mast near its base. The top of the mast was pushing against the seabed, and holding a good portion of the weight of the boat. There would be no moving it, but it seemed reasonable that if we got on the far end, and used the length of the boom for a lever, we might be able to slide the bottom of the broken mast up enough to clear the door into the cabin.

I motioned to Maggie and through a series of gestures, managed to make clear what I wanted to try. We got on the back of the boat and pulled as hard as we could. The boom was built to take a considerable beating from wind gusts and looked strong enough for what I had in mind. The spot where the mast lay was only a couple feet from the base of the boom, and it gave us the leverage we needed. It was still all the two of us could do to raise our end of the boom up a few feet, which in turn, slid the mast up the side of the cockpit. We pushed and pulled with everything we had, then slid the boom sideways and locked it behind one of the stern rails.

I felt the boat shift slightly, and I should have paid more attention to that subtle warning. I knew that the Caroline was resting on the keel and its leeward side, and I thought it had settled against the ocean floor. Had I looked again, I would have been more cautious.

We had managed to lift the fragmented mast up about a foot, enough for me to get under it and try to pry open the cabin door. The hinges were twisted and the door wouldn't budge. I wasn't sure the broken mast might not move, and I pulled back. Maggie tapped me on the arm and handed me the bang stick, shrugging as best she could in all of her gear. I pointed at my ears and handed it back, then picked up my bolt cutters and went to work.

It took me fifteen minutes, and a lot of air, but I finally twisted, pried and beat my way through the cabin door. The mast hadn't moved and I felt reasonably confident that it wouldn't, but I motioned Maggie away from the entrance. She wasn't happy, and we pantomimed our way through a small argument. Should the worst happen, I didn't want us both trapped in that tiny cabin.

I'd been in a lot of wrecks over the years, even pulled out a couple of bodies. Compared to finding your way through a Russian destroyer, searching the Caroline was nothing. I checked all the bunks first. No bodies, just a couple of unfriendly eels. There was a lot of storage, and it took another fifteen minutes of searching to recover the only treasure the Caroline had to offer. When I entered the cabin, I'd spotted what appeared to be a gym bag lying in plain sight. I checked every cupboard, closet, and hiding spot I could find, and that was the only personal article I found on the whole boat. I picked up the bag on my way out, and pushed it ahead of me as I swam up through the door opening.

The sensible thing to do, would have been to go to the surface and examine the contents of the bag topside, but I was curious. I swam over to the back of the boat, sat on the edge of the cockpit, and opened the bag. Maggie swam up and looked over my left shoulder, suspended a few feet above me. I opened the bag, and dug through a couple of shirts and a pair of sweats. At the bottom of the bag, I found a small ornamental box, bigger than most jewelry boxes. It had a lock on it. Now we had a lock, and no key.

I've mentioned my fascination with the Butterfly, and it picked that moment to mess with me. I felt the boat shift slightly again, then it started to roll. Moving fast underwater is difficult, and I was in an awkward position. I didn't move fast enough.

The boat had been completely supported by the mast and the keel, and when it rolled the rest of the way onto its side, the bottom of the mast came up and slid straight at me. I lunged back out of the way, then laid back to avoid the boom which had jumped over the stern rail and swung back, nearly taking my head off. As the Caroline settled into her final resting place, the main mast came back down onto the deck and settled on the boom. The boom slapped down hard and landed on my right leg, half way between my knee and foot, pinning me down at the edge of the cockpit. At least it wasn't the same leg that Dinar had used for target practice.

Instinctively, I pulled as hard as I could, but couldn't budge it. The mast was wedged against the cockpit again, with the far end resting on the ocean floor, pushing the boom onto my leg. Unlike before, the mast lay closer to the middle of the boom. No leverage there. I was stuck.

I put the bag down on the deck, and Maggie circled around to the far end of the boom where she and I had lifted before. While she tried to lift the boom up, I pulled at it with my arms, since my left leg was useless. There was just no moving it without leverage, or more horsepower. I looked at my watch. Twenty minutes of air left, but there were more tanks in the boat. I wasn't worried, I had a partner.

Maggie didn't panic. She retrieved the bolt cutters and started trying to cut some of the rigging

273

lines loose. I had started looking for another solution when Maggie suddenly tapped me on the arm, her eyes wide. My eyes followed her finger.

A six-foot Bull shark ghosted up off the bottom and made a lazy approach. It passed by us at a considerable distance, then turned and made another pass, much closer. A school of sharks that size would have been a problem, but we weren't spear fishing and there was no blood in the water. The animal seemed more curious than aggressive. Still, it was a Bull shark, and they could be unpredictable.

I grinned at Maggie and held up my finger and thumb, indicating that it was just a small one. She tried to smile, then pointed to my predicament and raised her hands. I pantomimed a rope and pointed to the surface. She picked up the bang stick and started up, with her new friend a short distance behind her. Confident as I was, I knew that I was going to need air soon. I had used up more than I should have beating on the cabin door. In another fifteen minutes, I would need to be topside, or have another tank.

Once Maggie climbed into the boat, the Bull came back down, boring right at me, then spinning away at the last possible second. Normally, it wouldn't have bothered trying to make a meal of something as big as I was, but perhaps it sensed my helplessness. I managed to stretch out and get my hands on the bolt cutter. At least it couldn't shred that. As soon as Maggie entered the water again, it joined her, circling as she swam back down with one end of a line. She managed to keep the bang-stick in one hand and the rope in the other, all the while watching the shark. The repellant bands were working. The Bull stayed a short distance away from her.

Maggie pulled the slack out of the line and secured it to the far end of the boom, then swam over to one of the brightly colored buoy lines. I always dropped a couple, but I was glad I had put down several, for Jasmine's benefit. She tugged on the line, pulled the buoy under twice, then swam back to me. I gave her the thumbs up and waited.

The anchor line was just barely visible, and it angled quite a distance to the west and north of us. I saw the line start to tighten before I heard the whir of the electric winch. The shark heard it immediately, and disappeared in a flash, charging straight up to investigate. Maggie and I waited, watching the boat above us begin to move slowly toward the anchor. I crossed my fingers, hoping the boom would move before the anchor did. Turning Jasmine loose with the twin Mercs didn't strike me as a good idea.

Perhaps the noise of the winch somehow disrupted the effect of the magnetic bands. I understand the concept, but the workings of a shark's brain are beyond me. I glanced beyond Maggie's shoulder, and suddenly the Bull was right there, two feet behind her. It didn't move, just hung there, studying her. Had it been a dog, I'm sure it would have tipped its head.

Maggie saw it in my eyes. She turned slightly, peering over her shoulder, then raised the bang stick. She inched it back close to the shark's nose, holding it by the middle of the four-foot shaft. Suddenly, with a quick flick, she poked the animal in the snout, not with the business end, but with the blunt heel of Captain Tom's home-made device.

A shark's snout and head are sensitive, and being poked with the hard steel rod didn't make the Bull happy. If it were possible for a shark to look indignant, that one did. It turned and disappeared for a moment, then made two more fast runs past us before finally gliding away and disappearing in the distance.

The rest was easy. The weight of the boat was enough to raise the boom, and I lost no time getting away from the Caroline as fast as I could. At the last minute, I remembered to grab the bag from the deck, and we returned to the surface.

After supper with Captain Tom and his wife, a lot of reminiscing, and too much wine, we decided to rent a suite at the nearest motel. It was there that we finally opened the box. Without a key, I had to retrieve a large screw driver from the trunk of Maggie's car and pry the lid open. I wasn't sure what to expect, so I wasn't surprised.

There was a small quantity of pot, sealed tightly in a sandwich bag with two small pewter pipes, an assortment of cheap jewelry, two pictures that had been ruined by the salt water, and a silver bracelet with a tiny inscription. *'To my best friend in the world, love Isla'*

"Probably not Isla's box," I said.

"Must belong to the other girl, the one that was with her when Jack saw them."

"Her best friend. Jasmine, did Jack say if he ever saw those two together before?"

"I was going to call him anyway, I'll ask." She disappeared into the bathroom to make her call.

I was slightly offended. "Does she think we're going to listen in?"

"She knows you will. Let her live her life, Slater. I think Jack's in it for the long haul."

"I just keep seeing Marcus and that other idiot, in my head."

"Time to let that go. Besides, I think there's another girl to save." She picked up the baggie with the marijuana in it.

"What do you mean?" I asked.

"Just one bag, one set of clothes, and it doesn't seem like they're Isla's. Is it possible the second girl was the only one on the boat?"

"Isla stayed behind? Why would the other girl risk her life to take Isla's boat out in that hurricane? And if that's what happened, where the hell is Isla?"

"I wonder if there's any way to fix these pictures? I say we give everything to Susan Foster and have her work her magic. That pot looks dry. If the bag stayed sealed, it's possible they could retrieve some DNA from one of those pipes."

"Good idea." I pushed the box away and leaned back, next to her. "I'm glad you didn't kill that shark today."

"I felt bad enough, jabbing her in the nose. She was just curious, I could tell that."

"She? You're giving a fish a lot of credit it probably doesn't deserve. Most likely it was trying to decide if your hair was edible."

"Anyway, I wasn't that worried. It helped me get over my phobia."

"You're so brave." I wrapped an arm around her and pulled her closer, then started kissing her neck. "I wish Jasmine had her own room."

"She does, at Maryanne's, and we'll be home tomorrow." She slipped out of my grasp. "So you can wait." She studied me for a moment. "Were you ever afraid down there?"

"With you for a partner?" I was serious, and she knew it.

"Let's make a promise to always be there for each other, okay?" She leaned in to kiss me again.

"I'm in it for the long haul." I assured her. "Wait, was that a proposal?"

She giggled in my ear. "I think that's your job, and it's still too soon."

"We don't want Jack and Jasmine walking down the aisle before we do."

"Are you crazy?" Jasmine objected loudly. Neither of us had heard the bathroom door open. "This girl isn't walking down any aisles, for years, and years. And years."

Maggie laughed and leaned against me again. "Just one years for me." She said.

Jasmine scowled in our direction. "I'm going to bed. Please keep in mind that we're all sleeping in the same room and I have ears like a bat."

I grinned at her and decided to play nice. "Night, Blue. You did good today."

"Night, Slater. Love you, you too Maggie."

Chapter Eighteen

"Are we going to show Roland the box?" Maggie asked as we drove across town to our client's Jacksonville home.

"He is the one paying us, and we need him to understand the need for his DNA. Hair follicles are good according to Susan. We're supposed to have him put them in an envelope, so we don't contaminate them."

"Do I get to meet Ginger, or is she playing tennis again."

"Roland said he has her running errands, but that she'll be back by the time we get there. He was in a meeting with Ross."

"Ross still has twenty percent of the company, right?" Maggie asked.

"Not sure, something like that."

"If...when Roland passes away, those shares are going to be worth a lot more, he might have control of the company."

"I don't know how many shares Ginger has, but if she and Ross team up, it would probably be enough to have a controlling interest. Roland doesn't want Ginger to have to deal with Ross, but he doesn't want to saddle Ginger with having to run the company either." The best thing about having a partner is being able to bounce ideas off each other, and it's especially great when Maggie and I are on the same page.

She continued, expanding the theory. "The shares are privately traded, so Ross or Ginger would be in the best position to buy out minor shareholders, and get more control. I'm sure it's all spelled out in the Articles of Incorporation, but with Roland gone, everyone's shares will be worth more."

"Right, so maybe he sets Ginger up as best he can and leaves Ross enough of a share to run the company. Carlos and most of the other engineers would quit, sell Ross their stocks, and he'd be free to peddle Roland's company to the highest bidder."

"In today's market, he'd stand to make, who knows, a couple hundred million dollars, maybe more."

"That's presuming Roland gives him control, or he can get Ginger to go along. Roland talked like he's worn out, to the point where he might just give Ross the stock he needs, and walk away."

"Unless Ginger is whispering in his ear, trying to work the same deal herself?" Maggie pointed out.

"See, we are starting to think alike."

"But, then who sent the necklace?"

"It could be Ginger, buying time," I said with little conviction. "If Ginger wants to liquidate the company the way things stand, she would need Ross to have a controlling interest, and he's not a good person to trust. Maybe, with the time the necklace bought her, Ginger's been working on

Roland, and convinced him she's willing and able to run the company. Then she doesn't need Ross. Either way, once he's gone, she's going to sell out. She makes a fortune, Roland's company goes to some giant conglomerate, and the employees are on their own. Not the kind of legacy Roland wanted to leave behind."

"They won't do any better if Ross has control."

"Roland doesn't trust Ross, but he's tired, he's ready to just give up. Could there be some legal restraints? Maybe Ross gets the controlling shares, but he can't sell the company for a certain number of years. I have no idea if it's even possible to stipulate that in a will. We're going to have to talk to Tommy as soon as we're done here."

"Nice car, "Maggie commented as we pulled into Roland's circle drive. The sporty BMW parked there looked new.

"Considering he doesn't work, Ross seems to be doing pretty well."

"Is Roland okay with us interrupting his meeting?"

"He said to come right in, that they're almost done."

I rapped on the door, then opened it for Maggie and we walked into the living area. I could see Roland sitting behind his desk, and he called to us and waved his hand. We had the jewelry box in a bag, and I had no intent of pulling it out in front of Ross.

Ross Dunbar look considerably younger than I expected. He was five years Roland's junior, but he could have passed for forty. He had the same bushy eyebrows and long jaw, and the same blue eyes that assessed you while he talked. He stood and shook my hand, then Maggie's. He assessed her a little longer than I cared for. I already didn't like him.

"Roland tells me he sent you on a wild goose chase," he said.

"Oh, I wouldn't say that. We've done some digging, and found a few things."

"Still, pretty obvious what happened to her." It didn't seem like he was trying to be unfriendly, but I didn't like that he was discouraging what little hope his brother had.

"Maybe, but that's why they call it investigating."

"Seems like a waste of Roland's money, to me." Now, that sounded unfriendly.

"Roland's money."

He smiled slyly, and let his eyes roam the redhead again, down to the bag with the jewelry box in it. "What's in the bag?"

"None of your business," Maggie spoke up. "Maybe some good news for Roland."

"He could use some of that," Ross said dryly.

Roland cut him off. "Ross, you should let Maggie and Slater share their news?" He nodded toward the door. "I'll talk to you in a couple days.

We can meet at the beach house and get all this settled."

"Sure. I'll be in Miami anyway, tending to some...personal business."

I took the opportunity for a dig. "I've heard you spend time there. A friend of mine mentioned your name. She's in law enforcement."

Ross gave me a saccharin sneer, then ignored me as he stood and nodded to Maggie. "Nice to meet you, Beautiful, I hope I get to see you again." As he left the office, the front door opened, and Ginger walked in. When she saw him, she held the door open and followed him out.

"My brother's a real dick, Slater," Roland said, and chuckled. "Don't let him get under your skin. He loves to push people's buttons, and he thinks he's God's gift to women. I used to make excuses for him, but after the shake-up at the company there was some unpleasantness, and I got to see just what he's capable of. I would never trust him again, but I have to deal with him."

"We've heard some stories." I tried to be noncommittal.

Roland hesitated, then shrugged and told us what we already suspected. "Yeah, it was him I caught with Caroline that first time. I was still young enough back then to give him a good beating, but from what I understand, it didn't change his behavior. He enjoys hurting people, me more than most."

"Then why trust him with the company?" His sudden caution told me I'd crossed a line.

"Who said I am?"

"The meeting?"

"It's business, Slater, and nothing I can talk about. Not a word to anyone about that, is that clear?"

"Absolutely. No leaks in our organization." I assured him, and Maggie nodded.

"Sorry, but we're working on something, and I can't have a word of it getting out."

"We? You and Ginger?"

He dismissed the question with a swipe of his hand. "I said enough about her. What's in the bag?"

"We had to pry it open, because we think the key that disappeared was the one that fit it." Maggie pulled the box from the bag and set in on Roland's desk. "Does it look familiar? We opened it so we could dry out the contents."

"I can't say that I've ever seen it before," he said, easing the lid up. The bracelet lay face up, and I saw him read the inscription. "The pot and pipes look dry, but I doubt there's any DNA on the bracelet after all this time. Is that what you're thinking?" He closed the lid and pushed the box back in Maggie's direction.

"It is, and there's something else," I said.

"Good, bad, or indifferent?"

"Hard to say," I admitted. "I don't want you to read too much into it."

"I have resigned myself to the fact that Isla is most likely dead, Slater."

"This probably doesn't change that, but there is a possibility that Isla wasn't alone on the Caroline when it went down. We found out that a man dropped Isla and another girl off at the boat, the day before the hurricane. They were both on the Caroline when it left the marina, but we don't know if they were both on it when it went down. It seems likely, but we can't be sure of that. This box was the only thing we found, and we don't think it was Isla's, mostly because of the inscription on that bracelet."

"That's why you want my DNA, to see if those pipes were Isla's?"

"Exactly." I didn't connect the dots, but I knew he would.

He studied my face, then Maggie's, then turned back to me. "You told me the odds that my daughter was alive are a million to one. If I understand what you're telling me, I'd say those odds just got a little better."

"Don't go there, Roland. As your investigator, I had to tell you that. But as a friend, and I'm trying to be that right now, don't get your hopes up."

"Most likely it just means two girls died that day, I know that. But keep digging. And don't tell Ginger this. She would get her hopes up."

I doubted that, but I didn't say a thing. Maggie pulled out her envelopes. "We need you to

286

pluck some hairs from your head and put them in these, for the DNA test. Blood would work, obviously, but we're trying to get this done as fast as possible."

"I have a contact that can expedite the test," I said. "If the DNA isn't your daughter's, we can guess that there was another girl on the boat when it went down. We can't be sure, because it's possible she just left her bag there by mistake. All we know is that it was a shorter, dark-haired girl. Do you remember any of Isla's friends that might have matched that description?"

"She never brought people home, and that last year she avoided me as much as she could. I wouldn't have a clue. By now, I'm sure you know about Jessie Forester. He was one of her best friends, he might know."

"We've talked to him, and we're going back down there in a couple days, if it's alright."

"Ginger and I are going to be there this weekend, but we'd love to have guests. She has been after me to take time off from work, and for once, I'm going to listen to my wife. I'll tell Carlos you're heading his way, but I'll have to take the downstairs bedroom this time."

"No problem. I can handle those steps now. We'd better run, we have to meet my contact and give her this box and your DNA sample."

"Remember, not a word to Ginger."

When we left the house, Ginger was leaning against the roof of Ross's car, smiling and talking.

When she saw us, she touched his arm and waved as he drove away, then walked over. She extended a hand. "Maggie, right? Jasmine told me so much about you. She worships you, and I can see why."

Maggie's cheeks colored, and they went on about how pretty the other one was for far longer than I thought was necessary. I finally told Ginger my plan to be at the beach house over the weekend, and she let us go after another five minutes of gushing and giving us both a substantial hug.

"What the hell was all that about?" I glanced in the mirror. Ginger was still waving and watching us drive away. "She was positively giddy."

"You didn't say how nice she is."

"She's our prime suspect! Just because she spent half an hour telling you how great you are, doesn't mean she's not conspiring with Ross to take over the company."

"I don't see that, and Jasmine likes her."

"She's on my list, Jasmine's too."

"She did spend quite a bit of time outside with Ross, but maybe they're both just worried about Roland."

"No, they're both worried about Roland's money. I'll admit, she seems to care about Roland, but that doesn't mean she isn't out to get the company. I'm calling Tommy, right now and get the details of Roland's will."

"I'm going with my gut, and I like her," Maggie insisted. "Let me drive, so you don't get a ticket or crash my car."

After we switched seats, I made the call to Tommy Ackerman.

"I can't tell you that, Slater, and this time I'm being serious. The terms of a will are completely confidential, and Roland would have me disbarred if he ever found out. I can say that there are some changes pending, but not what they are."

"But it has to do with the investigation."

"Have Roland call me, then I can tell you anything you want to know."

"Okay, I'm not doing that. How about something your office did a few years ago? I just need the date, and to verify a couple of facts I already know."

"I might be able to do that, depends."

"You, or someone in your office, arranged to bail out Roland's brother Ross four years ago in Miami. He supposedly beat up a hooker."

"I remember that, but if you want the details, I'll have to look it up and call you back."

"Okay, I'll take what I can get. And keep in mind, the Butterfly has his eye on you."

"I think you're mixing up your philosophies, Slater, and my Karma is just fine. I'll call you shortly."

Shortly was five minutes later. "We did arrange bail for Ross. The computer says he was released at four o'clock in the afternoon, August eleventh, 2015."

"And Caroline died on the twelfth, at one in the morning. I was told he wasn't released until the next day. Either my informant was lied to, or he's lying to me."

"I keep very good records, and I remember now, that was a Sunday. I wasn't happy about having to come into the office."

"Woody was wrong about Ross being in jail the night Caroline died." I told Maggie, after I hung up.

"Another reason to go back to the Keys?" Maggie asked as we drove across town to meet Susan Foster and deliver the DNA material.

"I doubt Woody would lie. It might have been a simple paperwork screw up, but it means Ross could have been the person Isla saw that night. Doesn't mean he killed her, but it makes it feasible. I'm not a Ross fan."

"Me either. Not that I'm opposed to going back, but what else is there for us to do down there?"

"I'm not sure, I think there's something we're missing. Plus, I want to spend some time with Roland and Ginger and be around when Ross drops by. Maybe we can talk some sense into Roland before then. I'm afraid he's being manipulated by your new girlfriend."

"Ginger?"

"Top of my list."

"If it came right down to it, don't you think Roland would just give her the company if she asked?"

"Maybe he is, nobody will tell me!" I threw up my hands. "Tommy said there are changes pending, but Roland said he would never saddle Ginger with the company. I'm afraid that means the company might be going to Ross."

"Bottom line, Slater, that's not your choice to make."

"I just want Roland to have the best outcome he can."

Maggie smiled at me. "You're such a softy. You didn't like him when we started all this."

"He did things he shouldn't have, and now he's living with the consequences."

"The Butterfly thing again?"

"No, nothing that profound. He should have worried more about his marriage than his business, and it kills him that he didn't. Everyone says he and Caroline were as much in love as anyone ever could be, yet it all went wrong."

"And you're worried that could be us?"

"I can't imagine how it could be, but yeah, aren't you?"

"There are no guarantees, Slater. One of us could find out we have cancer tomorrow. I can't imagine ever not loving you, but that happens to people all the time. We just have to be willing to work at it when we need to. Oh, and you need to always do what I tell you."

"I was being serious."

"Too serious." She laughed. "You're not Roland, and I'm not Caroline. We'll probably have our challenges, but I'm not ready to throw in the towel, so cheer up."

"Against all odds, I hope we find Isla alive. I would love to give Roland that."

Susan Foster met us at the usual spot, a restaurant ten minutes west of Point Road. Often as not she was dressed in sweats and sunglasses, sometimes a blonde, sometimes a brunette. I had walked right past her on more than one occasion and not recognized her. Considering what she did for a living, being visible was sometimes a liability. On this day, she was easy to spot. She had her blond hair tied back and was wearing a print dress. And, unless I was mistaken, she was wearing eyeshadow.

"Wow Susan, you're looking especially nice today. But then you always do." I had grown cautious with my compliments in the last few years. 'Tough night?' never went over well, but there was a time when I actually thought 'who is this good-looking woman?' was acceptable. When I thought about it, I realized that could never come out right, no matter how well intentioned.

"Thanks, Slater. I don't always dress like a homeless person, although sometimes it helps me fit in. Maggie, how are you?"

"Good, I faced down a Bull shark and lived to tell about it."

"She was very brave, seriously. She and Jasmine rescued me after I got caught under the boom of Isla's sailboat. The only things we found are in a bag in the car. We have some of Roland's hair, follicles included, and there are two pot pipes in a sealed baggy that look like they stayed dry."

"Plastic isn't the best, but the FBI lab can detect DNA in spots you wouldn't believe. It'll take a week or so."

"Can you twist somebody's arm, and make it happen faster? Roland Dunbar is making life changing decisions, and that DNA could make a big difference in what he does."

"Alright, I'll call in a favor. You're lucky I'm in a good mood today. I'm taking a couple days off, and I'll be hanging around Jacksonville, so I'll run the samples over to the main office myself."

"Days off? I didn't know you did that?"

"The perverts never stop trying to drag kids into the life, Slater, but I needed a break."

"How's your sister?" We spent an hour having a meal and talking about the mundane and the important, then I paid for lunch and we walked out. We transferred our cargo, then got into our cars.

Maggie dropped her window. "Have fun on your date."

"Thanks," Susan called back. "Just a walk and some ice cream, but it could turn into something."

"How'd you know she had a date?" I asked, once we were under way.

"Have you ever seen her in a dress before? Think about it."

That sounded condescending. "I told her she looked nice, I'm not completely oblivious."

Maggie sighed, as if the truth was self-evident. "But you're a man."

I leaned into it. "Thank you."

Friday, we made the drive back to Big Pine Key. We took Maggie's car and Jasmine followed us as far as Miami. We stopped there and had supper with her and Jack, then drove the rest of the way down. It was dark by the time we pulled into the circle drive, but a light was on, and Carlos walked up from the guest house when he saw us pull in.

"Roland let me know you were coming. The room Jasmine had is all set up for you, and Teresa will be over in the morning to make breakfast."

"She doesn't have to do that, Carlos. We're just staying a couple days."

Carlos unlocked the big front door and swung it open. "I know, but she insisted. Roland explained that you're actually private investigators."

"Sorry for the deception, but we wanted the locals to think we'd be their neighbors."

"No worries, it wasn't you that didn't trust us."

I covered for my client. "I asked Roland not to tell a soul, even Ginger, so it was all me. I didn't know you then, now it would be different."

"Thanks, good to know. We're heading up to Jacksonville next week, maybe I can give you a tour of the plant, and the four of us could go out to lunch."

"That would be great." He said goodnight, and we carried our bags up the stairs to the bedroom, unpacked, then went back down to the great room. We turned on the television and curled up together on the couch.

"Slater!" I woke up an hour later. Maggie was tugging on my sleeve, and whispering urgently in my ear. I opened one eye and looked at her cautiously. She put a finger to her lips and pointed.

The moon was full, and although the television made the kitchen area hard to see, there was enough light to make out the Captain's wheel. Eli was up to his old tricks. The wheel turned slightly, an eighth of a revolution this way, then a quarter back. We sat quietly and watched for a full five minutes, and the motion repeated itself, sometimes a quarter turn, once a full revolution. I searched the darkness for the ghostly shape of the old fisherman I had imagined after too many pain pills, but there was no sign of him, and no reason for the wheel to move.

"Magnets." I whispered to my partner. "Someone is controlling it with electricity."

"Let's go to bed and give Old Eli something to think about." Maggie snickered. We got up quietly and turned off the television. A cloud had covered the moon, and the room was too dark to make out the wanderings of the Pirate's wheel. Maggie pulled me toward the stairs. When I reached for the light switch, she stopped me. "Don't," she whispered, "let this one be a mystery."

I have the best partner ever.

Chapter Nineteen

Teresa had breakfast ready for us the next morning, and the pancakes were back. She and Carlos were polite to each other, but there was still some tension. Carlos talked with Maggie and I, but Teresa was all business. She made us breakfast, then complained of a stomach ache and left through the front door.

"She is still unhappy with me," Carlos said as he rinsed his plate and opened the dishwasher. "It's nothing you did. She's worried about the company and the fact that Ross is coming. I'm sure you heard, they're having a meeting here today."

"I heard, but is that bad?"

"Roland hasn't said what it's about, but if Ross is involved, it's not good."

"We'll take care of the dishes." Maggie volunteered. "I'm sorry Teresa's upset."

"She doesn't think Roland listens to me, or her. She says it was Roland that lied to us, no matter if you suggested it or not. She's worked for him for so long, I think she gets her feelings hurt when he doesn't treat her like family."

"I'm sure he cares what she thinks, but he has a lot on his plate right now."

"She'll come around. Bottom line, it isn't up to us what Roland does with his company."

"We're going to finish up, then go for a walk." I flexed my leg. "My leg is just about a hundred percent."

"He's starting to worry about the race," Maggie shared.

Carlos laughed as he walked out the door. "Can't say that I blame him."

"Didn't you just trim those hedges?" I asked Carlos when we got back from stretching our legs.

"I want everything perfect for when Roland gets here later today. He deserves to be able to take it easy. Maybe he can beat the odds."

"He told you? I wasn't sure."

"I knew there's been something wrong for a long time, and he finally came out and told me about the diagnosis. Terrible deal, all that happened with Caroline and Isla, now Roland. It's like the whole family is cursed."

I watched him run his trimmers for a minute. "That one's electric, it works from either side."

He looked at me quizzically. "Sure, either side, it doesn't make any difference."

"It wouldn't, unless you were still doing it the hard way." Sometimes little things escape your notice in the moment, then something triggers a memory, and everything falls into place.

"What is it Slater?" Maggie asked as I hurried toward the house.

"Grab your keys, you'll see."

"Is Jon going to take a shot at us if we stop out there?" I asked Jessie. "He promised Maggie some clippings of the good stuff, and she wants to get them before we go back home."

"It should be fine, but I'll call him and tell him your coming. Dad could go with you, but it's getting busy. I'd like to keep him behind the bar."

"He probably won't shoot at Maggie, he likes her."

"No surprise." Woody's eldest son laughed and gave Maggie a nod. "My brother has good taste in women, just not much luck."

"What are you up to Slater?" Maggie asked, after Jessie left the table. "I don't really plan on growing pot."

"It's just an excuse to go out there."

"And why are we going out there again?"

"I said, you'll see." I weakened. "I'll explain it on the way."

It really didn't trouble me that men found my partner attractive, and in this particular case, it was helpful. Jon Forester walked up to Maggie's convertible as we pulled up and opened the door for her.

"Jessie called me. I did start those clippings for you, Maggie, just like I said I would."

"That's great, Jon. Slater thinks I'm just going to kill them, but I'll bet I can get them to grow. Can I call you if they start looking sickly?"

Maggie and Jon walked side by side toward the greenhouse and I followed a couple of steps behind. I checked out Jon's gun as we walked. Some holsters have straps that cross over the hammer to keep the gun in place when you're working. And by working, I mean roping cows or wrestling steers, not growing cannabis. Jonathan Forester, and very possibly, Clint Eastwood, didn't have a strap to keep their guns in place. They needed to be able to whip them out easily and quickly to defend themselves against rustlers, bad-ass bikers, and in Jonathan's case, other pot farmers, and his own paranoia.

When we reached the greenhouse, Jon reached out to unhook the latch, exposing the handle of the Colt. Maggie was on his left, and it was a simple task to reach out and pull the revolver from the well-oiled holster. Maggie moved away and I took a step back, leveling the pearl handled gun at its surprised owner. He turned, eyes wide, and looked like he might run. I cocked the Colt.

He lifted his hands. "What is this bullshit? My Dad said I could trust you."

"Just take it easy. We don't want your money, and we won't hurt you. Just don't do anything stupid."

Maggie spoke up, "We need to talk to her, Jon. We're here to help her, not hurt anyone."

"Talk to who?" He tried. "What are you talking about?"

"Isla. We know she's here." I pointed at his empty holster. "You wear your gun on the right side, because you're right-handed. The old casting reel on that pole in the boat is set up for a lefty. The extra pruning shears in the greenhouse are left-handed, that's why I thought they looked funny. There's a picture in the bar of Isla and your brother offering a toast, and she's holding her drink in her left hand. I don't know who was sailing the Caroline the day it went down, but it wasn't Isla."

"I promise," Maggie said quietly. "We don't want to hurt her. Her father is dying, and he deserves to know that she's alive."

"Deserves? He murdered her mother!"

"If she was murdered, it wasn't Roland that did it. She took too many pills, maybe it was an accident. We're still trying to figure that out."

"But he sent people after Isla. They ran her off the road, and when that didn't work, they shot at her. She took my truck up to the market one day and someone started shooting at her. Thank God I plated the doors. That's why there are bullet holes in it, not because I shot at a wolf."

"Why was the other girl on the Caroline, instead of Isla?" Maggie asked. I kept the gun leveled.

"How could you know about that?" He struggled for a moment, then dropped his eyes. "It was all a huge mistake. A giant, horrible, mistake."

"And there's about to be another one." I emptied the Colt, dropped the shells into my shirt, and shoved the gun into my side pocket. "Roland is giving up. I think he's about ready to sign the company over to Ross, and I know Isla wouldn't want that."

"It was all a mistake," he muttered again. "Isla was so sick and upset that night, so confused and terrified. She was sure her father had hired someone to kill her. Sometimes when she gets like that, she hears voices from the beyond, and talks to her dead mother. The herb helps, it calms her down."

"Probably not," Maggie said. "She needs real medical attention. We need to talk to her. Is she hiding in the house somewhere?"

Jon shifted his gaze fearfully, looking up at the second story. "This isn't a good time, she's bad right now. Please. Please, just go away. You'll make her worse. She's sick, don't you understand? She's like her mother was, confused and scared. I'm helping her."

"She needs more help than you can give her, Jon," Maggie said. "We have to talk to her. This is no way for her to live, hiding like this for two years, and letting people think she was dead all this time."

"We'll be careful to not upset her," I added, "and we won't tell Roland where she is yet. Just knowing she's alive will be enough for now."

He started toward the house. "You absolutely can't say anything to her about Annie. Isla has blamed herself ever since it happened.

302

When I finally told her the boat went down, she tried to run into the bay and drown herself, to follow Annie. I've had to lock her in her room for weeks at a time so she wouldn't run away. I have to be with her all the time, because I'm afraid she'll try to hurt herself."

"Annie, that was her best friend?" I asked. "How did Annie end up on the boat instead of Isla?"

"They were going to take the boat up north together to save it from the storm, then go to Annie's parents place in Charlotte and hide out where Roland couldn't find Isla. But they waited too long. Annie was a descent sailor, but not good enough, I guess."

"Why in hell did she go alone?" I asked.

"Annie loved Isla so much, she would have done anything for her. Isla had one of her episodes, the worst one I'd ever seen. She was screaming and crying all night, worried about the hurricane coming and saving the boat. She kept talking to her mother like she was in the room with us. It was almost morning when we finally all fell asleep. When we woke up, Annie had taken the boat and was gone."

"We found a box on the boat, and a locket with Isla's name on it."

"Annie probably wanted to take that stuff to the after-life, if she didn't make it," Jon said soberly.

"Makes sense," I agreed. I wasn't going to argue the logic of that with a pot farmer.

He unlocked the front door of the house and we walked into the small living room. As expected, the place reeked of cannabis and patchouli oil. Jonathan put a finger to his lips and we climbed the steps to the second floor. There was a window beyond the landing, and a single door to the right. He knocked softly.

"Isla, Honey? There's someone here, someone you need to talk to. It's very, very important. It's okay, they're here to help you."

I wasn't sure what to expect. Isla had been in hiding for two years, hoping her father and everyone would think what they had, and leave her alone. I couldn't imagine who she might have trusted, or how many visitors she had welcomed into that squalid house. It seemed entirely possible that the only person she had seen for the last seven-hundred plus days was Jonathan Forester. That alone would unhinge most people.

We stepped quietly through the door. The room had a different odor, but it was just as pungent. It reeked of sweat and unwashed bedding. Isla Dunbar was on the bed, crowding back into the corner in a defensive position with her knees pulled up to her chest, and her forearms covering her face. She wore a tattered pair of pajama bottoms and an oversized tee-shirt that had once been white. Her bright red hair hung onto her shoulders and across her face, a matted tangle that hadn't seen a brush or water in an indeterminable amount of time. She squinted at us and lifted her head just enough to see around her arms, peering into the brighter light of the window behind us. Then suddenly, her blue eyes widened and her mouth fell open. She crawled quickly across the bed and lunged forward, wailing loudly.

"Mommy?" she wrenched out. Maggie stood in front of me with her auburn hair and blue eyes, her tall silhouette outlined in the door frame. Isla vaulted off the bed, and plunged into the redhead's open arms, screaming incoherently; then she buried her face against Maggie's chest and started crying softly. After a minute, she choked out a few more tortured words. "Mommy, why did you have to leave me? She took it, Mommy. She took the necklace you gave me. I'm sorry. I'm so sorry."

The salient misery in her voice tore through me like a knife as she continued sobbing and mumbling apologizes to the woman she mistook for her mother. Worse perhaps, was the plaintive hope in her voice, and the certainty that her mother had finally returned to rescue her. I stood there dumbfounded, unable to imagine what help I could offer the broken wretch.

Through some depth of maternal wisdom, Maggie knew what to do. She sat down on the bed, still holding onto Isla, who had fallen to her knees on the floor in front of her. Isla buried her face in Maggie's lap, and continued to cry softly as Maggie combed her matted hair with her fingers and made soothing noises. I backed quietly out of the room, pushing Jon ahead of me, closed the door, and stumbled down the dimly lit stairwell.

I took a few deep breaths, trying to process what I had just seen. Legally or otherwise, what Jon had done wasn't quite the same as what Marcus had tried to do to Jasmine, but it didn't feel that much different, and the Neanderthal in me wanted to react the same way.

Maggie was right about men, or about me at least. Blame it on testosterone or my years in the Navy, but it wasn't justice I wanted for Isla Dunbar. Jon's stupidity had deprived Isla of the help she needed and stolen two years of her life, time that she could have spent with her dying father. Maybe the doctors couldn't have helped her, but he had taken that opportunity away from her.

I stood at the base of the stairs looking at the unwashed degenerate, trying to slow my pounding heart and control my impulses. I wanted nothing more than to drag Woody's youngest son outside and, at the very least, give him a good beating. Isla, even more than Jasmine, was completely defenseless. All I could think about was the helpless, broken girl, huddled in the corner of her bed, crying out to her mother for protection from the demons in her head. I really wanted to lash out at someone, and Jon Forester was the most obvious choice.

It took considerable willpower on my part, but I managed to stop myself from doing that. Jonathan wasn't the same as Marcus. He may have kept Isla locked in his house to stave off his own loneliness, or truly believed her father was trying to kill her. However misguided, he may have even thought he could help her with his medicinal herb. But I really didn't think he intended her harm. No matter how angry I was at Jon and the insouciant Butterfly for letting the world go so terribly wrong, I knew I had to do as Maggie had said and try to be better than my impulses. Jon made it a little easier.

"Is she going to be alright, Mister Slater." He wiped at his eyes. "I care so much about her, and I really thought I could make her better."

"She needs more help than you can give her, Jon. A lot more, I would say."

"Sometimes she would seem okay, and I would let her help me, or we'd fish in the bay. I thought maybe it would go away, but she just keeps getting worse. What about her Dad? If we take her to the hospital, he'll find her. Are you sure he doesn't want to hurt her?"

"Jon, do you know what Lou Gehrig's Disease is?" He nodded. "They're giving Roland a couple years, and I've gotten to know him. He's made some terrible mistakes, but trying to hurt his daughter has never been one of them. He's a really good man, and they both deserve the chance to make things right between them before it's too late. For now, we won't tell him where she is, just

307

that she's alive. But she needs a lot of help, and Maggie and I are going to see that she gets it, whether you like it or not."

"Annie and I were together, and she left, then I fell in love with Isla. I don't want to lose her too, Mister Slater."

"She needs to get well, Jon, that's what's important. Locking her in that room wasn't right, even to protect her from herself." Being better was a real struggle. I sat on the dirty couch and closed my eyes so I wouldn't have to look at him anymore.

Half an hour later Maggie came quietly down the stairs. "She's resting, then she's going to pack a bag."

Jonathan stood quickly. "Where are you taking her?"

"Somewhere safe. She finally understands that I'm not her mother, and she realizes that she needs help. Slater?"

"You say, Red. What do you want to do?"

"I want to take her home, right now, back to Jacksonville. She's not ready to see her father. She can stay with me until we get her lined up with a doctor and in the hospital."

"Long drive. I need to go back to Roland's and stop him from signing those papers."

Jonathan spoke up. "Jacksonville? That's nine hours."

"I'll stop in Miami and get Jasmine to help drive and keep an eye on her," Maggie said. I knew that was for my benefit.

Jon was on the verge of tears. "I know I should have called someone, but she was so terrified. She was sure her father would kill her if he found her. She would scream, and cry, and beg me not to take her to the doctor." He looked at me, then at Maggie. "I could go with you. She trusts me, and I'm good at keeping her calm."

"Are you kidding me?" I looked at Maggie and I could see she was considering it. "Maggie, he all but held her captive for all this time. I don't trust him."

"I love her, Mister Slater. I do. As soon as I know she's safe, and in the hospital, I'll come back down here and wait until she's well, like you said."

"Who's going to watch your crop?" Maggie tipped her head toward the greenhouse.

"Isla's a lot more important than a few pot plants. I could care less."

"Good answer, kid," Maggie said, then looked at me expectantly.

"What? I still say it's a bad idea. He should be in jail."

"It'll be okay, Slater. He can keep Isla calm in the back seat while I drive. It will give me some time to tell her how much her father really loves her. It's not therapy, but it's a start."

"I'm really sorry, Mister Slater." Jonathan added. "I just didn't know what else to do."

"Dammit!" I finally gave in. "You owe me one, Red."

"You get to tell Roland his daughter is alive, that counts for a lot."

"Yeah, that will feel good. Jon, give me the keys to your pickup. And you better behave yourself on the way to Jacksonville, or I'm coming to find you."

I climbed into the old Bronco, then felt the weight of Jon's six-shooter still in the side pocket of my pants. I pulled it out, dropped a few shells into the cylinder, and laid it on the seat next to me. Maybe I'd see a Key-wolf on the way to Roland's place. Or not.

Chapter Twenty

What some people consider coincidence might indeed be attributed to the actions of the Butterfly. That seems like a pretty good first line for the book I intend to write. Then again, I may not get to it, it's all up to the Butterfly. I had just reached the end of what Johnathan Forester called his driveway, when my phone rang. It was Susan Foster.

"Hey, Slater. I had to lean on some people at the FBI lab, so you owe me."

"Put it on my tab. Things are getting interesting down here."

"Interesting here too, looking at these results. We found a match, but it wasn't from the sample you gave us."

"It wasn't Isla on that boat, but I already knew that."

"You did?"

"We just found her. She's a real mess, in need of a hot bath and a whole lot of psycho-therapy, but she's very much alive. Maggie's taking her up to our house."

"That's incredible! Really great, right?"

"Great for her and Roland. Not so great for the girl that must have died on that boat. Annie something, I didn't even ask her last name."

"Annie Roberts, and I can tell you who her biological father was, thanks to the miracles of modern science. His DNA was already in the database. Ross Dunbar, Roland's brother."

"That raises a few questions."

"DNA doesn't lie, Slater."

"Anything else the wonders of modern science can tell us?"

"I'm reading...genetically predisposed...not definitive..."

"Bottom line, Susan," I muttered impatiently.

"There's a lot of double-talk, but it says there's a high degree of certainty that her mother was of Asian descent."

"This just keeps getting better and better," I said into the phone, as I rearranged the theories that were floating around in my head.

"Was that sarcasm, Slater?" Susan asked.

"Yes, and no."

"Her DNA was in the data-base, and her parents, her adoptive parents, have been notified that she was almost certainly on the Caroline when it went down. The timing was right, she was reported missing almost two years ago."

"No doubt. At least they finally know what happened to their daughter. Thanks for your help, again. Stop by the house next time you're up our way and I'll buy you a beer."

"I'm in Jacksonville a lot lately, Slater. I'll be seeing you soon. Good luck with the case."

Ross's BMW was parked in front of the house when I got back to Roland's. I wasn't invited to the meeting, but I wasn't going to let that stop me. My leg felt great. I took the steps two at a time.

Roland sat in his wheelchair in the great room with Ginger beside him, smiling. Ross Dunbar sat on the other side of the coffee table, also looking smug. There were a dozen stacks of paper spread out in front of him, presumably giving him control of the company. Once those papers were signed, he could sell out to the highest bidder and walk away a very rich man. With a very rich accomplice, if my theory was correct.

Ginger had been the one encouraging Roland to walk away from the company. I knew the prenup was iron-clad, but I imagined the payoff, once Ross sold the company, would be substantial. I was guessing mostly, but it made sense. It wasn't something I wanted to believe of Ginger. She didn't seem like someone that would steal a fragile girls most precious keepsake of her dead mother, but Isla's tormented words still echoed in my head.

I couldn't be sure that Ross had been involved in Caroline's death, and it was possible that that had truly been an accident. But once Ross knew about Roland's ALS, Isla was the only person stopping him from getting the company back. He had run her off the road, and then tried to shoot her when she took Jon's truck to the market. If Isla had seen him, she mistook him for Roland. I had it

313

all worked out in my head, and it all seemed reasonable. I still didn't know why Ginger put the necklace in the mail, but I didn't care. I was about to return Roland's heir, and save his company.

"Slater." Ginger stood, still smiling. "Sorry, but this is a private meeting."

"I'm sorry too, Ginger, but I have news. Really important news. We just found Isla, and she's very much alive." I was feeling pretty smug myself, and I couldn't wait for the reaction.

"Bullshit." Ross said. "Her boat's at the bottom of the Gulf, and it's been two years."

"Slater? Are you sure?" Roland asked cautiously. "It can't be."

"I saw her with my own eyes, Roland. She's very sick, schizophrenic like her mother if I was going to guess. Maggie is taking her somewhere safe right now, then to a hospital."

"Oh my God," Roland exclaimed. "Oh my God."

"That's the best news, Rollie! I'm so happy for you." Ginger threw her arms around her husband, and they both started crying. Not the reaction I was expecting from Ginger.

Ross leaned forward and bounced a finger off the stack of papers in front of him. "That's great, Rollie, but a deal's a deal, right?"

"She's alive, Ross. Can you believe it? Can't you just be happy for me for one second?" Ross glared at me, and started shuffling through the papers. This was more what I had expected, and it made me smile; or maybe it was the look of pure joy on Roland Dunbar's face.

"Are you absolutely sure it was her, Slater?" Ginger finally asked, between hugs.

"Absolutely sure. But she was very confused. She thought Maggie was her mother at first, because of the red hair. I don't know much about mental illness, but she acted completely irrational, and terrified."

"Oh God," Ginger lamented. "She must have been sick all along. I should have realized, and been more understanding."

"Roland?" Ross broke in again. "Does this change our deal or not?"

"No. The deals done. You'll have your money by the end of next week, then I'm through with you for good."

"I'm lost." I admitted.

"We're going to find the extra money, somehow, and buy Ross out." Ginger explained. "I convinced Roland to let me help him, and to offer more shares to some of the engineers, so they'll stay on and help run things. But now with Isla back, when she gets well, we'll have to reorganize. Roland will want her to have control of the company." She paused and looked over my head. "My God! What is it, Teresa?"

If I hadn't already been sure, I was when I turned to look at the small woman. Her face was a mask of grief, tears streamed down her cheeks, and her lips trembled as she tried to talk.

"My Annie." She sobbed. "Her parents, the people that adopted her, they just called me a few minutes ago. She's been missing since the hurricane, and I prayed that she wasn't on that boat, that there was some other explanation. But it was…it was her. It shouldn't have been her." The last wasn't grief, it was rage. I looked down. She held Jon Forester's revolver in her right hand. She lifted it and pointed it straight at Roland Dunbar.

"You killed her! You, your damn money, and your damn company. I should have kept her all those years ago, but no! You had to protect your brother, and the business. I gave her up because you convinced me it was for the best. She was my daughter, Roland, and you made me give her up." She screamed the last, waving the gun in the general direction of Roland and Ginger. She was too far away for me to reach her, and I couldn't see the front of the gun. I had only loaded four cartridges, but I really didn't want to play Russian roulette. Teresa was completely irrational, but she knew enough to have the gun cocked.

"How did she find out that Isla was her cousin?" I asked, hoping that talking would keep her from shooting, and that she might calm down enough to put the gun down.

Teresa kept waving the gun at Roland, watching Ross and me from the corner of her eye. "When she turned eighteen, her parents told her about me, and I went to visit. She hated me. She didn't understand why I would give her up. She hated me Roland! But she asked about her family, and I told her who her father was, and about Isla." She drew a shaky breath. "My own daughter couldn't stand the sight of me, because you made me give her away."

"I really thought it was for the best, Teresa, you were so young." Roland said quietly. "I'm so very sorry."

"My Annie should've had a part of your company, not this piece of shit." She motioned at Ross. "He wanted Isla gone, either scared away, or dead. I tried to chase her away with Eli, but she was crazy enough to believe he was real. She liked the idea! Then Ross started playing rough. He ran her off the road, then took a shot at her. Some brother you have Roland, he was screwing your wife, then he tried to kill your daughter. I'd rather you gave all your money to this gold-digging bitch, than that murdering bastard."

"Shut up!" Ross started to stand. "Another week and the deal will be done. I helped start the business and that money belongs to me. She's lying Roland, the bitch is crazy."

"Crazy?" Teresa stopped shaking, and turned the gun toward Ross. She wasn't crying any more. "Our beautiful little girl, Ross, your own daughter is dead, and you don't care at all. You're a sick, selfish, greedy, bastard."

I knew she was going to shoot, and so did Ross. He lunged forward and rushed at her, trying to reach her before she could pull the trigger. The

Colt roared once, then again as Ross fell. The second shot missed him completely and buried itself in Ginger's left shoulder. She had thrown herself on top of her husband, and probably saved his life.

Teresa stumbled back, screaming and crying hysterically as she raised the gun again. Ross fell against me as I threw myself at her. I'd never hit a woman before, but there wasn't time for anything else, and I didn't hold back. The blow knocked her against the wall, and she dropped the gun before falling to the floor, out cold. I kicked the gun across the room, made sure Teresa had a pulse, then dialed 911.

I ran to the bathroom and grabbed towels. There was a hole dead center in Ross's chest, and he didn't have a pulse. I moved on and tried to staunch the bleeding from Ginger's shoulder. Even in as much pain as she was in, she asked me why I kept apologizing. I think I apologized for apologizing, because I didn't want to admit how wrong I had been about her.

Chapter Twenty-One

"Ginger's out of the hospital." I said, returning my phone to my pocket. She says you're forgiven for thinking she's a gold-digger, and the one behind everything."

"I don't think I ever said that, that was you and Tommy." The redhead handed Jasmine and me each a beer and returned to the kitchen. I tried to snatch Jasmine's bottle away from her, but she was too quick.

"All that time, Isla was hiding out upstairs in Jessie's brother's house?" She asked.

"Kind of like you and Jarrod. Jon kept her locked in the bedroom most of the time. He said he was afraid she might kill herself. That may be true, but it's no excuse. I guess the difference is that Isla was too afraid to go outside, and you're not afraid of anything."

"Damn right." She tipped her beer up and steered it away from my reach. "Okay, the ocean creeps me out, but that's about it. Did you ever figure out who sent the necklace to Roland?"

"Teresa. She decided she couldn't trust Ross, and wanted to buy time. We were right about the motive, but not the perp. She thought Ross or Roland owed her, because they made her give Annie up for adoption. She had just started cleaning for Roland, and she was only sixteen. If she couldn't get money out of Ross, she wanted

Roland to turn the company over to Carlos and some of the other engineers when he died, hoping eventually she would be able to buy her way back into her daughter's life. I guess Carlos finally went to see her, but I don't know what's going to happen there."

"It does seem like she got a raw deal," Maggie said. "Roland's paying for a lawyer to defend her. Justifiable man-slaughter, if you ask me. That's a real thing, just so you know." She smiled sweetly at me.

I continued explaining the whole mess to Jasmine. "The key was for the box we found. Isla must have had it, and Teresa got it when she stole the necklace. Once she realized no one knew what it was for, she took it off the chain to try and figure out what it fit."

"Why did she take the necklace in the first place?"

"Spite, or just to make Isla more unstable. She spent enough time with her to know how bad her mental state was. She hated that Caroline's daughter was going to run Roland's company someday, and hers wouldn't even talk to her. She knew losing that necklace would drive Isla off the deep end, because her mother had given it to her. In a way, that's what ended up getting her daughter killed. You can't mess with the Butterfly."

"Stupid Butterfly," Jasmine complained, and took another drink.

"Alcohol is a gateway drug." I cautioned.

"You would know," She snorted. "You were the one seeing ghosts when we were down in the Keys."

"I wasn't seeing ghosts, but I still say that Captain's wheel moved. Eli sent me out there to help you that night."

"Thanks again, Slater." We bumped fists, and both took a drink.

"What did Woody say when you told him his son is a rotten kidnapper?" Maggie asked.

"Kidnapping's a strong word." She raised a brow. "That's what he said. I agree with you. But it's his kid, what else is he going to say? I guess that's for the lawyers to figure out. I'm hoping we can work with Woody again someday, he's a sharp guy."

Jasmine leaned back. "Maryanne tells me your case got tossed, and Marcus and Mick got a slap on the wrist."

"At least I got to break Mick's nose." We bumped fists again, but stopped snickering when Maggie sat down with us.

"Janet got her money back, thanks mostly to Jasmine," she said.

"Glad to hear you're earning your pay, Blue. What did you do?"

"I just presented her with some other options, to help with the breakup."

"What kind of options?" She just smiled, so I took a guess. "Were these legal, or romantic options?"

"Both. Think about it, Slater. You know the person."

I thought, then I shrugged.

"Susan Foster."

"No way!" I looked at the redhead.

"I didn't know she was gay either," Maggie admitted. "But it's not like I see her that often."

"She did tell me once that she doesn't date guys with girlfriends," I confessed.

"Or any, I guess." Maggie paused and gave me one of her looks. "And now I'm a little curious how that came up?"

"Told you, I can always tell," Jasmine crowed. "Susan went and had a chat with the Lanes, and Janet had a check the next day. She's letting them off the hook, because nobody else lost any money, but Stacey is going to have to stick closer to home from now on."

"Maybe it's safe for you to leave the house now, Slater," Maggie joked. "The main thing is Susan and Janet are getting along very well."

"Here's to Slater and Partners." I raised my beer. "We solved the case and made a love connection."

Jasmine lifted hers and peered at the bottom of the bottle. "Damn, I'm out of beer."

"You've had enough." Maggie and I both said at the same time.

***

Hurricane season was over before we made the trip back down to Big Pine Key. Roland Dunbar was completely wheelchair bound, still able to lift his hands and talk, but little else. He and I sat a short distance away from the net, where Ginger, Isla, Maggie, and Jasmine were playing a half-hearted game of badminton. Beyond them, the sun was creeping toward the horizon, and a slight chill blew off the water.

"I owe you more than I can ever repay, Slater," Roland said. "We'll never be sure if Ross gave Caroline too many sleeping pills or if she just got tired of the struggle, but you gave me my daughter back. Maybe sometime soon I'll get to see Caroline. She was so tortured in life, I hope she's happy now."

"She's probably up there right now, having a cold one with Old Eli."

"You a believer?"

"No, not really. Maybe. All I can say is that I know for sure I saw that Pirate's wheel turn, three different times, and I haven't been able to budge it since."

"Eli's gone, at least that's what Isla tells me. It could be the treatments and the medication she's on chased him away. It's too bad Caroline couldn't have gotten that kind of help."

"How are Isla and Ginger getting along?"

"Ginger's my wife, but that doesn't mean she's trying to replace Caroline. Isla's finally figuring that out. They're getting there. I'm guessing they'll do fine once I'm gone, maybe help each other through it. Isla has big plans for the company and she wants Ginger to help. She'll keep everyone working and slowly transition into high tech products. She gets to save the planet, and my company will keep going. It's what I wanted all along."

"Woody says you let Jonathan off the hook. He appreciated that."

"Isla gave him the money to fund his medical marijuana business, but she claims they're just business partners now. I'd like to see his ass in jail for fraud or kidnapping, but she said if I want things to work out between us, I have to let it go. There's absolutely nothing I wouldn't do for her."

"I know how it feels. I almost killed the two guys that hurt Jasmine."

"I'm hopeful there's something after this. But when it comes right down to it, my daughter's the only immortality I'm sure of."

"There's quite a few of us that'll miss you, Roland. That counts for something."

He laughed and extended his hand. "Don't get maudlin on me, but I'm glad we crossed paths, Eric. All the money in the world won't buy you real friends."

"Are you really going to sell this place?" I'd seen a real estate sign.

"Yeah. Isla is going to take a few of her mother's treasures with her when she leaves tomorrow. Ginger and I are going to stay for another week and watch the sun fall into the sea. She and I need some of those sunsets I was telling you about."

"I really misjudged her." I admitted. "She's quite a woman."

"That she is, Slater. We're both very lucky men." The game had stopped for a moment and the redhead waved to me. Roland looked over. "That big race is coming up, and my money's on you. Can you take her?"

I watched Maggie toss her auburn hair to the side and stretch her elegant frame to reach a shot, feeling very lucky indeed.

"Sorry Roland, but there's not one chance in hell."

End

Slater and Maggie will have another mystery to solve very soon.

Reviews are like oxygen to this writer, and I am fond of breathing. Please let me know what you think. T.J. Jones